how much
IT MAY
Storm

A. N. WILLIS

How Much It May Storm

Print ISBN 978-1-7343597-5-6
Cover design by Ana Ristovska

Produced by Observatory Books
Denver, Colorado

First edition October 2020

For Kevin and Mom—Always my first readers

HOW MUCH IT MAY STORM

Dinah
November 1943

For as long as I can remember, people have said that our town is dying. But today is the first time that I've really felt it. Today, my brother is leaving. He's boarding a train that will take him away to some faraway place—whether a battlefield in Europe or an island in the Pacific, he can't yet tell me—and I might never see him again.

"Hurry up," my mother says. She drags her fingers through my short hair as we walk. "You have gravel behind your ears. You didn't even stop to wash?"

"Nate doesn't care." My breath comes out in white wispy clouds. Makes me crave a cigarette.

"He cares if his sister looks decent. You're nearly grown, too old for this tomboy foolishness."

The train whistles. It's pulling in. She grabs my wrist and makes me run. We're a sight, the two of us; Mother running in her nicest pumps and me shlepping along, holding up Nate's old trousers so they don't fall off my hips. It's my fault we're late. I was cleaning out the shed, like Mother had asked me and Nate to do a million times, but I picked today. As if mind-numbing chores would somehow slow this moment from coming.

On the platform, Papa is talking to Nate. My brother bends over Papa's chair to listen. Nate's dark green uniform is handsomely pressed, and his hat is set at a jaunty angle. I want to run over to him, grab that hat, muss his hair. Used to be, he'd have a laugh. Now that he's an army Joe, I'm not certain. He's off to do more important things.

He used to promise he would never leave me behind.

Nate comes over and hugs me tightly. "You'll be OK," he says into my ear. Even though he's the one we're all worried about.

"Sure I will. I've got your record collection to play with."

He groans. "Go easy, will you? I don't want to come home to a bunch of scratched up—"

Mother interrupts us, and Nate lets me go.

I'm not the only girl in town to watch a brother take that train to war. Nate is the last one left: the very last male in Powder Ridge who could be drafted. But to me, Nate's not some number on a card. He's the only part of my life that's not bleak. Without my brother, who's going to talk me through the endless days up at Cherry Mountain? Or the monotonous nights at home? I can't do it without him, I just *can't*.

I reach out to tug on his coat, but the fabric slips from my fingers.

A porter steps off the train to help Nate carry his bag. It's happening too fast. The past two weeks that Nate's been home, I've been pretending this day wouldn't come. Suddenly I want to hug him again, tell him I love him. Tell him to be careful. There's so much I didn't say —didn't know *how* to say. And now there's not enough time.

"Nate," I call out, "wait, please—"

The whistle shrieks. He leaps up and waves at us from the stairway, grinning like this is the best day of his life. The train begins to pull away. Mother is bawling, and that's the only thing that keeps my tears inside.

We stand there in the cold until the last car is gone, until even the white puffs of steam from the engine have disappeared. My heart has a scratch down the middle of it and it's skipping, skipping, skipping.

A week later, the first real storm hits. It's a rager. Snow flying sideways at the windows, wind screaming in the eaves. I'm up half the night from the noise. In the morning, Jim Gainsbury stops by to shovel us out. I could've done it myself, but I'd hurt Jim's feelings if I said no.

I trudge my way up to the mine in my snowshoes. There's not a single footprint ahead of me on the mile-long path. Everything is quiet, like the snow is a thick goosedown blanket and the world hasn't quite realized it's morning yet. Flocked evergreens line the path on one side. On the other is a steep drop-off. Every once in a while, a mound of snow slips from a branch and thumps onto my hat. I swear, it's like the trees are aiming.

Finally, the path curves around and the view opens up into a panoramic vista. Craggy mountain peaks reach up into the clouds. The old mining encampment lies before me. The sun is shining in from behind, casting the whole expanse in shadow: ramshackle buildings, rusted mining carts, and a scattered field of debris. The gigantic piles of waste rock are iced with white.

Nate and I have eked out a living up here for years, ever since Papa's accident. We scavenge ore for the mining company so they can squeeze every last drop of money out of the mine they abandoned.

I pass through the cluster of buildings that used to be the main drag. Farther on about a quarter mile, there's a bunkhouse that once housed three hundred men a night. Now it's boarded up and its red paint is peeling. I walk toward it on my way to the waste rock piles beyond.

Something moves in one of the few remaining windows—third floor, last one on the left. I stop and stare. There shouldn't be anybody in that boardinghouse, especially not up there. I must've imagined it.

But as I watch, two handprints appear on the glass. Like whoever's in there is looking back out. At *me*.

My skin burns with heat. The feeling of violation is like a punch in the center of my chest. Somebody's up there messing with our stuff. Nate's and mine.

I pull the scarf back up over my face and hurry toward the boardinghouse.

The building has been rotting a little more each year. Last winter, a glancing blow from an avalanche collapsed one side. Now, the only safe way to get inside is to climb —which you would've thought was enough to keep nosy parkers away.

I unstrap the webs from my shoes, and they drop heavily into the snow. I reach for a vertical slat of wood at the corner of the building, pulling myself up. Splinters scratch at my gloves. Ice crystals prick at the inside of my nose.

I reach the third floor and carefully edge my way over to the window. The two handprints are still there on the glass. As I watch, they fade away like fog on a mirror. I peer in.

The wooden crate where Nate and I store our things —it's pulled out into the open. Somebody's taken off the lid.

Since we were little, Nate and I have been keeping some of our possessions in that third floor room. Just stuff that matters to us. Books, comics, souvenirs that we didn't want Mother to find and throw out. We certainly never thought some low-life would be prowling around up there, trying to filch our childhood memories.

It's probably McGrady. My brother's only been gone a week, and already McGrady has been complaining that the mine's no place for a seventeen-year-old girl on her own. *It ain't my job to look after you.* That old scumbag thinks he can force me out. But I can hold my own.

I push up the window and ask, "Hello? McGrady?"

Nobody answers. Then I remember—there weren't any footprints in the snow. Even Terrance Jameson isn't up at the mine yet, and he's usually the first one. My brother likes to say, *You never look before you leap, Dinah.* Guess I still haven't learned.

I squeeze inside and land gently on the floor.

The room seems empty. Whoever was up here is gone.

This used to be a common room of some kind. A couch tilts toward a hole in the center of the floor, where rotting planks have given way. In a nearby corner, an abandoned bookcase lies on its side. The room smells like an old icebox. Stale and cold. A tattered curtain flutters. The door to the hallway is closed. Ages ago, Nate locked it, but who knows if the lock still works.

I crouch and pull the crate toward me. Our copy of *The Time Machine* rests on the top. I glance quickly through the rest, but there doesn't seem to be anything missing.

The light shifts, and I look up, my rapid breathing the only sound.

"Hello?" I ask again. Not a peep.

My nerves are starting to hum. I don't like this. Not one bit.

My hands are still resting on the crate. There's a half box of Lucky Strikes that Nate left here at some point, and I pocket those before replacing the lid. I'm ready to get out of here.

I get up and go to the still-open window.

There's a soldier down there in the snow, staring up at me.

Nate, I think immediately, though it couldn't be my brother. He's miles away in some army camp. And this guy isn't even wearing the right uniform. His coat is heavy, olive-colored. Old-fashioned. The pocket flaps are torn.

I put my head out. "Hey, smart aleck! Was that you up here?"

I expect him to say something back. Or, if he's been sneaking around and doesn't want to get caught, to run. But he does neither. Instead, he comes *toward* the bunkhouse. I can hear his boots scrape against the boards.

He's starting to climb.

2

Millie
November 1918

I've seen death many a time, more often than I like to count. I know its face. So when I see the soldier in the dining car, I can tell right away that he's in danger. There's a distant look in his eyes, a gray pallor in the poor lad's cheeks as he grips his coffee. But it isn't just that. Any nurse worth her keep could read the warning in those signs, even a girl of mere one-and-twenty like me.

No, it's the shadow lying over him that tells me death is nearby. A shadow, although there's a sconce hanging right above his head. The light shines, but it can't reach him.

"I'll sit here, thank you," I tell the porter. "Tea and toast, please." I slide into the booth across the aisle from the soldier, smoothing down the white skirt of my uniform. There's a faint tinkle of crockery as we round a bend. The train sways to and fro, and wind blows through the open windows of the car.

The soldier glances up, then back to his coffee. He's wearing an olive drab army uniform. His small suitcase rests beneath the table next to a cane.

"Hello," I say. "Are you headed for Powder Ridge?"

He looks up, surprised. He has to clear his throat before he speaks. "Why, yes. Good morning, miss. How did you know?"

So he's a polite one. Well bred, which goes with the lieutenant's insignia on his shoulder. Impressive for a boy who couldn't be a day older than I.

"Powder Ridge is the first stop this morning," I explain. "We're the only ones braving the dining car." The few other passengers are keeping their distance, despite the efforts at ventilation.

It isn't fair that death would choose this boy—a soldier who's survived the war only to be doomed on his way home. Could it be influenza, I wonder?

I can't say I don't fear the illness. Nurses and doctors have died already. But they keep doing their duty, and so shall I. Though my methods are undoubtedly unique.

The porter brings my toast, and as I eat I study the handsome soldier, hoping I'm wrong about his fate. Sometimes the darkness fades, and death retreats for reasons beyond my ken. The darkness alone never reveals the source of the danger, whether it will be sickness or melancholy or cruel accident that cuts short a life—only that death is stalking him. I cannot stop fate. But my talent allows me to ease it.

My mother used to tease that I'm too curious for my own good. No doubt she was right, but that fact doesn't change my nature. It's what makes me so skilled at what I do. If I do say so m'self.

I nod my head at the cane lying on the ground. "Where were you wounded, if I may ask?" Some people would call me bold, but boldness has never steered me wrong in the past.

He sits up straighter. "Cantigny." He speaks softly, like he hasn't used his voice this much in some time. "Shell fragments to the left knee."

"Good gravy! The devil himself must have aimed them." It would've been terribly painful. *Morphine*, a voice whispers in my head. I wonder how much they had to give him. And for how long.

A smile sneaks into the corner of his mouth, and the shadow over his face begins to dim. "The devil indeed. It's nearly six months ago now, yet sometimes I still forget it's gone, if you can believe it."

"Still hurts too, I wager? Even the part that's missing?"

"They call it a phantom. The name fits. It haunts me."

The shadow drifts back across his features, like a cloud covering the sun. But I do not think it's related to the war wound. No, this is something else. Some new darkness on the horizon. *I see you there*, I tell it. You think you can skulk about, but you can't hide from me.

The shadow doesn't give any sign of hearing my warning. But sometimes, I wonder if death sees me, too. And if it recognizes me right back.

"I don't want anyone's pity though," the soldier says, regaining his smile. "I'm on my way home, and that's reason enough to celebrate."

I hesitate, thinking of what I've heard of Powder Ridge. The town is still under quarantine, just now recovering from an outbreak of this plague. Surely he must know already and have cleared his permissions to enter. I hope his family is unscathed. But it's not up to me to bear bad tidings, especially when I know nothing specific.

The porter announces, "Next stop, Powder Ridge."

I stand to gather my coat and few belongings.

"Would you mind too much…" The soldier trails off, but I know what he's asking. I scoop up his suitcase, hand him his cane. He stumbles when he tries to get up, and I place a hand on his arm to steady him. He is still getting used to his prosthesis. I feel the rapid thrumming of his pulse all the way through the wool.

"Thank you, miss," he whispers with a smile. A blush brings back color to his cheek. "I imagine that the soldiers you've tended count themselves very lucky."

Contrary to his assumption, I'm not in the Army Nurse Corps. My patients tend to be much older. And far less appealing.

Oh Millie, I tell myself. *You have patients already. You don't have time for this boy.* Yet I dearly wish I could help him. So much about death is still a mystery to me, but I know enough to provide comfort when the dreaded moment comes.

The porter repeats loudly, "Powder Ridge," and we break apart. The train has stopped. Outside on the platform, someone's calling my name.

I disembark and see my best friend, Briony Jameson, waving from behind a barricade. No, I've forgotten— she's Briony Spencer now.

An official steps forward, straightening his cap. "Are you Nurse Boylan?"

"That I am." I find the letter authorizing my presence here, but the man is already turning toward the soldier.

I step to one side and am immediately swallowed up in Briony's arms. I should've expected that no barricade could hold back my friend.

"Millie, you're here! It's so wonderful to see you!"

"I don't know how you can see me at all," I try to say, but I'm crushed against her ample bosom. She stands back and holds me by the shoulders. I haven't seen her in a year, but she's just the same as I remember: six feet tall in her heels, long blond hair coiled atop her head, and a dusting of freckles on her nose and cheeks. I met Briony in Denver, back when she led quite another life. She's a married woman now, and a rich one to boot. She's the reason that I'm here in Powder Ridge. There's a local family that needs a private nurse, and Briony begged me to come. She arranged everything. Since the epidemic is already fading in Denver, I agreed.

"Have you heard anything from Terrance?" I ask. Briony's brother is over in France.

"He's not much of a letter writer. But how was your trip? I know it's not such a long way, but with all the snow I wasn't sure if—" Then Briony stops speaking, her mouth hanging open. She's fixed her eyes upon my soldier—ha, *my* soldier, I flatter myself—who has finished with the town official.

He smiles, and I realize that he's patiently waiting for his suitcase, which I am still holding. I'm about to apologize and hand the poor lad his case when Briony interrupts me.

"Stars in heaven. Edward Gainsbury, is that really you?"

I take a small gasp of cold air. *Gainsbury.* It can't be. Oh, not that name.

He laughs. He hasn't noticed the shock on my face. "Most of me anyway. Good to see you, Mrs. Spencer."

"You remember me! I'd only just arrived when you left."

"I'm just glad you remember *me*. I haven't told anyone I'm coming, and to be honest, I'm a little nervous about turning up this way. They know I was wounded and in the hospital, but not that I was released."

"Then I'd better start the welcoming party!" Briony looks like she wants to launch herself at him as she did me. But she shows restraint, which might be a first for the notorious Mrs. Spencer, and shakes his hand vigorously instead. "It's just marvelous to see you. Wait until they hear you're back! And you were on the train with Millie? Of all the luck…"

Briony looks from Edward to me, then from me to Edward, and then the realization dawns. "*Oh*. But you probably don't know, do you?"

The whistle sounds. The train begins to pull away. The town official steps forward again and says, "You're both headed to the same place, so I trust you can find your way, Miss Boylan? You'll need to follow these restrictions." He hands Edward and me each a pamphlet, marked at the top with the words *Powder Ridge Public Health Regulations*. Schools, theaters and churches are closed; gatherings are banned.

"We're going to the same place?" Edward asks. "What is it I don't know?" He sways and leans against his cane.

Briony stares at the ground, wringing her kid-gloved hands. "I'm sorry, Edward. It's just awful. It's why Millie's here."

He looks at me, a plea in his expression. I'm about to give him the worst of news.

"Mr. Gainsbury, my name is Millie Boylan. I told you that I'm a nurse. Well, I'm sure grieved to tell you this, but I'm here to care for your mother and your sister Lydia. They're very ill."

"Influenza," Briony adds. "Town's been rife with it these past weeks. We thought the worst had passed, but for your family…" She shakes her head, a few blond curls escaping.

He blinks rapidly. "Thank God Miss Boylan's here to help them recover. We'd better go see them right away."

"I wouldn't advise that," I say. "The contagion could place you in danger as well."

"I've survived worse. I haven't seen my family in nearly a year; I tell you I'm going."

He won't be dissuaded. Briony takes Edward's suitcase, and the three of us set out toward the Gainsbury home.

I don't have the heart to tell him the truth—that I'm not the kind of nurse that helps patients recover. I provide care for those near death. The Gainsbury family only hired me because they don't expect Edward's mother and sister to survive.

But the dark cloud over Edward worries me even more. I fear that, even now, I may be walking him toward his doom.

3

Dinah
1943

The soldier is getting closer. I can't see him, but I hear him breathing as he climbs.

"What do you want?" I ask.

There's no answer.

I refuse to panic. I'm not the kind of girl who screams at the slightest scare. I don't even know why he's coming up. Maybe just to talk.

But he knows I'm in here. *Alone.*

I try to think of something menacing to say. *I'm armed. Don't trifle with me.* But instead I panic and slam shut the window. I try to set the lock, but it's rusted to pieces. I turn around, scanning for someplace to get away or hide. Across the room, the door taunts me. I want to run out into the hallway and escape down the stairs. But the floor might not hold me.

Nate, I need you. This would never have happened if he were here.

I decide to risk the door. I slide along the wall, keeping to the edges of the room. One step. Then another.

A floorboard gives way with a loud snap. My foot goes into the hole. My hands slam against the ground. I crawl backward, my ankle throbbing. My vision gets fuzzy and everything starts to blur.

I find myself back at one of the windows and, out of options, I throw it open.

"Terrance!" I scream, praying that he's arrived on the mountain. "Terrance!" My voice echoes across the basin, and I'm shocked at the terror I hear in it. I'm supposed to be braver than this.

He comes running from the stable. Just seeing him makes me calmer. It takes a few endless minutes for Terrance to reach the building. The floor keeps creaking beneath me as I watch his approach, hugging my elbows.

"The hell you yellin' about, girl?" Terrance asks, craning his head at me.

"Down there," I say, pointing. I'm still breathless. "Somebody. Down there."

Terrance looks around. He's got his usual floppy hat, waxed canvas coat, and rubber boots. "Nobody here but us two. You drop all your marbles and forget to pick 'em up?"

Terrance is wiping at the front of his coat. He's spilled something on it. *Coffee*, I realize. *He was making the morning coffee.* It's such a simple, normal thought that all the panicked energy drains out of my body. My knees go weak. I sink onto the floor, lean back against the wall, and close my eyes.

Terrance doesn't believe me.

"Jiminy Christmas, you're imagining things," he says. "That brain of yours is missing your brother, that's all."

I'm back down on solid ground, shivering with my arms hugged across my torso. My ankle still aches. I'm worried I twisted it.

"He was wearing a wool military jacket," I tell Terrance again, "and not like Nate's. It was old. The pockets were ripped." It looked like it was from the Great War. A coat that had already seen its share of battles.

Terrance shrugs at me. "You sound like McGrady, going on about ghosts up in that bunkhouse. Hearing strange music and all that."

Those stories are ridiculous. Until today, I've never seen a thing out of place in the boardinghouse. "McGrady is an old coot. He's probably sleeping off a bender right now. I really saw somebody." I point at the snow. "What about his footprints?"

"Looks like just a big mess of snow to me. Which *you* made by coming over here."

I look around. He's right, it's all a big mess now. But I'm sure there are more tracks here than just mine. Could Terrance have made them himself by coming over?

"What exactly was so important in that room, anyway?" Terrance asks. "What you got up there?" He's standing back, peering at the third floor window.

"Nate and me keep our comics up there. That's all."

I walk along the side of the building, my shoes sinking into the snow. I spot something on the ground—a brown leather glove. I scoop it up, holding it aloft. "Here," I say in triumph. "The guy dropped it."

"Anybody could've lost a glove. You *wish* there was some boy after you."

"Do not."

Terrance is laughing at me now, and I guess it does sound far-fetched. A soldier boy in a Great War uniform who follows me and then vanishes without a trace. Like some kind of ghost. I don't believe in those kinds of things. He was *real*.

I stuff the mystery glove in my pocket.

The day goes just as badly as I expect. McGrady does turn up after an hour, but it takes us half the day just to clear enough snow that we can reach the waste rock piles.

We have to break up the larger pieces, searching for ore that might still hold valuable minerals. On occasion, we even find a cache of high-grade. We bring anything decent back down the mountain. Then it'll get shipped off to a mill and smelter in another town, where modern technology can extract more from these rocks than the mine could in years long past. It's not much of a living. And once winter really sets in, we won't be able to work up here at all. It'll be odd jobs on Main Street until spring melt.

At least my ankle is feeling better. I end up going back to town with a single rock rattling around in my pocket. Hip, hip, hooray for me.

By late afternoon, Main Street is deserted. Many of the storefronts are dark, and I see distorted reflections of myself as I pass.

Powder Ridge used to be something. Or so they say. The bank is a grand edifice of sandstone, complete with a pointed tower that stands out over the rest of the street. But there's no bell inside anymore. I pass the former opera house, which these days is just a run-down movie theater. Once, there were over three thousand people who called this place home. Now it's more like five hundred.

I've heard about girls working in factories building ships and airplanes. I've seen those *Rosie the Riveter* posters, with her curvy bicep and perfect makeup. Women are even signing up for Uncle Sam and shipping out overseas—Army nurses, Coast Guard Reservists, the WACS and the WAVES. It's no surprise to me that us gals can hold our own, though I doubt we'll get much credit in the end. I've thought about joining up myself. But I'd probably wash out. I've never been one to take orders from strangers.

In Powder Ridge, women have been taking over men's jobs too. The only difference is that the men's jobs here weren't all that desirable to begin with. Plenty of guys and gals alike have left for better horizons. When the war started two years ago, there were only a couple dozen guys between eighteen and forty-five left in Powder Ridge at all. They enlisted or got called away one by one. Until only my brother was left.

For many reasons—both personal and political— Nate would have been first in line to give Hitler a kick in the blitzkrieg. For years, we've heard about the unimaginable things happening to Europe's Jews under the Nazi regime; the news has only gotten worse as the war wears on. Nate has never backed away from a fight. But he wouldn't leave me and our parents by choice. We all rely on him. Or, we did. Now my parents rely on me. The little sister, the second fiddle. The girl who has never been good enough on her own.

Nate, I wish you'd come home.

Down the middle of Main Street, there are two deep furrows in the snow where somebody's driven through. I walk in one of the ruts to the assay office. The bell tinkles as I come in. Abby Spivak looks up from her game of solitaire. There's music playing from a radio set; a Billie Holiday tune.

"Hey, Abby," I say.

Her father ran the assay office until his draft card got called. The mining company didn't bother to send anyone else, so Abby covers the desk now. She seems distracted today, but as soon as she sees me she smiles.

She pushes her playing cards to one side of the counter. "Hello, Dinah. How was today's take?"

I show her my rock. She grimaces, but goes through the motions of weighing it on her fancy scale and peering at it through her eyepiece. Dusty balances and equipment sit on the shelves behind her. She sets two dollar bills on the counter and slides them over.

"That's too much," I say.

Abby smiles and winks. "There's a little extra from Terrance, too. He knows it's been hard with Nate gone."

I sigh, both thankful and embarrassed. Terrance shouldn't have to pick up my slack.

"By the way, how *is* Nate?" Abby asks.

She already knows that my brother wrote me. The assay doubles as the Powder Ridge Post and Telegraph, so Abby has a leg up on all the gossip in town. Also, I think she's been stuck on Nate since we all were in diapers. He's always been too busy taking care of me and our parents, never had much time for a girl. I probably should feel guilty about that.

I tell her about my brother's letter, which was long on pages but short on substance. But in my head, I'm thinking about the soldier I saw at the boardinghouse. I consider reporting him to Abby. Whoever he was, he shouldn't have been up there, and she's the closest we've got to a rep for the mining company. But what she says next derails my train of thought.

Abby leans her elbows on the counter. "Say, you know who got a telegram last week? Mrs. Gainsbury."

There's a sinking feeling inside me. We both know what that means.

"Last *week*? I didn't hear a peep about it."

"I was keeping mum to give her a chance to share the news. But I don't think she's told anybody."

I shake my head. Mitchell Gainsbury worked the waste rock at Cherry Mountain with Nate and me. He's a jokester, always laughing. *Was.*

My heart has lodged in the bottom of my throat, and I need a few moments before I can speak. "Is it official? They know for certain?"

She nods. "The telegram said he died a hero. He was a mensch if there ever was one. I'm sure gonna miss him."

"Same here."

"I'll let you know if I hear about a memorial." Abby looks down at the counter, and her eyelashes splay prettily. "But come see me if you ever want to reminisce."

There's a warm feeling in my stomach. I nod. I just might do that.

Mitchell, Nate, and Abby were close friends growing up, and they always let me tag along. Abby taught us all to shoot. Mitchell's mother forbade guns in their house, even toy ones. I remember how Mitch's hands shook when he fired off that peashooter. His kind, easy smile.

Jim Gainsbury, Mitchell's brother, shoveled the steps at my house just this morning. And I had no idea. I pick up the money from the counter and say goodbye, my mind still on the Gainsbury family. I wonder if there's a way to help them.

I find Mother at the kitchen table with a glass of gin and apple juice. "I was wondering where you were," she says. As if my schedule was some grand mystery. I set the bag of groceries on the table. There's a couple of carrots and onions, a packet of grayish chicken, and a potato with so many eyes that you can feel it watching you. Mother gets up without another word and starts on dinner, sipping her gin along the way.

I consider telling her about Mitchell Gainsbury. But there are some names we don't mention in this house. Actually, come to think of it, it's just the one name. Gainsbury.

I start taking off my gear and stowing it in the assigned cubbies. Mother keeps the house moderately clean—we must always be *decent*, she likes to say—so I try to oblige.

Papa is sitting on the sofa with a blanket over his lap. He's listening to the radio voices drone on and on, staring towards the window but not really at it.

"How's the world today, Pop?" I give him a perfunctory kiss on the cheek, hoping it'll brighten his mood.

No such luck.

"It's all going to shit," he says hoarsely. "Not like your generation gives a damn."

My pop's a regular armchair general. "Some of us do," I say.

"I didn't mean Nate," he adds.

I wish I could say that my father and I are close. That his mining accident five years ago made him realize the true value of his family. Turned his shriveled heart to gold. But the real world doesn't work like that. My father was a mean, demanding philanderer then, and a lot of the time he's a jerk now. The wheelchair has nothing to do with it. I don't even know why Mother married him in the first place.

Now that Nate's escaped, I wouldn't blame my brother if he never comes back.

Scratch that. I'd blame him forever. But he *will* come back. Even if it's just to get me. If I stop believing that, then I'm really out of hope.

Later that night, I find my mother asleep in an armchair, an empty glass in her hand. She's already put my father to bed. I move the glass and help her up.

"Mom, you should go to your room," I say. "You'll end up with a crick in your neck." I have no interest in hearing her kvetch about it tomorrow.

She murmurs something and stumbles off to her room. I follow to make sure she gets there. She slides into bed beside my father, and I tuck the blankets around her. I kiss her on the forehead. She smells like cheap gin and primrose toilet water. Her colognes of choice.

I'm turning off the lamp in the living room when I see Mother's photo album. It's lying open on the side table. She must have been flipping through it. It's full of photos from her childhood. It's one of her favorite pastimes; reminiscing to herself about all the things she's lost.

I pick up the album to put it away. She'll get in a lather if she can't find it. But the photo on the page stops me. I've seen it before without paying much attention, but today it makes an entirely different impression.

It's a soldier, one of those posed pictures that the army takes for the guys to send home. He's wearing an army uniform and helmet from the Great War. He has a clean-shaven face, a slight smile. The brightness in his eyes makes it seem like he's about to laugh. My mother's handwriting is beneath: *Edward Gainsbury, 1918.*

I know this face.

It should be impossible. But I'd swear it's true: this is the soldier who was outside the boardinghouse this morning. He hasn't aged a day.

4

Millie
1918

Gainsbury House is far grander than I'd expected. It's a lovely Queen Anne, complete with a wrap-around porch, colorful wood trimmings, and a round turret. I'm sure that to any other person this home would seem cheerful, especially given today's clear blue sky.

But the view stops me cold. There is a coal-black shadow looming over the house like a permanent storm cloud.

As we hurry up the front steps, Edward looks up and frowns. Almost as if he can see the shadow, too. But that's unlikely. I've never met any who see the things that I do—excepting of course those facing imminent death. For them, the veil is lifted. But Edward cannot be so close yet to the end.

Can he?

While I consider these unpleasant thoughts, Briony rings the bell. We're greeted by an apple-cheeked girl of about thirteen. She's the spitting image of Edward, only with a rounder face and long chestnut hair. But there's an air of exhaustion about her.

"Hello, may I help—" Her hands fly to her mouth, covering a delighted scream. "Edward! Edward!"

She jumps into his arms in a burst of renewed energy. The both of them are laughing and crying at once. Edward steps back, regaining his balance.

The girl returns to her feet. "How did you get here? You didn't tell us they were letting you come home from the hospital!" Her eyes are running over him again and again, as if she can't get enough. "How are you?"

"I'll answer all your questions, Grace, I promise. But Mother and Lydia—what's happened?"

"They're sick." She closes her eyes and shakes her head, like she's trying to focus. "They've been in bed for days, and the doctor's come every morning. He's already been here today and said they haven't worsened. They're sleeping now."

Edward sighs. "Thank God." He nods his head politely at Briony. "Mrs. Spencer, I think you've met my younger sister?"

Briony does a little curtsy. "Lovely to see you again, Miss Gainsbury. But I'm going to fly before I cause any new scandals. Give me a ring if you need anything, Millie. We have a telephone at my place. Just ask the operator." She squeezes my elbow and trots down the stairs.

Grace's apple cheeks turn rosy. I don't know what scandals Briony is referring to, but knowing her, there've been many.

"And this is Miss Millie Boylan," Edward tells his sister. "She's a nurse."

Grace's expression grows serious again when she realizes who I am. "Oh. Miss Boylan. We've been getting ready for you."

"I wish I were meeting you under happier circumstances," I say. "I'd best go inside and see to your mother and sister."

Grace leads us into the house. The home is lovely inside as well, full of plush carpets, exotic wood paneling, and chandeliers. Although the artwork on the walls is a bit more rustic. There are old photographs of mining scenes—men with pickaxes, horses turning great wheels.

Mr. Gainsbury must own some of the mining interests here in Powder Ridge. From what I've learned, the precious metals up on Cherry Mountain are the primary industry in this town.

We leave the suitcases in the foyer. Grace leads us up a grand staircase to the second floor.

"Where is Father?" Edward asks. He's out of breath from the climb. I myself feel my heart racing—Powder Ridge is much higher than Denver, and the air is thinner here than I'm used to.

Grace's eyebrows wrinkle. "Working," she says, as if this should be obvious. "But Rachel was here this morning! I nearly forgot. Do you want me to send word to her that you're back? I'm sure she'll come at once."

"That's all right," Edward says. "Perhaps later on."

I wonder who this Rachel might be. Not that it's my business to be getting into. I'm here to work, after all. Nothing more.

Grace stops at a closed doorway, nervously pulling at a lock of her long brown hair. "This is the sickroom. Mrs. Bishop is inside with Mama and Lydia while they're sleeping. That's why I had to answer the bell for you."

I glance at the door, checking for shadows. Signs of the nearness of death. But nothing seems out of order. "Have they suffered any nosebleeds?" I ask quietly. I'll get a full update from both Mrs. Bishop and the doctor later on, but I'm loath to disturb the ailing if they're resting peacefully.

Grace bites her lip and looks at her buckled shoes. "I don't think so," she says in a very small voice. "Mrs. Bishop and Rachel take turns sitting with them."

"And I hope precautions are being taken? Ventilation, face coverings and gloves?" I've brought supplies with me—more gauze for masks, paper cuffs to shield sleeves—but it'll do little good if the others have already been infected.

"Oh, yes. At least I think so. I'm not allowed in the room, but I stay out here and I always call Dr. Durham right away if they ask me."

Edward puts a hand on her shoulder. "You've done an admirable job," he tells her. "Miss Boylan is the only nurse who could possibly take over, and that's because she's world famous. She came all the way from Ireland to help us." He gives me a wink.

"Indeed," I say, touched by his affection for his sister. So he noticed my accent. I've lived in America for a dozen years and naturally picked up the local inflections, but sometimes I still let slip my origins. "But please, call me Millie. Both of you."

Grace manages a small smile. She points to the door directly opposite the sickroom. "This was supposed to be your room, Miss Boylan," she says. "I mean, Millie. But…"

I open the door, and immediately I understand the problem. There are trophies on the bureau, school pictures on the walls. A baseball and glove sit on the desk. And above the bed, in a display case, hangs a Colt revolver with a decorative ivory grip.

This must be Edward's room.

"There's no trouble, Grace," he says.

The bed has striped pillow cases. I can't help picturing Edward's head there as he sleeps. "No, I'll find another room, of course," I say, unable to meet his eyes. I back away from his bedroom and knock into him. I feel my cheeks flushing and curse myself. I'm rarely moved enough to blush, but when I do, my face turns red as Colorado sandstone.

"I won't hear of it," he says. "My room's the closest to the sickroom. I'll find a cranny to store myself. I take up less space than I used to, at least."

"Don't make a joke of it!" Grace emits a sudden sob and wraps her arms around her brother's neck. "I was so terrified when I got your letters. I thought you might die from your wound. And now with Mama and Lydia being ill…"

Edward murmurs a comforting response. I stare at the pointed toes of my boots, unsure if I should slip away. But Grace breaks away from her brother, wiping her eyes and putting on a brave face.

"I'll go find someone to bring your suitcases upstairs. Oh—and one more thing, Millie. Don't mention Briony or Mr. Spencer to my father, OK? Thanks."

She bounds down the stairs before I can respond. Edward just shrugs at me. "I don't know what that's about," he says. "But I'd do what she asks. The less my father knows about anything, the better."

"As you say." Grace is a sweet girl. Now that I'm here, I hope she can get some rest. I'm sure she's eager for a long kip. That, or time alone with her brother.

For the moment, I'm the one alone with him.

I'll admit, Edward has made a strong impression on me. I wish I could rid him of the shadows. And not *just* because he's a handsome soldier. Although, can you blame me for noticing? I've always had a weakness for a cleft chin. His brown hair is cropped close to his scalp on the sides, but it flops playfully over his forehead on the top.

I should urge him again to stay elsewhere, away from the sickness. Already there are too many people being exposed to Mrs. Gainsbury and her daughter. But I know that Edward will again refuse, and in truth, I cannot fault him for his steadfastness. I've been told I have a stubborn streak myself.

His light gray eyes are studying me closely. I search for something to say. "You could tell that I'm Irish? I thought I'd hardly any accent left."

"There's a lilt in the way you speak. It's quite nice." He lifts a hand toward my face, though he doesn't touch me. "And your hair—it's rather striking, if you'll forgive me."

I smooth my hair back into its bun. It's dark red, the same vivid color that my mother had. "Ah, so that's what gave me away." It's not that I'm ashamed of my origins. I'm from the village of Sneem in County Kerry, the loveliest, greenest stretch of mountains and farmland in existence, though I left when I was just nine. But I usually prefer to keep my personal story to myself when I'm on the job. Given my line of work, I try not to get too intimately acquainted with my charges.

I should use the same caution with Edward Gainsbury. Yet I've never encountered someone who so makes me want to flaunt my rules.

"I'll let you in on a secret," he says, his voice lowering. "Since you'll probably discover it anyway now you're staying in my room. My dream has always been to play professional baseball. I'm going to be the first one-legged man defending the Yankees' outfield."

"That's…ambitious."

He laughs at my surprised expression. For an instant, I see the boy he was before death cast its shadow upon him: vibrant, adventurous. Easy to laugh, even easier with a grin.

"No, that was a joke," he says. "I did want to be a baseball player, once upon a time. Anything to avoid working for my father. That's why I enlisted last year the moment I turned eighteen."

So he's only nineteen. I'm two years his elder. Yet he's nearly a head taller than I, with broad shoulders creating an admirable frame for his lean limbs. His nose is long and sloped; his cheekbones are angled, though there's no trace of whiskers on his chin. My face begins to warm.

Edward glances across the hall at the closed sickroom door. "My mother and Lydia..." His eyes blink rapidly with their ample lashes. "I thought I was leaving the danger behind me. Nothing is the way it's supposed to be."

"Then you and I both need to find our way here," I say. "Perhaps we can help each other."

Too bold, my girl, my mother's voice says in my head. Though she sounds more smiling than scolding. *You've always been too bold indeed.* But I cannot resist. Surely there's a way to banish those shadows from his brow. He has so much life in him yet. There must still be time.

Edward nods emphatically. "I hope that's so." He gestures toward the bedroom. "I can take my grandfather's gun from the wall if it makes you nervous. It was my thirteenth birthday present. My father had high hopes of making me a man."

"Looks like you succeeded on your own." I realize I've been staring at his chest, and my cheeks start to burn again.

I put my hand on the door knob, expecting Edward to withdraw. But he stands there looking at me until I return his gaze. His gray eyes are still burdened with worries, yet full of gentle humor.

Gather your wits, Millie. You have work to do. This is already shaping up to be my toughest assignment yet, and it's entirely because of the dashing lieutenant before me.

5

Dinah
1943

The next morning, I stop by Gainsbury House. The curtains are drawn over all the windows, and I'm not sure anyone's home. Actually, except for the shoveled sidewalk, the house looks far more neglected than I remember. Shingles are missing from the turret roof. The paint is chipped and peeling. The front window has a long crack. I can't even recall when I last came down this street.

Truth is, I've been damned selfish. I was sorry when Mitchell got drafted—he'd always been nice to me, a second big brother almost—but I didn't really give him much thought after he was gone. Nate was still here, and that was all I really cared about. I didn't come by Gainsbury House to see Jim or their mother. I didn't make sure that they had enough to eat. But now, the Gainsburys are all that I can think about. I guess it helps to have someone to look after—especially when I haven't got my brother to look after me.

I ring the bell and Jim answers. His hair is ruffled, and his shirt is untucked. "Hello, Dinah. Do you need more shoveling?"

"It's not that. I heard the bad news."

He nods, frowning. "Mama doesn't like talking about it, but I miss my brother. He's never coming home."

"I'm awfully sorry." I feel a twinge in my chest, a hint at the deeper panic Jim's statement gives me. *He's never coming home.*

"Can I come inside?" I ask.

"I don't know…Mama said…"

I can hear voices in a different room. "I'm here for another reason, too. I want to offer you a job. Would you like to work with me up at the mine?"

His face brightens. "Like Mitchell used to do? I think…I think I would like that. It's best to keep busy. That's what Auntie Liddy calls it—keeping busy."

"Exactly. You'd be plenty busy. We just need to convince your mom."

Mitchell and Jim are twins. But Jim was born with his umbilical cord wrapped around his neck and didn't get enough air for several minutes. The doctors said he'd never be able to live on his own. His mother's always been protective of him.

Jim lets me into the foyer. I keep my pack slung over one shoulder. The front rooms are dimly lit. I have to blink a few times, letting my eyes adjust. The air is shockingly cold.

"She's in the kitchen," Jim says.

I haven't been inside Gainsbury House in years. Mother forbade Nate and me from playing with the Gainsbury kids—something about her ugly history with the family—but of course we didn't listen. We went over anyway. As a child, I remember being impressed by the sheer size of the place, the cavernous quality of the rooms. I thought rich people's houses must all be like that; empty, quiet, full of old pictures like a museum. But now that I'm older, I can see what's missing. There's no sense that people actually *live* here. Just sparse furniture. Undisturbed dust.

We pass the staircase. It leads upward into darkness.

In the corridor, there's a beautiful painting of a woman. Heavy brush strokes of blue, green, and purple paint make her look both vibrant and sad.

Jim takes me to the kitchen, where his mother and another woman are sitting with cups in their hands. It's much warmer in here, almost oppressively so. There's an old-fashioned coal stove in the corner, and the walls around it are stained with soot. The smell of burned coffee stings my nose.

The two women look up. Jim's mother has obviously been crying. She stands and says, "Dinah! My goodness, what are you doing here?"

She's smoothing down her rumpled dress, trying to make herself presentable. *Decent,* Mother's voice intones in my head. *We must keep things decent.* But Mitchell's death is so far from decent that it makes me want to scream.

"I heard," I say awkwardly, "and I just wanted to say I'm sorry. Mitchell was a good friend to Nate. And to me. I wish there was some way…" My voice cracks and I feel like a sap. Who am I to walk into this house and be sad?

But his mother comes over to me and wraps me in a hug. She's crying. Sobbing, really, which embarrasses me. I hug her back tightly so I don't have to see her tears. "I'm so sorry, Mrs…." I realize I don't even remember her last name. Everybody just calls the whole family "Gainsbury," even though she must have a different surname from getting married.

She sniffles and wipes her face. "Mrs. Tate. But you can just call me Grace."

Jim is crying too. He's standing next to the stove. The other woman at the table gets up and puts her arm around him. "Oh Jimmy, my dear boy. Life has not been fair to us, has it?"

She looks like an older version of Grace—the same long nose, sturdy hips, and tanned skin, only her brown hair is graying at the temples.

"I'm Dr. Lydia Gainsbury," she says to me. "But I go by Liddy these days. Came the moment I heard the news." She lets go of Jim to shake my hand in both of hers. "You're a boyish one, aren't you?"

I tuck my messy hair behind an ear. It's chopped into a chin-length bob; I'd have cut it even shorter if Mother wouldn't pitch a fit. I don't care if folks think I look like a boy just because I wear my brother's old clothes. But I *am* a girl, whatever they may say. I'm just a different kind of girl.

"Don't mind me," Lydia says, laughing, "my mouth tends to run. You're the first person to come offer condolences, you know that? I don't know what's wrong with the people in this town."

"That isn't fair," Grace says. "We haven't made any announcements. I wasn't ready."

"It's just like what happened all those years ago. After we lost Edward. Tragedy struck our family, and all our friends scattered."

"Liddy, *please*. Plenty of families lost someone then. Dinah Weller doesn't want to hear about our troubles."

Liddy looks at me sharply, and there's a new scrutiny in her eyes. "Weller? I remember your parents. How is Rachel doing? Been a very long time."

Doesn't sound like the memories are very fond. "My mother's fine, thanks. Who was Edward?" I ask, trying not to sound too interested. I think of the photo book in my pack. It's my mother's, the one she was looking at last night in the living room. Should I take it out? Show it to them? But now that Liddy's mentioned my mother, I hesitate.

"He was our brother," Grace says. "Mitchell always admired his uncle, though they never got the chance to meet." She clears her throat and goes to the stove, fiddling with the kettle.

"Edward was a lieutenant in the army at just nineteen," Liddy says. "Won a field commission, which is rare, you know. And he was so kind to us, too. Why are the best men taken so soon? No offense to our dear Jimmy, of course."

Grace is noisily filling the kettle at the tap. It's clear that she doesn't want to discuss Edward anymore, though Liddy doesn't seem to realize it. I quickly bring up my other reason for coming today.

"Now that Nate has gone to war, I was hoping that Jim could work with me up at the mine."

"I'd like to," Jim says. "It'll be like Mitchell used to do."

We discuss the idea for a few minutes. Grace is hesitant, but Jim is enthusiastic about the adventure of it, and that helps convince her.

"I just hate for you to be gone so often," she says to Jim.

"It's better for young men to have freedom, though." Liddy pats Grace's arm. "They need time to themselves. I'm here now, so I can keep you company."

Grace sighs. "We can try it for a week and see how it goes. Thank you, Dinah. I think I'm going to lie down for a bit." She hugs me goodbye, which surprises me. But it's welcome.

Liddy offers to walk me out. "How long will you stay?" I ask her.

"For good, I expect. There's only the three of us left in the Gainsbury clan now, so we'd better stick together."

In the corridor, Liddy sees the way that my eyes pause on the painting.

"That's a portrait of our dear mother," Liddy says. "She's passed. Our father too, though Grace didn't paint any portraits of him. He bought us this house, but he was a cheat—in every aspect of his life."

I can understand how that feels. "I'm sorry."

Liddy takes my arm and steers me into a sitting room. "You were asking about Edward earlier. Here, I'll show him to you."

There are family pictures here, a whole wall of them arranged over the fleur-de-lis wallpaper. Liddy points to the same portrait that's in my mother's album: Edward Gainsbury in his lieutenant uniform, his eyes still lively despite the age of the photo.

"He is a charming one, isn't he?" Liddy asks.

I can't suppress a chill as I think of him out in the snow yesterday. The sound of him climbing the wall of the boardinghouse. But that's silly, I tell myself. It wasn't the same fella. Just someone who looks like him.

Wearing the same uniform.

"Did he have any children?"

Liddy laughs. "I certainly hope not! Our father would've been livid. Edward never married and never mentioned any mistakes. He's too smart for that." Her brow wrinkles. "*Was*, I mean."

"How did he die?"

Liddy touches Edward's collar in the picture, as if she's straightening it. The pause lengthens, and then finally she answers my question. "It was the Spanish flu. He came home wounded, already so weak. Our mother and I were sick with it, and within days Edward had contracted the illness and died. It was a very rough time, as you can likely imagine. I'm sure I would have died from the grief alone if it wasn't for Grace. I'm here to return the favor. No matter how hard it is, she'll have to let go of what's passed."

Then Liddy smiles and glances around the room. "Perhaps I can spruce things up a little, too. My sister is clearly not one for decorating."

We say goodbye at the door. I'm halfway down the block before I realize the strangeness of something she said. *He is a charming one, isn't he?* She was speaking in the present tense.

6

Millie
1918

My mother was a nurse before me, and she's the one who realized my talent. She worked at a charity clinic in Denver providing care to the city's most unfortunate. The clinic occupied a second-floor space in one of the buildings along Larimer, one of Denver's roughest streets. So we saw mostly fallen women, orphans, chronic alcoholics and the like. It's where I met Briony. Where I learned from a young age about humanity, about suffering. And I began to see another face shadowed over those who would soon die.

I remember her very clearly; the woman I first helped to pass over. Ester. She was carried in from a local brothel with a cancer in her belly. The pain was nigh unbearable but we had little ether or morphine to give, and I'd sit with her of a night to distract her from it. She had long red hair like mine. Ester had taken a liking to me because I looked like a sister she once had, long ago. I was thirteen years old.

"I wasn't always like this," she often said. "If you could only know what troubles led me here." I would ask her to unburden herself, though she never did, at least not to me. But day by day, a shadow grew over her, as if her mental anguish had manifested in the air. It was like a spot of spilled ink that slowly bleeds into a sheet of paper. A dark caul that hung over her, blocking her from the light. Yet when I asked my mother, she claimed not to see it.

Each day, Ester's face got harder to see. Yet I noticed that, whenever I touched her cheek, the caul would shift to avoid my fingers. It always returned and was even darker the next time I would see her. I began to see the shadows over other patients, too, though far fainter. I did not know yet what these shadowy portents meant: that something monstrous was lurking, hoping for a chance to strike.

Ester died on New Year's Eve. I was brushing her thin hair—she liked that especially—when the pain seized her. This time, it wouldn't let go. She was a poor wounded creature trapped in the jaws of some relentless, vicious thing. I watched her remaining strength drain away along with the color of her skin. I called out for my mother to come, but Ester closed her fingers around my wrist to keep me at her side. It must have taken every last bit of her strength.

"Don't leave me alone with it," she said. "I'm afraid."

The room was already dark, though light spilled in from the window with the New Year's celebrations in the street below. The shadows had grown so thick over her head that I could barely see her. But as I bent over her, two pinpricks of ghostly light appeared on her face. They were eyes.

But they were not Ester's eyes.

Appalled, I put my hands on either of her temples, trying to wave the thing away. The eyes closed and disappeared. The shadows fled. I could see the relief that overcame her features. Ester looked at me with her own hazel eyes—eyes that were still beautiful despite all her sorrows—and she smiled.

"Thank you," she whispered.

I kept my hands upon her face. She held my gaze. We stayed just like that until the fireworks began to crackle outside, and she was gone.

When I stood on wobbly knees, I found my mother in the room. She'd heard my calls for her and witnessed what transpired. She couldn't see the shadows, of course, but she had seen enough. I fell crying into her arms and told her everything.

"You have a gift," she told me that night. "It's up to you whether to use it. But such things always come with a cost, and you're too young yet to fully understand that price."

I've thought of that night often. The warning in her words. But I had eased Ester's suffering. Of that, I was sure. How could I not use such a gift?

Just a few years later, I helped my own dear mother pass over. Cancer took her, too. I am old enough now to better fathom the costs of what I do. It takes a great toll to know death on intimate terms. But I have never regretted my choice.

Not yet.

My first day in Gainsbury House, the mood is tense but quiet. I familiarize myself with Mrs. Gainsbury and Edward's sister Lydia: their histories, their humors, their sources of comfort. Dr. Durham stops in, checking over my work with a critical eye before heading off to other patients.

The mother is a pretty brunette of around forty years old and seems to have a delicate constitution. Beth is her name. She has a kind smile and whispers many "pleases" and "thank yous" despite her coughing fits. The poor mite is so weak that the coughs shake her nearly out of bed. Her eyes are bloodshot and her skin is lightly tinged with blue, a common symptom of this disease. Blood-tinged sputum foams from her mouth and nose, and I must replace her gauze mask frequently.

There are shadowy cauls over both sick women, but they are thin yet. I think there is some reason to hope for a recovery, which surprises me. It's not what Briony led me to believe. But of course, now I'm here, I'm committed to doing everything for them that I can. Perhaps I can help banish the darkness from this house entirely. I begin to let myself hope.

The morning after I arrive, Edward comes to the doorway of the sickroom. I've just been singing "When Irish Eyes Are Smiling." Beth loves the song; I heard her trying to hum it earlier between coughs. My own mother used to adore singing it too. She purchased the sheet music and would play the melody on a neighbor's piano. The song brings back memories of her, both fond and bittersweet.

I've urged Edward to stay away for his own sake, but he says he's already been exposed to influenza in the army, which has been rife with the illness. I've convinced him to confine himself to the hallway, though he refuses to stay away altogether. It helps, actually, because Lydia asks after her brother constantly whenever he's not visible.

I worried at first about the shock that Edward's sudden reappearance would cause for my patients. But instead, he's raised their spirits. He's shown them his prosthesis, and he often jokes about his time in the army camps and the hospitals. I listen to his stories just as raptly as his kin. The glances of his pale gray eyes give me a private thrill. He doesn't hint at the hardship he must have endured. But I see it there in his every faraway look; every cringe when he stands too long. When he stares with concern at his ailing mother and sister. Thankfully, they don't seem to guess at how much he's hiding. I wonder if he might share these secrets with me, if I asked him. But I don't know if I should. I still wish to help Edward, yet I'm doubtful about how best to proceed. Especially when I already have responsibilities to his family. I worry that my attraction to him is clouding my judgment.

"How are my ladies this morning?" Edward asks through his face covering. He sits in a chair that Mrs. Bishop placed for him on the landing.

"We're brilliant, now you're here," Lydia rasps, and then begins to cough. She is both good natured and quick with her opinions. A girl after my own heart indeed. This morning, she is propped listlessly against a pillow. Like her sister, Lydia is a feminine version of Edward, even down to the small cleft in her chin.

Edward has just settled into his chair when he bangs his fist against the arm rest. "I was going to read aloud, but I forgot the book on the kitchen table. Of all the damned—" He bites down on the curse and casts a hateful glare at his cane.

"I'll get the book," I rush to say. Edward nods gratefully, relaxing back into his chair.

I squeeze past him to head downstairs, carefully leaving my apron in a box I've designated for this purpose.

When I enter the kitchen, I find the elder Mr. Gainsbury pacing there. "Nurse," he says. "I want an update on my wife's condition. Remove that blasted mask, will you?"

For five minutes, he drills me with questions. Again, I have the sneaking suspicion that Mr. Gainsbury is not aware of my specialization in terminal patients. I remind myself to ask Briony about this later—possibly there's been a miscommunication? He seems to think I'm a regular private care nurse. I expect he didn't want to entrust his family to the same emergency hospital to which the common folk of Powder Ridge have been assigned.

He doesn't even ask about Lydia. But I assure him I'm doing all I can for both my patients. Finally he releases me, and I grab the book from the table.

As I pass through the entryway, there's a knock at the front door.

I pause, wondering if I should answer it. Grace comes running down the stairs. She throws open the door, revealing a girl in a wide-brimmed hat.

"Rachel!" Grace exclaims.

Ah, the mysterious Rachel that Grace mentioned yesterday. She's tall and pale-skinned, with her black hair in a short, wavy bob. She's wearing a simple green blouse and a narrow, long skirt, but a peacock-blue sash shows off her slender waist. She's nowhere near dowdy, yet not too fashionable either. She's lovely.

"Millie, would you get Edward?" Grace begs me. "He'll be so excited that Rachel's here!"

I go upstairs. "I believe you have a visitor," I say, unable to hide the disapproval in my voice. The Gainsburys seem determined to bend the town's health regulations. But I suppose Rachel was already here frequently before I arrived.

Neither Lydia nor Beth responds, but I sense their sharpened attention.

Grace calls up from downstairs. "Edward, come down! It's Rachel!"

His eyes are a bit panicked. "Won't you join me, Miss Boylan?"

"This seems like a family matter," I say quietly. "I've no wish to intrude."

"Rachel? Oh, no. She's not family exactly. I mean…" Edward walks with me farther down the hallway. He pulls down his face mask and lowers his voice. "Her father used to work for my father. After her parents died when we were fifteen, she lived with my family for a year until an aunt came to be her guardian. But now, well, there's a certain awkwardness."

So she was his sweetheart, perhaps? And he's nervous about their reunion.

"Please," he whispers, squeezing the top of his cane. "You said we could help each other, didn't you?"

I can't say no to those eyes. "All right."

I go to the bathroom for a thorough wash-up. My hair has escaped its bun, and I carefully tuck it back into place. I know I'm being vain, but I can't help it with a beauty like Rachel around.

In the parlor, Rachel stands up from the sofa when we enter. She puts a hand to her chest. "Oh, Edward. I can hardly believe it. It's so wonderful to see you!" She rushes over to him, perhaps to embrace him or take his hand, but she stops short when her eyes land on his cane.

I expect Edward to make some kind of joke about his missing leg, but he only smiles and nods a greeting. "Rachel, this is Millie Boylan," he says. "The nurse who's helping my mother and sister. Miss Boylan, this is Rachel Kohler."

"You were caring for them before I arrived?" I ask Rachel.

"I was," she says stiffly, not meeting my gaze. She only has eyes for Edward.

"That was kind of you. I hope you've taken precautions to limit your other contacts? In my experience this influenza is quite—"

Rachel waves a hand. "You're new to Powder Ridge, so I don't blame you for not understanding. Near everyone's been exposed. I already recovered from a bout myself, a couple of weeks ago. We've been lucky so few here have died. The worst is past."

But is it? I think. I may be bold when the situation warrants, but I know how to be cautious, too. Hard-won experience has taught me that.

For several minutes, they discuss the health of Mrs. Gainsbury and Lydia. Soon, Rachel steers the conversation back to Edward. "You'll join me for dinner soon, won't you?" she asks him. "I mean, once your mother and Lydia are well. It's just that I want to hear everything about what it was like over there. It must've been thrilling. You have no idea how much I've—I mean, we all have missed you."

Edward looks down at the rug. Grace puts her small arms around him. "Tell her how you got your field commission," the girl begs. "He led twenty-seven men to safety after all the officers had been killed."

Reluctantly, Edward tells the story for the third time today. Despite my promise to stay, I slip out of the room at the first opportunity. I've seen these kinds of reunions before. There's awkwardness at first on both sides. But before long Rachel will assure him that she doesn't care about his injury, and Edward will fall in love with her all over again. Admittedly, my imagination is writing an entire story when I barely know the prologue.

And the only refuge I have was once Edward's bedroom. Truly, there is no escape.

I ready some soiled masks to boil in the kitchen. Then I retreat upstairs, flop onto the bed and close my eyes. I was awake all last night watching over my patients. I just need a few moments' rest.

I dream I'm inside a spider's web. Everything is dark, too dark to see, and it's absolutely silent. But I can feel silky filaments spinning around me. Fixing me in place. The mandibles of some horrible creature poke and prod at me. Looking for a way inside.

I wake up gasping. There's a sharp rap at my door.

"Millie!" Grace says. "Millie, help! Mother can't breathe. She's turning purple!"

7

Dinah
1943

On our first day of work together, Jim and I hike up
to the mine. Turns out, he has an impressive baritone.
We duet "We'll Meet Again," which brings a sting to my
eye even though the song is cornier than cornbread.

When we get to the stable, Terrance and McGrady
are already there. I feed BT a few carrot ends that I
brought with me and rub his lumpy snout. BT is short for
"Bear Turd." But don't look at me, I didn't name him.
That's Terrance Jameson's weird sense of humor. BT is
seventeen, just like me, which for a donkey is middle-
aged. But he's still spry. Every day, no matter the weather,
he climbs up and down this path carrying supplies and
equipment.

"Jim's gonna work with us for a while," I say.
Terrance offers Jim a cup of java, which Jim gratefully
accepts. McGrady only grunts.

"Hear you've seen the ghost over at the bunkhouse,
Dinah Weller," McGrady says in his gravelly drawl. He
always calls me by my full name, and it always sounds
sarcastic coming out of that toothless mouth. Either he
doesn't know that there's snot frozen in his beard, or he
doesn't care.

McGrady's been working up here at the mine since
he was a child, breathing in the dusty air in the mine
shafts. Back then, they used children to squeeze into tiny
spaces that the grown men couldn't reach. He's got a
persistent, phlegmy cough from those days. Terrance said

that McGrady's family used to be important around here, but they shunned him because he was illegitimate. I used to feel sorry for him. But that was before I got to know him.

"There's no such thing as ghosts," I say.

"Don't get your titties in a twist," McGrady quips. "Oh wait, I forgot you don't got any."

"Now that's goin' too far, Sean," Terrance says disapprovingly. "Let her be."

I finish my coffee and set down the cup. "C'mon Jim, let's get started." Jim gives BT another pat and then we head outside into the cold.

"That man doesn't seem very nice," Jim says.

"You mean McGrady?" I choose a sledgehammer from the stack beside the stable for myself, then a larger one for Jim. "You're right. He's all wet. Stay away from him, all right?"

"Sure," Jim says. "You too."

I laugh. "I usually try to stay as far away from that smelly S.O.B. as I can." When Jim asks what "S.O.B." means, I change the subject. Instead I tell him about the ore we're looking for, how small to break up the rocks, that kind of stuff. But as we head over to the mountainous waste piles, I'm watching the boardinghouse from the corner of my eye. Waiting for something to move.

I don't see anything, but still, yesterday's events are gnawing at my stomach just as much as Terrance's acidic coffee. I remember those two handprints on the third-floor window. Almost like they *wanted* me to see them. Was it a taunt? A question? A warning?

Nate's and my belongings are still up there. Suddenly I can't stand the thought of it. That crate is filled with all the stuff that we've collected since we were kids. And it's just sitting in that rotting third-floor room for any no-good nobody to steal. Or for McGrady to paw through, if he somehow hauls his girth up to that window. Ghosts my ass.

No. I can't leave it there. Nate deserves better than that.

"Say Jim, think we could take a little detour?" I ask.

"Shouldn't we get to work?"

I head toward the boardinghouse. "I just need to make a quick stop over here. For Nate, you know?"

"OK, if it's for Nate. But Dinah." He's stopped, his boots buried to the ankles in snow. "Isn't that the bunkhouse? That man said there are ghosts there."

I glance forward at the old building. It looks more tilted today than ever. Patches of dark red paint remain here and there, as if blood is seeping from the wooden siding. The glass in the last few windows is the same fathomless black as a raven's eye.

I laugh and the sound is stilted. "Oh now, there's no such thing as ghosts. McGrady was just pulling your leg."

But I'm carefully examining the snow bank at the building's base. There was fresh snowfall last night, so if that soldier came back, I'd see his footprints. But there are none.

We tromp closer through the snow, trying to keep our balance along the way. I take off my pack.

"I left some things up in that room," I tell Jim. "I just have to climb up and get them. When I give you the signal, stand clear—I'll toss them down." I point to the deep snow bank that's in the building's shadow.

"All the way up there? Are you sure?"

"This is just something that I have to do." Nate would understand—I get this way at times. An idea starts buzzing in my head, and the only way I can swat it is to follow it through.

I start to climb. Jim is sniffing his nose, the way people do outside in the cold. I'm glad I can hear him. It makes me feel secure. Nobody's going to sneak up on me this time. If that Edward Gainsbury look-alike is really out there, he didn't seem anywhere near big enough to be a match for Jim.

The building creaks as I make my way up. I reach the third floor, edge across to the window, and look inside. My breath makes a circle of fog on the glass, but I can tell that everything's just as I left it the other day. My crate is tucked out of sight.

"Still OK, Jim?" I call out.

"Yes, Dinah. Please come down soon?"

"I'm planning on it." I slide up the frame and shimmy inside.

The room is even darker today without the sun shining through the opposite windows. The smell of frozen dust threatens to make me sneeze. At first, I don't move away from the wall. I bend down slowly to look beneath the furniture, but the floor is in shadow.

I let out a slow exhale, forcing myself to calm down. I'll just make this quick. Then I'll never have to come back here again. I crawl over to the brass bed frame and reach for the crate.

There's a creaking sound. I go still.

It sounded like a foot stepping on a loose board. I'm holding my breath. I hear the sound again: the long, slow groan of the wooden floor as a foot treads upon it.

It's coming from the next room.

I squeeze my eyes shut briefly, then open them again. There's nothing in the next room. *You're imagining it*, I tell myself. Old buildings creak. Nothing to it.

But the lump in my throat is so big that I can't swallow around it.

I slide the crate out from beneath the bed frame. I lift off the lid. Nothing's been disturbed. *The Time Machine* is still lying on the very top. I take an armful of books and go to the window.

"Jim!" I yell down. "You ready? I'm going to throw down the first few books. Shake off the snow, OK?"

He stands back, nodding. I toss down the stack of comics and pulp novels, cringing when they scatter everywhere. But Jim runs to collect them.

Nate would probably be laughing his guts out if he could see me right now.

When we brought that crate up here, we never would've thought that the building would get so bad. We were just twelve and thirteen, savoring our new freedom. Our father had worked at the mine since before we were born, and after the mine finally closed about a decade ago, he kept working as a scrounger. Then one day, he fell on the site—dropped straight into a vertical mine shaft where the barriers failed.

When we took over Papa's job, Nate and I spent half our time exploring. Terrance, McGrady and the other men working the waste piles didn't have any patience for minding kids, so they left us to ourselves so long as we kept away from the more dangerous areas. The boardinghouse was our favorite. We were small enough to squeeze past the boards that had been nailed over the ground floor's doors and windows. Most of the furniture had been left behind; there were pictures of ladies in nightgowns on the walls, pillows still on the beds, even a stray boot or pair of overalls hung behind a door. The stairwell doors were padlocked, but we found a cupboard staircase behind the kitchen. We had the run of the place back then.

In the third-floor common room, I gather another armful from the crate. "Look out!" I yell to Jim, and throw down what I've gathered.

These aren't just things that we've collected. They're memories of my life with my brother. Our collection of *Captain Marvel Adventures* is here. Nate's first baseball glove, and my rag doll that Mother said I was too old for. I find the spyglasses that we ordered from the Sears & Roebuck catalogue. I think of Nate wearing them, making me laugh with his secret agent act, and I smile for a brief moment.

I turn around for more, and there's the creaking again. Louder this time.

I stand very still. My nose is starting to run, but I don't dare move to wipe it.

There's another creak. It's coming from the next room, just like it was before. Then I hear slow, plodding thuds. Like the sound of boots walking across a wooden floor.

There is someone in the hallway.

I feel a scream coming out of me, and I clamp my teeth down against it. I heft the entire wooden crate up into my arms. I bring it to the window. My arms are trembling, and books are spilling out and careening into the air. It won't go through. Dammit, it won't go through. I force myself to pause, even though I'm breathing so hard I can barely think. I can't even tell if I hear the footsteps anymore. My blood's moving too fast, rushing in my ears.

I grab the lid and fit it onto the crate, snapping it closed. I push the window up as high as it will go. This time, I turn the box on its side and it slides easily through.

"Dinah?" Jim asks from below.

"Stand back!" I push the crate into the air, hoping that its remaining contents will survive the fall. I'm about to climb onto the windowsill—to get the heck out of there—when the window pane comes crashing down. It almost smashes my fingers before I jump back out of the way. My behind lands on the floor. There's a cracking sound, and this time I *know* it's me causing it. The floorboard underneath me is buckling.

I scramble toward the window, gasping. I spin around so my back rests against the wall. Cobwebs are starting to knit at the corners of my vision. All over the room, the sofas and chairs look like hulking monsters in the dark. I can imagine shoulders hunched, heads lowered to pounce. But nothing moves. The door is still closed. If someone was out in the hallway, they haven't come inside. I'm all right. Jim is waiting for me right outside. I just have to stay calm.

"Dinah?" I can hear Jim calling my name, even though his voice is muffled through the glass.

Resting my hands on the windowsill, I get up onto my knees, then stand. I try to push the window open. But now it won't budge. I try to wrap my fingers around the wood frame, searching for a better grip, but the windowpane is stuck in place. My breaths are coming quick and shallow, making circles of condensation on the window.

As the fog of my breath dissolves, two handprints appear.

"What—" I take a step back. The floor creaks in protest.

The handprints are still there, firm outlines on the glass. It's as if someone's pressed his palms to the window. But I can see through the glass, and nobody is out there. A funny squeak comes out of my mouth.

I glance over my shoulder, and two more ghostly handprints appear in a window on the opposite side of the room. And then in the half-broken window beside it. Small hands, no bigger than mine.

8

Millie
1918

Beth Gainsbury is not breathing.

I rush to the sickroom. Edward, Grace, Rachel, and Mrs. Bishop are all crowded around her. They aren't even wearing masks.

"Out," I say, retrieving the rest of my uniform. "Please, you all need to leave. Call Dr. Durham." Edward ushers them to the hall.

Lydia is crying in her bed. "Help her, for God's sake."

I lift Mrs. Gainsbury higher in her bed and attempt to clear her airways. Her face is indeed a bluish purple, giving her an appearance of cold, but her skin is burning to the touch. Her fever has spiked. She begins coughing violently, her little body seizing. I hold a handkerchief to her mouth. The phlegm is bright red with blood. She moans, dragging in a ragged breath.

"Will she make it?" Lydia asks weakly.

A stream of blood trickles from Beth's nose. I wipe it carefully away.

"Don't you worry yourself a moment," I say to Lydia. I soak a towel in cool water and lay it over Mrs. Gainsbury's forehead. The fit is over for now, but another will no doubt follow.

I go over to Lydia's bed to tuck in her quilts. Her fever is at a low simmer. "You musn't stress your mother or yourself further," I whisper to her. "Both of you need your rest."

The truth is far more dire. Beth Gainsbury will be lucky to see the morning. And if Lydia begins to panic, she won't last much longer.

I discard my paper cuffs, go to the bathroom to wash, and remove my apron before venturing out into the hallway. Edward and Grace are hovering by the door. Rachel has gone. Grace rushes to me and clutches at my hands.

"Oh Millie, will Mother be all right?" Grace asks.

"I can't say, dear." I wish I could reassure the poor lass, but I must reserve my energy for what's ahead. "Edward, I'm afraid Lydia must be moved. She shouldn't see this."

He nods slowly, and his gray eyes are intense on mine. He has seen enough hospitals and death to understand my meaning. "I'll see to it. I've sent word to Dr. Durham."

I return to the sickroom, leaving Grace sobbing on the landing.

The doctor comes and goes, advising me on treatment. I work through the night by Mrs. Gainsbury's bedside. Her coughing fits have increased until the poor woman's lips are constantly blue from the lack of air. Pillows prop her up to open her lungs, but it hardly helps. I retrieve a cotton pneumonia jacket from my supplies and place her into the padded fabric to keep her warm. Her face covering goes into the growing pile of soiled fabric in the corner; it'll all be burned later.

It's all I can do to keep the blood from her nosebleeds off the floor. It's shocking how quickly she's worsened. But this new influenza—Spanish flu, they're calling it—can take even the strongest patients in a matter of hours.

Then the vomiting begins.

Over Beth's head, the shadowy caul has grown thick. I don't pretend to understand these mysteries. But I've noticed that the shadows are especially drawn to those patients with the greatest doubts, regrets or fears. I think they feed off of suffering. And Beth is surely terrified.

I sing "When You Wore a Tulip" to her, letting the Irish lilt return to my voice. I know the comfort that a friendly word can bring, so I speak soothingly to her and stroke her hair as she vomits into the pan.

Her hands search for mine. The smell of bile and blood is overpowering in the room. The shadow is thick over Beth Gainsbury's face. The only light comes from a lamp beside the bed, and I can hardly make out Beth's features. She coughs. It sounds like she's choking.

"I'm here," I whisper to her. "I won't leave you. Don't be afraid."

But I don't know if she can hear me. Beth's hands are trembling. The shadows shift and move about her face, crowding together eagerly.

The second set of eyes begins to open.

9

Dinah
1943

I lunge at the window closest to me and try to pry the frame up from the sill. Open, please let it open. The handprints begin to move. First one hand, then the other. Repositioning on the glass. And then, slowly— as if it's swimming through thick mist—a face starts to appear. Looking in at me.

I scream just as the window slides up.

Jim is there, clinging to the outside edge of the sill. "Dinah? Are you OK?"

"Jim, what are you *doing* out there?"

"You didn't come out. I got worried. I climbed up just the way you did."

Jim could've fallen climbing up here—he still could —and it would be all my fault. Grace is trusting me to watch out for him. "Go back down," I say. "*Slowly.* I'll be right behind you." I grab a loose board and use it to prop open the window.

As I watch Jim climb down, I can still feel eyes on my back. I wonder if those other handprints are still in the opposite windows. But I don't dare look behind me. The moment that Jim reaches the snow, I climb out of the window and head down.

It was only Jim outside the window. His face that I saw.

But that doesn't explain those other handprints. Or the fact that, just before Jim opened the window, someone else's features were starting to emerge from the mist. Curved lips, a thin nose, wide eyes.

That face belonged to a girl. But it was no one I've ever seen before.

When I get back to the ground, Jim helps me gather up the rest of my scattered belongings. Somehow the crate survived the fall.

"Why did you scream when you saw me?" Jim asks. "Did I scare you?"

"I'm just jumpy today, Jim. Sorry about that. Thanks for helping me."

I find *The Time Machine* and brush the snow off. From over by the slag heap, there's the sound of metal clanking against rock. Terrance and McGrady must have gotten to work. Jim and I should too if we want to make any coin today. I can't seem to catch my breath, though.

Jim dumps a stack of books into the wooden crate. "I didn't know where the footprints were coming from," he says, "so I walked over to the trees, and that's when I realized you hadn't come down yet. So I decided to climb up there and check, and—"

"Wait, what footprints? Where?"

Jim frowns, and I regret using such a sharp tone. He points to the other end of the boardinghouse. "Round that corner over there. I thought I saw somebody before. When you were high up inside that window."

"Was it Terrance, checking up on us? Or that big hairy guy, McGrady?"

"No, he was younger. He had a sort of green coat on."

Hurrying, I stuff the last of my things in the crate and fasten the lid. On impulse, I grab my small rock hammer from my pack and stow it in my coat pocket.

"Could you show me?"

I follow Jim around the corner of the boardinghouse. The snow has packed down a bit since yesterday. Sure enough, there's a fresh set of bootprints here, leading off into the woods.

As I'm staring into the trees, I see a flash of olive fabric. Dammit, it's him. It was probably him walking around in the boardinghouse too, scaring me half to death. He's still following me, and I'm sick of it. With Jim next to me, I feel a whole lot more confident. In fact, I'm embarrassed to think of how scared I was inside the boardinghouse.

"Hey," I yell. "Stop!" I start to run after the army coat. I'm going to give him a piece of my mind—and while I'm at it, I'm going to find out who the heck he is.

"Dinah, wait," Jim says.

I stop at the edge of the trees. "There's some guy hanging around here who doesn't belong. We gotta go after him." Jim catches up with me after just a few paces. I add, "if we get separated, you follow our footprints back here and get Terrance, all right?"

We run headlong into the woods, following the trail.

10

Millie
1918

Quickly, I place my hands on Beth's cheeks. The gauzy darkness retreats from my touch. But the pinprick eyes do not close. Instead they open wider.

I feel them looking *into* me.

Tears spring into my eyes. I bite my lip so hard that I can taste blood, not just smell it in the room. Inside my head, I hear a rasping voice. It says my name. It's a thousand voices brought together into one.

"Beth, listen to me." I'm speaking haltingly. Gasping for breath. But I will not fail her. I will not. "Let my voice guide you."

Finally, the shadows begin to slide away from Beth's face. The coughing eases, and her expression relaxes. Her eyes lock with mine. I see so much sorrow there. But no fear.

"Tell my children I love them," she whispers. "Rachel, too." And then the change happens in her eyes, that loss of focus, and she is gone.

The shadows disappear as quickly as smoke.

I sit back, panting. A cold draft runs through the room. I still feel those pinprick eyes upon me. *We see you, Millie Boylan,* they seemed to say. *And we never forget a face.*

It is near midnight. I wash Beth Gainsbury's body and prepare her as best I can for tomorrow. In the morning I'll have to call the undertaker. But for now, I am spent.

I go to the bathroom to clean myself up a tad. The mirror shows me a grim visage. My eyes are bloodshot. My lips, chapped and dry. Did I really hear that voice speaking to me from the shadows? I don't know. Whether it is death itself, or some creature that keeps death's vigil, I can't say. But I felt its malevolence. I remember a line from the Bible: *My name is Legion, for we are many.*

And now, that creature knows my name. It has never looked at me with such cruelty, such recognition, before this night. Why was Beth Gainsbury different? I can't understand it.

Perhaps my mother was right; I still have a price to pay for using this talent of mine. Or it may simply be that I couldn't hide from those eyes forever. But now that they've seen me, should I continue on as if nothing has changed?

Out on the landing, I see light beneath a door at the end of the hall. I worry that either Edward or Grace is still awake, waiting for news. I pad quietly toward it.

The door is open by a crack. After a quiet knock, I push it farther inward. Edward is walking back and forth across the small study. One arm is crossed tightly over his coat, the other a fist around his cane. His hair and eyes are wild. That horrid shadow hangs over him, even darker now. I can tell he is in pain. But still, he keeps pacing.

He rushes toward me when he sees me, and I must put my hands on his shoulders to halt him.

"Is she?" he asks hoarsely.

I nod. "It was peaceful. I made sure of that."

"What do you mean, you made sure?"

I shake my head. I'm too tired. I'm forgetting myself. "I just mean, I made sure she was comfortable. I sang to her."

"She always loved to sing." Edward's face twists with anguish. "Oh God, Millie, how can this be?" He covers his eyes with his hand to hide the tears.

"I'm so very sorry."

He is falling forward onto me. I help him over to a wingback chair. "Where is Grace?" I ask. "She needs to know."

"Grace went to her room."

The lass is probably sitting awake, dreading the news. I know from experience that she'll want the truth as soon as possible. I go to leave. But then Edward speaks up again.

"I hate to ask your assistance, but I must," he says. "I cannot take this much longer."

I think he refers to his sorrow. But then I see what is laid out upon the desk, and I realize he refers to more than simply grief. There is a syringe kit, a rubber strap, and several amber colored vials.

Morphine.

I study him more closely. He's shaking, sweating. His brown hair hangs into his eyes. I'm beginning to understand. "When was your last dose?" I ask.

"Before breakfast. I usually have a dose in the morning, and again at night."

"How much have you been taking?"

"Only enough to—"

"*How much*, Edward?"

He tells me. It is bad. But morphine is a powerful substance, and its grip upon a man can take hold devilishly quick indeed. I know little about treating an addiction, but I've seen the way it works upon a person—whether strong or weak, young or old. The drug is like Spanish flu, laying low too many in its path.

"You'll need to be weaned from it," I say. "It could be dangerous to stop all at once."

"They already tried at the hospital. It didn't work."

"So Dr. Durham is writing your prescriptions?"

He hesitates. "I don't have a prescription. I can't get one anymore. I...stole these supplies before I left the hospital."

Oh, dear. This is worse than I thought. It used to be, anyone could buy a bottle of morphine-laced patent medicine at the local pharmacy. But in recent years the laws have changed. Now a patient needs a doctor's prescription. More and more people have been turning to illicit means to quell their need.

"Perhaps you shouldn't stop your doses just yet," I say. "You should talk to Dr. Durham first. You've just lost your mother."

"You don't understand. I'm not trying to cure myself. I'm not such a hero." He turns his face away from me in shame. The gauze-like shadows settle on his forehead like probing fingertips.

"The pain is more than I can bear," he says. "I see terrible things. Death is lurking everywhere, watching from the darkness. I wake in the night with my leg on fire, and *it's not even god-damned there.* 'Be a man about it,' that's what they told me at the hospital. But all the time I just wanted my mother. She didn't want me to enlist, you know. 'You're just a boy,' she said. 'You're my boy.' And now she's gone, and I know she was right. I'm so afraid. That's why...I need you to..."

The light in this room is already dim, but little of it reaches Edward's face. His cheekbones stand out in harsh relief. His eyes are just dark wells. Like the sockets of a skull.

"Edward, what are you asking me?"

11

Dinah
1943

There's another flash of olive between the trees. "That way," I whisper, pointing. But Jim's already falling behind me. I dash forward, desperate not to lose the soldier. He's been trying to get my attention since yesterday, and he's damn well got it. He's made it clear that I won't get any peace until I find out what he wants. I'm putting an end to this, now.

I follow his tracks in the snow. I clamor over an ice-slick boulder, then over a downed tree. When I reach an old ruined cabin, I pause and step carefully around it. Three of its walls have collapsed inward. There's a pile of splintered wood, rusted bedsprings, and rotting furniture. At first I think I've lost the tracks, but then I spot them on the other side of the cabin.

I run into a clearing. But there, the tracks abruptly stop. I whirl around, realizing too late what he's done.

He leaps out from behind a tree and tackles me.

We fall into the snow. I get a face full, and it burns in my nostrils. The soldier and I grapple with one another and with the snow, rolling again and again. I break away from him, pulling out the rock hammer. The soldier is standing now. We're both covered in ice and snow. His brown hair sticks up wildly. His eyes are wide, ringed with damp eyelashes.

"Wait," he says. "I'm like you."

That doesn't mean anything to me. I can hear Jim calling out, "Where are you?"

"Jim," I say, but my voice is just a croak.

"Please," the soldier says in a whisper. "I don't want any trouble."

I take a step toward him, hammer held high. He puts up his hands, warding me off. Only one of them is wearing a glove.

"Then why've you been dogging me? Why were you in the bunkhouse?"

"The—" He looks confused. "That old building? I wasn't in there. I was going to climb up the other day, but I ran when you started yelling."

"Liar."

"Dinah!" Jim calls. I wonder if he's lost the tracks.

"Dinah?" the soldier repeats. "You're a—wait, you're a girl?"

I scowl at him. The hammer droops in my grip, and that split second is all he needs. The soldier lunges. Both of his hands close over the hammer, wresting it away from me.

"Jim!" I scream. I put my arms up instinctively, ready for the blow, but instead he winds up his arm and launches the hammer away from us into the trees.

He backs up a few steps. He has the same hunted stare as a rabbit who's been caught away from its den.

"I thought you might be hiding, too," he says. "Avoiding the draft. I see that I was wrong. Please, just forget you ever saw me." He turns to go.

"Hold on, who are you? One of the Gainsburys?"

He spins around, his mouth open. I see the recognition in his eyes. The fear.

"Dinah! Dinah!" Jim careens into the clearing. He's panting, bending over with his hands on his knees. "Are you OK?"

"Sure, Jim. Everything's jake. Thank you for finding me."

When I look to where the soldier was standing, he's already fled.

12

Millie
1918

"My mother is gone from this world," Edward says. "And I am afraid I will try to follow her."

I look again at the vials spread across the desk. There is enough here to put him to sleep forever. Finally, I understand—he's asking me to stop him from giving in to grief. It's no wonder the shadows have plagued him. How can I turn away from such a plea?

I open the vial and prepare the syringe. Edward has already removed his coat. He's unbuttoning his shirt. I gasp slightly, not because I haven't seen a male patient undress—rather it's the shock of seeing *him*, Lieutenant Edward Gainsbury, in such an intimate state. He takes his arm out entirely, rather than just rolling up the cuff. The veins on the lower part of his arm are quite red and sore from prior injections. His skin is pocked with round scars. He points at the inside of his upper arm, where the veins are blue beneath his pale skin.

"Do it here," he says. "Please."

I slide the rubber strap just beneath his shoulder and tie it off. The dark hairs on his skin raise at my touch. His chest and arms are lean, well muscled. My eyes trail involuntarily from the hollow between his pectorals down along his stomach, where more fine, dark hairs meet his belt.

He sighs when the needle goes in. Closes his eyes. Leans his head back against the chair.

I am breathing fast, my heart thudding against my ribs. Turning away, I clean up quickly and wait until he is alert. It doesn't take long. He's well used to his dosage. I feel the wrongness of what I've just done—injecting an addict with the very drug that's controlling him. And not just any addict, but a man I cannot pretend to view dispassionately. No, I feel my attraction to him in the rapid coursing of my blood. The flare of heat at my core. I've doubted many things in my life, but I've always been able to trust my own intentions. Until now. Until him.

I stow the rest of his amber vials in my pocket.

Edward sits up and says, "Thank you. I *do* want to free myself from this." His cheeks color as he rights his clothing. "If you could help me."

"Dr. Durham might be a better choice." I stand, knowing it's past time for me to have left. I'm a nurse, but I shouldn't be *his* nurse. I lack a professional detachment when it comes to Edward.

"Don't go," he says. "I know I've already asked too much. But I don't want to be alone."

Self-consciously, I straighten the front of my skirt. "Perhaps you should call Miss Rachel Kohler. I'm sure she would sit up with you."

Edward cringes. "Rachel has always been a good friend. When she lived with us that year, I'd have called her my best friend. But I'm not in love with her. Not the way that she hopes."

There's no appropriate response that I can possibly make, so I stay silent. I sit in a chair by the window, push back the curtain, and look out. The streetlights are dark. The moon is high and full and rising still.

I feel so drawn to Edward. It would be all too easy to surrender to that desire. I wouldn't be the first nurse to fall into the arms of a handsome, wounded soldier. The "lure of the khaki," some call it. But Gainsbury House has brought me closer to that awful, shadowed face than I've ever been. Those pinprick eyes have seen me. I'm afraid of what might happen if I choose to stay too long.

"Do you think Lydia will die too?" he asks.

"I really don't know." The shadows have marked her, but she could still recover. "Lydia is young and relatively healthy," I tell him. "But this flu takes the strong and the weak alike."

"I've seen that too," he says. "I survived it myself."

I lift my eyebrows in surprise. Newspaper articles say the illness has spread through military encampments and killed many soldiers. Edward did hint that he'd been exposed, but not that he'd actually fallen ill.

"It happened after I was wounded. Many of the fellows in my unit didn't make it through. This strain of influenza is like nothing the doctors have seen before, or so they said. Yet it spared me. So to come home and find Lydia feverish with it, and my dear mother...I almost feel as though *I'm* the one who brought this on them."

"You couldn't possibly have—"

"I know, I know. It's foolishness. They were sick already. But everywhere I look here, I see death. As if it's following me."

What can he mean? I come closer to him. His chest moves beneath his shirt as he breathes. I want to place my hand over his, but I don't dare.

"What exactly do you see?" I ask him.

He shakes his head, sitting up. His eyes move over the room, seeming to search for the words. "You can't imagine what it was like in the trenches. The mud and the stink and the suffering. I started to...see things. There were dark smudges hovering over the heads of some of the men. Many of these same men died soon after."

My breath catches. "The shadows?" I whisper.

He nods. "I know that it sounds like madness. I thought maybe it was. But I kept seeing it after I was wounded and through my time in the hospital. Smoke in the air, blocking the light whenever death was near. Sometimes it got so thick I could hardly see."

I place my hand over my mouth. I cannot believe it. He's describing exactly what I've witnessed.

"For a while, the morphine made the visions disappear," Edward continues. "But since I came home to Gainsbury House, they've returned. Even now, I feel something ominous hanging over me, darkening my thoughts. A curse—I don't know what to call it. But it's there. I feel the weight of it like it might suffocate me. And when I look into the mirror, I could swear that I see it." His fingers gesture at the air above his head. "Is it a delusion? Shell shock? Or could it be…real?"

Instinct compels me toward him, even as I know I shouldn't do this. For years, I've trusted no one with this secret. Yet my hands reach out for Edward's face.

His eyes widen. "What—"

I rest my palms against his cheeks. Immediately, the shadows around him begin to move away.

He looks at me in amazement. "I feel the difference," he whispers. "The room is lighter. My *mind* is lighter. How?"

"I don't know how to explain—" My answer cuts off abruptly when the air is pulled from my lungs.

The shadows—they're *touching* me.

At first they probe my fingers. Then the darkness rushes over my hands and up my arms. I can't move. My God, it *burns*.

I scream.

"*Millie*? What's happening?"

Edward reaches out for me, and somehow—perhaps by the same instinct that's driven me—he knows what to do. His hands find my face, imitating the way that I am holding onto him. The effect is immediate. The shadows on my arms vanish. I collapse forward onto him, sprawling across his lap. I'm shaking and crying, my skin still burning as if it's been scalded. But Edward doesn't let go of me.

"I saw them," he whispers to me. "You did too, didn't you? 'Shadows,' you called them? What are they?"

I can't answer him. There is some new force at work in this house, a darkness stronger than I've ever faced before. Those horrible pinprick eyes recognized me tonight; for the first time, the shadows have actually touched me. *Hurt* me. There's danger here, and not just for me. What if they attack Edward next time?

Since I lost my mother, this is a burden I have borne alone. And I *must* bear it alone, for my own sake. I know the danger all too well.

I push away from him and stand. "I didn't see anything."

Edward catches my hand. I cringe in pain, though he's holding me gently. My skin is bright red and raw. "You said we could help each other," he insists. "You've already done so much for my family. For me. But Millie, I've fought battles before. I've stared into the darkness. You needn't be alone with this. Let me help you."

"I…" I shouldn't. There are the risks I know—and others that I can't yet even grasp. The shadows have fled from Edward at the moment, but they'll no doubt return. I'd be a fool not to be afraid. If I'm smart, I'll get away from this house as fast as possible. Get away from Edward Gainsbury and whatever power the two of us share. The lad is addicted to morphine. He is facing intense struggles of his own. Death has its eye upon him.

But in Edward, I may have found someone—an ally, a friend, maybe even more—who might actually understand me. Could I really give up such a rare, precious gift?

Despite the pain, I squeeze Edward's hand, nodding my ascent. We're in this together now.

No matter where it might lead.

13

Dinah
1943

The next day, I don't see any sign of the guy in the army coat. *Forget you ever saw me*, he said. And you know what? That's exactly what I intend to do.

But all day, I can't shake the feeling that somebody's following me, just out of sight.

That afternoon, the house is strangely quiet when I get back to town. I take off my layers and leave them by the door. My boots are covered in slush, so I set them just outside. Mother will be furious if I let them melt into a dirty puddle in the kitchen.

At first, I don't notice that anything's wrong.

Dishes await me in the sink. My father is snoring in the living room while the radio patters endlessly. I don't bother turning it off. *Amos N' Andy* is like a lullaby to my papa.

There's no sign of my mother. Perhaps she's gotten a head start on her doses of gin today and gone to her bed. I shouldn't be surprised. McGrady dropped off his weekly delivery last night. He used to distill illegal moonshine during Prohibition, and now he makes cheap gin to sell to discerning individuals like my mother. They say he brews it up in his bathroom. I guess it's good that his tub is getting *some* kind of use.

After a quick wash-up and a change of clothes, I go into Nate's room. I have to stifle a scream at what I find.

I've been spending more time in my brother's room lately than my own. It's comforting. I thought my belongings would be safer here than they were in the boardinghouse. But now the wooden crate has been dragged out of Nate's closet, and its contents are scattered everywhere—books and comics lying open, pages torn, a box of cigarettes smashed. The spyglasses that Nate and I ordered from that catalogue? Broken into two pieces.

"Where is my memory book?"

I spin around and find my mother in the doorway.

"Those were our things," I say. "Mine and Nate's."

We're both whispering because we don't want to wake my father. But our words are every bit as venomous as if we'd screamed them.

"It's always *you*, poor *you*. But you're the thief. *Where is my memory book?*"

I've still got it in my pack. I didn't think to put it away. Why didn't I remember?

I'm trembling I'm so angry—both at my mother and at myself. The room is starting to tilt. I throw my pack at her.

"Have it, then," I say. "You've ruined everything else."

The bag hits her in the chest, nearly knocking her wizened frame to one side, but she grabs hungrily at the opening. She pulls out her photo album and gazes at it with relief.

When she's gone, I shut the door and turn to face the mess.

The spy glasses are beyond repair. But I tuck both halves into Nate's desk drawer. I gather the ripped pages and stack books. I hardly notice when my vision starts to blur; wet blotches appear on the cover of a comic. I wipe my eyes with my sleeve and sit on the floor beside Nate's bed.

I miss my brother. I miss when he'd wake me early on Sunday mornings to make flapjacks before our parents got up. How he'd make me laugh when I was feeling low, or after a fight with Mother. I'd trade all this junk in a second if it could bring Nate home.

The wooden crate squeaks as I drag it to me. I'm about to dump in the items I've collected when I notice the record.

It's sitting in the bottom of the crate. I don't remember any of the records from Nate's music collection being here, though. Did my mother tear through his box of jazz albums, too? But no, I can see his collection sitting right on his desk beside the record player, undisturbed.

I pick up the mystery record by the edges. Flip it over a couple times. The label is so faded I can't read it. It's a different size and color from Nate's other records, too. Looks old. I've definitely never seen it before.

I slide the record onto Nate's RCA. The machine hums gently when I flip the power on. I pick up the needle and set it down on the edge of the disc.

A tinny piano tune begins to play. The music is strangely slow. The notes sound like they're coming from someplace far away, yet they're so loud that each strike of the piano key makes me jump. I want to turn it off. But my feet are stuck in place, my hands frozen against my sides. Cold sweat begins to trickle beneath my arms. The music starts to speed up. The notes are becoming staccato. Wrong.

Someone cries out. But it isn't me. The door bursts open, and my mother's there, her eyes bulging.

"Stop it! Stop! What is the matter with you?"

She bats the needle aside, grabs the record, and flings it across the room. I run after it. I don't even know why I feel protective of the awful thing—maybe because my mother seems to hate it so much, and I'm committed to disagreeing with her. I scoop the record from the floor. There's a scratch down one side.

"You woke your father with that hideous noise! He was begging you to turn it off. Didn't you hear him?"

I didn't realize that it was Papa's cry I heard. I feel guilty for upsetting him. "I didn't know it would play that. But you can't just come—"

"No. I have had enough." My mother takes me by the arm and drags me through the house. She opens the front door and shoves me right out into the yard. My socks soak into freezing slush. I'm still holding the record.

"Get away from here," she shouts, loud enough for all the neighbors to hear. She's forgetting all about decency, and that's when I know that I've really done it.

I'm about to apologize when she throws my coat and my boots out, too. I suppose I should be grateful. "Don't come back until you can act like a *decent* human being," she says. Then she slams the door.

I knock at the Spivaks' front door. Their house is tidy and well-kept, its siding painted blue. There are flower boxes beneath the windows, though no flowers are growing there now. I trace a finger down the mezuzah that hangs on the doorframe.

Barbara Spivak answers. Her expression goes from curiosity to alarm when she sees me. "Dinah?"

"Can I speak to Abby please?" I've stopped myself from crying, but I know my eyes must be puffy and red.

They let me go into their bathroom to clean up. When I come out, my coat and boots are hanging by the door to dry. Abby hands me a cup of mint leaf tea. I sit down on a cushioned chair with a high back.

While I sip my tea, the record sits in my lap. I'm not sure what else to do with it.

"Dinah, what happened?" Barbara asks. She's wearing trousers and an oversized denim shirt that must belong to her husband. Her long black hair is pulled back in a tail. "Did you have a fight with your mother?"

My cheeks start to burn. I wish that my situation wasn't so easy to guess.

Barbara isn't a traditional mother. But she's the kind of mother I'd dream of having. She's an avid hunter, long board skier, and hiker. In the summer, she fishes in the local creeks. Any given day when we were growing up, Barbara would invite us to come along on her day's adventure. *And* she'd pack a kosher picnic basket. Abby would always groan and refuse to join. I don't think Abby realized how swell she had it.

"My mother sort of...kicked me out," I say.

Barbara's tongue clicks against her teeth. "That woman. I'm going to go have a word with her."

"No," I say quickly. "Please don't. She just needs to cool off."

Barbara shares a glance with her daughter. The two of them whisper a bit, and then Mrs. Spivak quietly leaves the front room.

Abby and I are alone.

Abby moves over to the chair right beside me. Unlike her mom, she's dressed in a swing skirt and a ruffled cotton blouse. Her dark hair is carefully curled and styled.

"What's the story with that record you're holding?" Abby asks. "Is it Nate's?"

I put my tea on a table. The words come spilling out. I'm speaking so quietly that Abby has to lean in to hear me. I half expect her to laugh. Or to dismiss it all as superstition or imagination or loneliness, the way that Terrance has. But she's nodding, and her eyebrows furrow in concentration as she listens. She's giving me that much, at least. And I *have* been lonely. Without Nate, I haven't had anybody to talk to. I never needed anyone else until he left. In fact, I got offended that Nate bothered to have so many friends when he had me. I think I'm starting to understand, though.

With just my mother and father at home, I'm suffocating. But what if, all these years, Nate was the one who couldn't get enough air?

I realize I've been quiet for a couple of minutes. Abby's eyes are unfocused, thinking. I can't tell if she believes me.

I think I'm being haunted. That's what I said, though I can hardly swallow it myself.

"I'll prove it," I say. "I could show you the bunkhouse. Or I'll play you the record."

"I don't have a player here. We'll have to go to the assay office."

It's late afternoon by now, and the streets are quiet. When we get to the office, Abby takes me into the back room. I set the record carefully atop the player on the desk. Neither of us goes to play it.

Abby cranks up the heater. "When you first turned up at my house," she says, "I thought you must've heard about the new letter."

"Letter?"

She goes over to the post office area, where there are labeled bins. Only a few of them have letters. She plucks one out and hands it to me. "Think it's from Nate?" she asks.

It's addressed only to me. The last one was addressed to my parents too. I rip open the envelope. Unfold the page.

Dear Dinah,

I'm either hot or cold over here where I am, and my buddies and me are either thrilled about it or cursing the stars. I'll let you pick, so the censors don't have to. I miss you. I love you. Say howdy to BT and don't let anybody get under your skin. Take some time away from Cherry Mountain. Love, P.F.C. Nate Weller, aka Your Big Brother

P.S. I hope this helps.

There's a twenty-dollar bill tucked inside the envelope.

I can't believe he's sent so much. I show the bill to Abby. She gawks at it. "Now ain't *that* a sight for sore eyes. Say, you want something to drink to celebrate? A smoke?"

The room is warming up quick, and the mood is considerably lighter now that I've got twenty dollars in my pocket. We shed our coats and sit down at a small table. We share a room-temperature bottle of Coca-Cola and a slightly-smushed Chesterfield that Abby had in her purse.

I notice a new poster pinned to the wall. "What's that all about?"

It's a caricature of Uncle Sam—complete with heavy brows and curling white hair—but with Rosie the Riveter's pretty face. The bold text reads, "Ladies, Powder Ridge needs YOU to volunteer for the Mountain Rescue Brigade! Now that our men are bravely fighting the baddies overseas, don't you think it's your turn to take up the fight at home? Contact Barbara Spivak to enlist!"

"My mother's latest project," Abby says. "It's admirable, of course. Somebody's got to do it. But she keeps pestering me to join. She won't even let me smoke in the house, but she's *more* than happy for me to smoke outdoors. Preferably while we're scaling some mountain or clearing an avalanche. Know what? I'd rather sit at home and knit hats for my pop overseas."

Abby's lips wrap around the Chesterfield. She's got dark eyes with flecks of gold in them. I never really noticed that before. Then her mouth hitches up on one side in a lopsided smile. She passes the cigarette to me. Her fingers brush mine, and a tingle passes from my hand to all my other nerve endings.

"You ever think of leaving?" I ask.

Abby is eighteen, already graduated. She did well in school—always top marks, fastest in the county when the district finally allowed a girls' athletic league. And she can shoot like Annie Oakley, even though she never seems to enjoy it. She could join up with one of the women's auxiliary programs.

"Leaving?" Abby says. "Only every second."

"But what about you and Nate?" I imagine the two of them taking off without me, and I feel a wave of queasiness that isn't just from the Chesterfield. Nate has never shown a particular preference for her. Yet I assume that they'll end up together. Abby is amazing. Who could stare into those gold-flecked eyes and feel anything else?

Abby's eyebrows knit, then she laughs. "Me and Nate? I don't think so. Your brother's swell, but he's not my kinda swell. No offense, I hope."

I'm too shocked to speak. "None taken," I stammer out. Nate's not her type? Then who is?

Abby is still looking at me, like she's waiting for me to say more. Then her eyes lower, almost bashfully, and takes a swig of Coke. "Now here's a real scoop: The mining company is thinking of shutting this place down for good." She glances around the back room. Her eyes linger on the crate for the ore rocks. There's hardly any there. "You didn't hear it from me. But if that happens, maybe none of us will have a choice about leaving. We'll have to park our tuchuses somewhere else."

I cough on my inhale and sit back in my chair. Smoke spews out of my nose. I shouldn't be surprised. But Powder Ridge has been dying so long that I got to thinking it would struggle on forever.

"Won't be long before Powder Ridge is nothing but another ghost town," Abby says. She takes the cigarette from my hands and stubs it out. "What do you say we listen to that record of yours? Find out if Powder Ridge already has some ghosts in it?"

Her tone is flippant, but she's put me at ease. She waits for me to turn on the player. Set the record spinning. I sit back down beside her, my shoulders tense. I'm clenching my teeth, waiting for the music to start.

But there's only a mechanical sound, like papers crinkling. No music.

"My mother scratched it. But it should still play." I get up and restart the record. The same happens. I restart it again. I'm starting to hyperventilate. I can't cry in front of her. I just can't.

Abby comes over and stops my hand. "Just let it play," she says softly.

We sit and we wait.

Finally, there's a voice. A girl begins speaking.

"I've seen death many a time, more often than I like to count. I know its face. So when I see the soldier in the dining car, I can tell right away that he's in danger."

14

Millie
1918

After Beth Gainsbury's death, Lydia's health takes a turn for the worse.

Lydia's new sickroom is downstairs in a small parlor. Edward had his sister moved here after Mrs. Gainsbury entered her final hours. So it's here that I sit now, reading a Jane Austen novel aloud as Lydia lies burning with fever. Her skin is translucent, and there are rings of red around her eyes that must be from crying, although she never seems to cry around me. At the moment, her eyes have fluttered closed. She is breathing shallowly but regularly. A dark pall of shadow hangs over her forehead like a veil.

Mrs. Gainsbury passed two nights ago, now. The skin of my hands and arms is still sore. Grace noticed it and asked what happened. I said I'd scalded myself on the hot tap in the bathroom. Edward overheard our exchange, and I saw the meaning in his glance. He wants to know more about this strange phenomenon that we've both witnessed. But I haven't been able to discuss the shadows with him further. In fact, Edward and I have discussed very little since that night.

Lydia still looks for her brother often. Right on cue, she says, "Edward?"

"He isn't here, dear. I think I heard him downstairs speaking to your father." Most of Edward's time has been taken up with arrangements for his mother's funeral. Twice a day I give him his morphine injections, each time slightly reducing the dose. But I haven't applied my hands again to his face, and Edward has not asked.

The truth is that I'm afraid. What if the shadows attack me again?

And if—or rather *when*—I must help Lydia with her own passing, what then?

Lydia blinks slowly. "I keep dreaming he's still at war. And we get a telegram." She turns her face toward the window, where the shades have been pulled back to let in some light. It only makes her features look more drawn.

In this room, there's a small sofa against one wall with framed pictures stacked on the floor beneath. An upright piano sits beneath a dust cover, and there's a gramophone box on a side table. Neither instrument looks like it's been played in ages. It's a room full of forgotten and unwanted things. I would have preferred that Lydia be moved to her own bedroom, but her father objected to that. Her bedroom is next door to his.

"Is Edward well?" Lydia asks. The cold compress has slipped from Lydia's forehead, so I re-wet it in a basin of water and lay it back over her skin.

"He's as well as can be expected," I say, which I hope is a fair answer while being suitably vague.

She scratches at her gauze mask. "But is there…any risk?"

"Any risk of him contracting influenza, you mean?" I turn the book over on my lap. She's right to be worried. I've thought about this many times myself. Officials have advised that patients with influenza be quarantined to prevent the spread of the disease. I wear my mask when I'm in the sickroom, but it's my stout constitution that I rely upon to protect me. I rarely even have a sniffle. But we don't yet know what sort of germ causes this disease.

"For now, I think that both your brother and sister are safe. They're strong." Grace seems robust. And Edward already had influenza at the army hospital a few months ago. In the past, I've been told by doctors that a patient who survives a flu is unlikely to fall victim to it again the same year, though it's certainly not infallibly true.

Lydia coughs. I remove her mask to replace it. The fabric comes away stained pink.

"And my father?" she asks.

Do I detect a new hint of sarcasm in her words?

"Mr. Gainsbury seems very healthy," I say. "I haven't noticed any signs of fever or weakness."

"Weakness?" Lydia says in a whisper. "Oh no, not him. He'd never let anyone call him 'weak.' It should have been him, not my mother, I—" A tear leaks from Lydia's eye. "I'm sorry."

I wipe her face. I am worried that Lydia will feel the same temptation that Edward did; the temptation to give up. "You've got your mother's strength in you. She'd be proud to see how you're fighting."

She closes her eyes. The shadows darken and swirl about her. I wish that I understood more about my own power. Why did the shadows burn me when I touched Edward? Was it just the contact with *him*, some alchemy between the two of us? Or has my talent fundamentally weakened? If I can't help my patients through their passing, I need to know.

Lydia looks so frail. The lass hasn't even had a chance to mourn her mother. Then, she says something that rends my heart.

"I *am* fighting," she tells me. "I want to live. Goddammit, I want to *live*." She shouts these last words so forcefully that she gags. I put a pan near her, in case she vomits, but she clamps her mouth shut. She keeps the bile down through sheer force of will. This girl is formidable.

Can I? Do I dare?

Without any more deliberation, I put my hands gently on Lydia's feverish cheeks. The shadows retreat. They do not touch me. I sigh with relief.

Lydia's eyes squint open. "That's...nice," she says. "Thank you."

She's studying me inquisitively. Did she feel the change? Does she realize what I just did?

I wonder if I've gone too far. What if I've only traded one danger for another?

I've long considered whether my talent might help the sick recover. When I first discovered the ability eight years ago—after I helped poor Ester pass over at the clinic on Larimer Street—I thought that perhaps God had given me the power to heal. It sounds arrogant, I know. But I'd heard of such things. The laying-on of hands. It had been too late for Ester. But what about others? I knew that I had to try.

I would trace my mother's steps when she made rounds at the clinic. Over her objections—based solely upon her concern for me—I applied my hands anywhere I saw the shadows gathering. I was able to give brief moments of clarity. Light could shine once again on a suffering mind. But I saw no real difference in the end. Some patients, those who were strong and sometimes lucky, survived. But too many didn't. Too many times, I cried as I saw the life drain away from a patient I'd tried to save. All I'd done was give the patient's family—and myself—false hope.

The efforts took a physical toll upon me as well. My hair dulled and began to fall out. Sores developed around my mouth. I looked so haggard that my mother finally locked me in our tiny apartment and demanded that I rest. I'll never forget looking in the mirror over my mother's dresser that day. I saw the hated shadows clinging like spider's webs to my own temples. They didn't burn me, not then. But still, that reflection frightened me.

And the most frightening of all? The attention that my efforts began to attract. When I ease the passage of the dying, they take my secret with them. But the living tell their tales. Rumors began to spread about me through the clinic. Some patients—those who'd felt the relief of my touch and then happened to recover—called me miraculous. Others said I was a fraud, or even hinted that I was inviting in the Devil.

In the end, my mother had to leave her job. She found a position across town for a private clinic, which catered to certain wealthy clientele at the end of their lives. You see, a few of the rumors had followed me. Enough that a friendly doctor put in a discrete word on our behalf. My mother and I worked side by side. I used my talent solely to help patients pass over at the very moment of death. If a patient managed to recover, then she wouldn't have witnessed my power anyway. I kept my own heart distant. Though I had no formal training, I learned all I could about nursing from watching my mother. And the physical toll upon me was held at bay. My reputation grew enough to support us, and—after cancer took my mother suddenly when I was seventeen —to support my own practice as a private care nurse.

The families who employ me know only that I ease the suffering of the dying. Though I'm not sure if Mr. Gainsbury knew even that when he hired me. But Edward knows my secret now. My intimacy with this family continues to grow. I've been facing temptations afresh.

And if Lydia learns my secret, too? Can I trust her?

That night, I stay by Lydia's bedside. But I must fall asleep at some point, because I wake up in the morning to shouts and cheers. I nearly fall out of my chair.

"What?" I ask, rubbing my face. I'm still half asleep. "What's going on?"

It's coming from outside. I run to the window and pull back the curtain—people are streaming into the street, screaming and hugging and cheering.

There's laughter behind me. I turn around and find Lydia sitting upright with Edward beside her.

"It's just been announced," Edward says. "There's an armistice. The war is over."

"We thought you'd sleep forever," Lydia adds. "Can I go outside and join the celebration? I can't stand being in this room another minute."

There's not a trace of the shadows upon her.

15

Dinah
1943

When the needle reaches the end, Abby lifts it off the record.

"I don't even believe in ghosts." I sound desperate. Like I'm begging her to make this go away.

The girl on the record is named Millie. She claims that she can see shadows over people's heads when they're near death. I've never heard anything like it before, and Nate certainly never mentioned it. If it weren't for all the familiar names, I'd think it must be fictional. Like one of those spooky dramas they play late at night on the radio.

Millie says that she met *Edward Gainsbury* on the train. What are the chances of an old recording with somebody named Edward Gainsbury just happening to end up in my brother's room?

Abby comes over and squeezes my elbow. Her hand is warm, and my nerves calm a bit. She says, "Whether you believe in it or not, something is happening to you. And it's not going to leave you alone until you figure it out."

I'm worried that she's right.

In the recording, Millie describes how she came to Powder Ridge to help the Gainsbury family during the Great War. She mentions Grace and Lydia, Edward's sisters, who're grown and living at Gainsbury House right now. Millie even mentions my mother, Rachel.

The recording isn't very long. It ends after Millie begins to help Edward end his morphine addiction. There's that big scratch in the recording, though. There are places where it skips or gets stuck. So I can't be sure how much of the story we're missing.

I think of that face I saw outside the boardinghouse window, materializing out of the mist. A girl's face. I try to picture her, but the memory is nothing more than a blur.

I can't ask my brother to explain what's been happening to me. Abby doesn't know, either. I'm the one who has to go searching for answers. Unfortunately, there's only one person I can think to ask: the fellow who looks like Edward Gainsbury. This whole thing started on the day he appeared.

I want to know who he really is. Why he's here. What he knows about the record and Millie's story.

I just have to find him.

I wait until Sunday, when nobody ever works the mine. Our usual day off. The Spivaks have been letting me stay in the back room at the assay office. Main Street is deserted when I sneak out after sunrise.

I've decided not to tell Abby where I'm planning to go. She'd probably warn me that it's a bad idea. But I'm bringing along a vicious camping knife that I found on one of the assay's back shelves. I won't let the soldier catch me unawares again.

No, not a soldier, I remind myself. Draft dodger. He admitted as much himself.

I know that he doesn't live in town. If he did, I'd have seen his footprints leading up the snowy path to Cherry Mountain. But there are old prospectors' cabins scattered in the hills all around the mining encampment. So that's where I'm going to look.

I strap on my webs and make good time up the path. The sun emerges from the clouds and I begin to sweat, so I peel off my outer jacket and stow it in my pack. When I come around the bend and see the Cherry Mountain encampment spread before me—the ruins all glittering with melting ice, the endless span of evergreens, white snow, azure sky—I stop to take a breath.

I pass an overturned mining cart. There's rubble from past rockslides and avalanches piled up behind it. The low-slung stable is off to my left; the boardinghouse is about a quarter mile ahead. When I reach it, I walk into the woods, trying to remember which way I chased the guy the other day.

I find a boulder and scramble up high enough to scan the treetops. I'm looking for faint wisps of smoke—some sign of a fire burning beneath a chimney. The glare makes my eyes water.

I'm still perched on top of the boulder when I hear the music.

My body freezes in place as I listen. There's a piano playing. No—it's a *record* of a piano playing. I hear the telltale skips and scratches of a recording. The tune is familiar, but it's set to a ragtime beat. The notes are like cold fingertips sliding around my neck, making my hairs raise.

It's the song from Millie's record.

I begin to shiver uncontrollably. I slide down the boulder and run, following the music. It's like I'm being drawn by some instinct deep inside of me, beyond reason or willpower.

I trip over a fallen log and land facedown in the snow. Ice goes straight into my shirt. But I right myself, grab my pack and keep going through the powder.

A ruined old cabin appears, and immediately I recognize it. I've seen it before. There's a clearing not much farther on—the same clearing where the guy jumped me a few days ago.

The music is louder here in the clearing. If it wasn't impossible, I would say that it must be *coming* from here. Speckled aspen trunks line the clearing like sentinels, their bare branches pointing at the sky.

As I stand there, the tune turns eerie and sluggish. The notes draw out too long.

Then finally…the music stops.

The woods are absolutely silent. I'm holding my breath.

There's movement at the far end of the clearing. Dark ovals are appearing in the powder. I blink my eyes, but still I see them—narrow boot tracks are sinking into the snow, as if a set of heavy feet is making them. Another appears, then another. And another.

They're coming toward me.

I fall backward into the snow, then launch myself up. I run blindly out of the clearing, pushing through the trees. The melody starts up again, growing louder and louder.

I gasp for breath, trying not to scream, and that's when I smell it: woodsmoke.

A dark shape emerges ahead between the trees. It's another tiny cabin, but not a ruin like the last one. Tendrils of smoke are rising out of its chimney. Footprints lead straight to its door.

I'm just standing there when the door opens.

A young man wearing a tattered army jacket steps outside.

His expression is angry, and he says something, but I can't hear it. My hands cover my ears, but I can still hear that ragtime music playing. It won't let me *think*.

I scream and fall to my knees, sinking into the snow.

The last thing I see is a green jacket and two furious gray eyes, standing over me.

16

Millie
1918

All of Powder Ridge must be out in the street celebrating the armistice. Except for Lydia, Edward and me.

I tuck Lydia beneath her covers. She's still too weak to go outside, so she couldn't go join the revelry. But she's gained enough strength to return to her own room, and I've been busy all morning with her move. Truly, I've rarely seen such a radical return to health. I've heard of strong men laid low for a month after defeating Spanish flu. Yet Lydia is breathing clearly, and her cheeks bear a rosy glow. You wouldn't believe she was so sick just yesterday.

Could it have been my intervention? I keep waiting for her to mention the way I touched her face yesterday. To ask me to explain. But thankfully, she seems distracted by other concerns.

"Where has Edward gone off to?" Lydia asks. "And Grace?"

"I expect that they're getting things ready for tomorrow," I say.

"Oh. That." Lydia sinks down against her pillow. "I don't want to think about tomorrow."

While Lydia's recovery has lightened the Gainsbury family's burden considerably, the funeral tomorrow could plunge them all back into despair. Lydia is still weak; Edward too is far from well. And Grace is even younger than I was when I lost my mother. I know how hard this must be for them all.

Mrs. Bishop suddenly bursts into the room. Lydia and I look over in surprise.

"Um, Miss Millie? You're wanted in the corridor. I'm to take over nursing duties for the rest of the morning."

I turn to Lydia. "Will you be OK?"

"I can manage alone. If I have to." The words are stiff, and I worry she's annoyed. But then she nudges my arm playfully. "Go on, then. You deserve a break."

The moment I step out of the room, I find Edward in the hallway.

"Don't just stand there, Miss Boylan," he says. "Get your coat and your boots. There's a foot of snow on the ground." He walks toward the stairs. I realize he's already wearing his heavy, double-breasted overcoat.

"But the quarantine, I thought we weren't meant to leave the house—"

Edward laughs. "Haven't you looked outside? The quarantine's on holiday today. The whole world's on holiday."

And Heaven help me, I can't resist. "But where are we going?" I ask, hurrying after him.

"To find Grace, naturally." He grins. "You'll never guess where she's run off to."

We come to a tall, wrought iron gate. Edward opens it and gestures me through. "This way, mademoiselle."

I curtsy and give Edward a wink. "I thank you, Lieutenant." Then I look up at the house we're approaching, and I stop with a gasp.

Before me stands a massive edifice of brick, stained glass, and sculpted iron. Marble and bronze statues line the walkway up to the porch. This can only be one place. And then the door opens, and my surmises are confirmed. Briony dashes toward me, her long blond hair bouncing atop her head.

"Millie, finally! We've been waiting all morning."

Edward has brought me to the notorious Mr. and Mrs. Spencer's house.

"And no lectures about masks or illness or any such depressing things. Today we're only celebrating." Briony links her arm with mine and leads me toward the door.

I look back at Edward, concerned that we're leaving him behind, but he just waves me onward. "I'll get there. A fellow never minds keeping up after a couple of pretty girls." There's a sheen of sweat on his forehead. But his eyes are insistent.

Edward has been flirtatious with me for the whole walk. And the shadows gathered around his head have faded. He didn't even ask me for an injection this morning, although I still keep his supply of morphine in a locked box in my room. His prosthesis obviously hurts him. The tightness around his mouth hints at his pain. Yet he's managing without the drug. I know how much this must mean to him. And he *does* look enticing with that flush of exertion upon his cheek.

Briony leads me into the entryway of her home.

Gainsbury House is grand. Luxurious, even. But Briony's home could be the Palace of Versailles by comparison. "That chandelier came all the way from Venice," she tells me. "And the carpet is from India. Isn't that marvelous?" There are silk draperies and gold-filagreed candelabras everywhere I look. Briony isn't stuffy about it, though. She's giggling like a little girl in a toyshop as she shows me the house. Edward catches up with us when we're in the dining room, admiring Briony's china cabinet.

"I was just about to show Millie the best surprise of all." She leads us down a hallway past the kitchen. A narrow door opens up into a huge room lined with windows. It's large enough to be a ballroom, but instead of staid furniture we find drop-cloths, easels and spattered paint. It's an artist's workshop.

Edward whistles. "Quite impressive," he says.

"Courtland is too good to me," she tells us. "I asked for a studio, and he gave me the whole ballroom. Not like we host many parties, anyway, which is a shame because I throw a good party. But Powder Ridge society doesn't seem to agree."

"These are all *your* paintings, Briony?" I remember the skillful drawings that my friend used to keep in a notebook, but these paintings are a far cry from such beginnings. There are mountain landscapes glowing with sunlight; a view of Powder Ridge's Main Street at sunset. And the portraits! Many of the people I don't recognize, but I spot Briony's profile on one of the canvases. She's mostly in shadow, yet the brushstrokes capture so much of her vitality and playful spirit.

"Some are mine," Briony says. "But not all."

That's when I notice that there's another painter working on one of the canvases.

"Grace!" Edward says. "There you are."

There are many exclamations of surprise—Grace did not expect to see us here today—and plenty of laughter from Briony, who apparently plotted it all with Edward's help.

"Is Rachel coming, too?" Grace asks.

Edward's smile falters. "I invited her. But she said she was busy today."

While Grace is showing her brother her artwork, I pull Briony aside. I'm thinking of her comment on the first day that I arrived in Powder Ridge, when Briony walked with Edward and I to Gainsbury House. *I'd better be going before I cause any new scandals.* That's what Briony said when Grace answered the door.

I supposed that Briony's background alone might be the cause of any uproar in town. She was—shall I say—a lady of the evening in Denver. I met Briony years ago, at the clinic where my mother worked. Briony was sick with a fever that day, but her sense of humor and sheer exuberance drew me to her. Our lives couldn't have been more different, but we bonded quickly. Briony and her brother Terrance were orphaned at a young age, and after my mother's death, they comforted me through the worst of my grief.

Then the mining baron Courtland Spencer, thirty years her senior, fell hopelessly in love with Briony and carried her off to the mountains. According to her letters, she didn't get an easy welcome here. But obscene amounts of money tend to smooth the road, especially in a frontier town like Powder Ridge where nearly all money is new money.

Now, I wonder if the elder Mr. Gainsbury wasn't sufficiently impressed. "Does Mr. Gainsbury know that Grace is painting in your studio?" I ask my friend quietly.

She weaves her arm through mine, and we begin walking slowly about the room, admiring the paintings. "Not exactly. Beth Gainsbury—God rest her soul—didn't mind that I was giving Grace lessons. There were some of my paintings on display in Courtland's buildings on Main Street, you see. The assay office, the hotel." She giggles again. A lock of hair falls over her forehead. "Plenty of the saloons, too. Though I don't think that Beth or Grace saw *those*. But Grace marched right up to my door, rang the bell, and asked me to teach her. I was happy to do it. When her father found out, though— there was a bit of a scene after church. Luckily I was wearing the most gorgeous feathered hat that day, so all the stares were more than welcome."

I squeeze Briony's arm. My friend is quick to laugh off society's disapproval, but I know that it wears on her. "I'm not surprised," I say. "Mr. Gainsbury seems very stern." The man is my employer, so I should be more grateful. But he seems to view his family as a problem to be managed, rather than a source of comfort and love.

"He had a right fit about it," Briony continues with another giggle. "He forbade Grace from seeing me. So we've had to rearrange our lessons. I'm always careful to stand off to the side when I give instruction, so that she hardly ever *sees* me at all."

We finish our circuit of the room and come up behind Grace, who is painting again. Edward stands nearby, resting against his cane and watching his sister with admiration in his eyes. Grace is working on a portrait of their mother. She has used heavy brushstrokes in the Impressionist style, weaving shades of blue and green into her mother's hair and skin. It creates the sense that her mother is underwater and looking out toward the surface. Grace has painted both her mother's beauty and her own sorrow onto the canvas.

I want to praise Grace's work, but instead I take Briony's hand and nod my head toward the door. This feels like a moment that should belong only to Edward, his sister, and their shared grief.

Briony has been my closest friend for several years now. Sometimes my *only* friend, and it's been hard living in Denver since she moved to Powder Ridge. We've had some unforgettable nights together—like the time that she persuaded me to dress up as Santa Claus on Christmas Eve, false beard and all, and visit every bordello on our block to hand out rubber condoms.

"What are you chuckling at?" Briony asks me.

"Memories," I say. "A certain Christmas." I will never forget running down Larimer Street with a parade of prostitutes singing carols behind me.

Briony bursts out with a loud guffaw of laughter. "Never again have I made it through 'It Came Upon A Midnight Clear' with a straight face."

She finishes giving me a tour of the house. As we walk, Briony tells me more about her husband, Courtland Spencer. Apparently he went from working as a child in a mine to owning half of Cherry Mountain's riches. Samuel Gainsbury owned the other half. But when it came time to sell their stakes to a rich foreign investor, Courtland held out longer and managed a far better deal than Mr. Gainsbury. Now, Courtland supervises all of the Cherry Mountain Mine's operations, while Gainsbury is merely the Assistant Superintendent. So perhaps there is animosity between the two men. But I'm still mystified about why Mr. Gainsbury hired me on the Spencers' recommendation at all.

Before I can ask, we end up outside a grand oak door. There's music coming from inside. "Courtland?" Briony calls, knocking. "Can I bring Millie in?"

We walk into yet another enormous room. This one is paneled in rich woods from floor to ceiling. In front of a marble-lined fireplace, Briony's husband is seated at a desk fit for President Wilson himself.

"Millie Boylan!" he exclaims, leaping up. "I've been waiting ages to meet you!" He's got a backwoods accent, which fits the history that Briony has told me.

There's a clock on the mantle that appears to be solid gold. A ragtime record spins on a brand new gramophone on his desk. Amazingly, it's playing "When Irish Eyes Are Smiling." Briony knows what the song means to me. How it reminds me of my mother.

I hold out my hand, but instead of shaking, Courtland catches me in a suffocating hug. "You've made my wife incredibly happy by coming to Powder Ridge, and that makes *me* just ecstatic. I owe you. Anything I can do for you, you name it. Anything at all."

"Courtland, set her down. She can't breathe."

Mr. Spencer releases me, and I laugh as I straighten my hair and my dress. "I'm all right. But I should be thanking you for recommending me to the Gainsburys."

"*Me?*" he scoffs. "Samuel Gainsbury wouldn't take my advice if I was trying to steer him away from a cliff. He'd go off the side just to spite me. No, that was all Briony and Grace and their machinations."

I raise an eyebrow at my friend. There's plenty she hasn't been telling me. And I certainly can't imagine that she told Grace the truth about my line of work. It's no wonder that Mr. Gainsbury assumed I was a typical private care nurse. Briony shrugs and smiles, as if saying, *Well, what did you expect? I got you here, didn't I?*

The record ends, and Courtland goes to switch another onto the gramophone. "Don't forget my offer, now," he says. "Anything you need, I'm your man."

I think of Lydia waiting back at the house. She's been left out of the celebrations, left out of this entire day. "There *is* something," I say. "I'd only be borrowing it of course. If it's not too much trouble."

Later, as we begin the walk home, Edward is quiet. Grace has stayed behind with Briony to finish up her painting lesson. She's promised to be home for dinner. While Edward and I slowly make our way down Main Street, I admire the freshly-painted facades of the buildings and the bustle that I see inside each window. American flags are waving everywhere. There are so many delivery trucks in the road and pedestrians milling about—and often stopping Edward with hoorahs and attaboys, even surrounding him and singing the Star-Spangled Banner—that we detour to a side street.

"Tired of celebrating?" I ask him. I've got the record tucked under my arm. I can't wait to play it for Lydia when I get back. Courtland didn't hesitate about giving it to me. *It's not a loan,* he insisted, *it's a gift.*

Edward shakes his head. "I'm elated that my fellow soldiers are coming home, of course. But people are acting like I'm personally responsible for Germany's capitulation."

"Well, thank you for braving the crowds today and inviting me along. My step feels lighter than it has in quite some time."

He grins. "The day isn't over yet. You just might find yourself flying by the end of it."

Instead of turning toward Gainsbury House, Edward points me to a secluded path. There are fewer houses here, more hilly slopes covered in white. We make it all the way up a steep hill. From here, I can see all the many rooftops of Powder Ridge. Chimneys are puffing pale smoke, and children are throwing snowballs. Down in the town square, chants and songs have broken out. The peppy strains of "Over There" roll merrily toward us on the wind.

Edward has stopped beside a rickety wooden sled. "Your chariot, m'lady," he says.

I assume he's joking. I burst out laughing. "You can't expect me to ride that tiny thing." If it were just Briony and me, I'd sled down this hill in a heartbeat. But I'll end up with my skirts over my head. It's not how I'd want the brave Lieutenant Gainsbury to see me.

"Actually, I expect both of us to ride it." He sits himself down on the sled and with a goofy grin says, "All aboard. No—wait." Edward tugs up his trouser leg, revealing his prosthetic limb. He unbuckles it. He hisses with pain when it comes off, and then he tosses the prosthesis unceremoniously down the slope. We both watch the limb roll all the way and finally bury itself in a bank of snow.

"Oh, that's better." He sighs with relief. "You have no idea how much I despise that thing. *Now* it's boarding time. Train's ready to leave." He pats his knee. He wants me to sit in his lap. But he can't meet my eyes.

"Lieutenant Edward Gainsbury, I believe you are blushing."

"Am not. It's just the cold. Are you coming with me, or are you going to watch a poor cripple careen down a hill for your own amusement?"

I can't hide my smile. I glance around, but I don't see anybody nearby. I set Briony's record gently by a tree. Gathering my skirt and petticoats, I sit carefully between Edward's knees. He puts his arms around my waist, drawing me closer. His thighs gently squeeze my hips. Now I'm definitely blushing too, and no doubt it's a red as furious as my hair. Thank goodness he can't see my face.

"Ready?" he asks. His breath is warm against my neck. I nod. He uses one hand to push off, and suddenly we are flying. I scream, half terror and half delight, trying to hold on to the sides of the sled. We end up crashing into the snow bank, both of us tumbling off the sled and laughing hysterically. I haven't laughed so much in years—maybe not since that memorable Christmas Eve I spent with Briony in Larimer Street.

Edward crawls over to me. He pulls me upright. I'm sopping wet and covered with snow. "Did you survive?" he asks, chuckling as he brushes snowflakes from my hair.

"That train was defective," I say. "I'm going to complain to management."

Edward's fingers move from my hair to my face. His thumb traces my chin. I think he's going to kiss me. Am I going to let him?

I think I am. And I think I am going to thoroughly enjoy it.

I spot movement over Edward's shoulder, which makes me inhale sharply and look up. It's already gone. Just a flash of color. But I remember the green of that blouse. And I think I saw the toss of her stylish bob; it was Rachel Kohler. She saw us.

I look back to Edward, but the moment is gone. He's searching for his prosthesis in the snow. "We'd better get home," he says. "I'm sure Lydia is getting lonely. She'll want to hear your record."

17

Dinah
1943

I smell coffee.

I'm lying on a narrow bed atop the covers. My eyes quickly scan the space—I'm in a one-room wood cabin. There's a few shelves laden with canned goods, a small icebox, a rough-hewn table. A brand new stove sits in the corner, pumping heat into the tiny room.

The guy in the army coat is turned away from me, fiddling with something in the corner. It's a shiny steel kettle. He sets the kettle down on the table next to two ceramic mugs. He dishes ground coffee from a canister into the mugs.

He's taller than Nate, but I figure they're around the same age. Nineteen or twenty. Old enough to be called a man, yet without the hardness in the jaw and the hands that I usually see in the grown men of Powder Ridge.

Then he glances over his shoulder and sees me watching. Long lashes frame his gray eyes, and his chin has a slight cleft.

"Who are you?" I ask, sitting up. I rub my forehead, still feeling the echoing hum of that terrible song. Did that really happen? But it must have. Because I'm here.

"I told you to forget about me," he says. His voice is low and hoarse. "I just wanted to be left alone."

"But you brought me inside." I think of the knife in my pack. It's sitting across the room at the guy's feet. Can I get to it? Do I need to?

"You were screaming," he says defensively. "You passed out."

"It was that creepy music. I was..." *Terrified*, I think. But I don't want to say it. I'm still scared, right here and now. I don't like that he touched me while I was out. But aside from my headache, I seem fine. Making coffee isn't exactly an act of aggression.

His expression hasn't changed. "Music?"

"You couldn't hear it?" I squeeze my eyes shut. What is happening to me?

When I open my eyes again, he's staring at me warily, like *I'm* the one who seems threatening.

He's grabbing my pack from the floor. "If you're better now, then you should go."

"Wait," I say. "Not yet. I came all this way to talk to you."

"But I don't want to talk."

He's reaching for the door. I struggle to get my thoughts together. If he pushes me out of here and closes that door, I'll probably never get another chance.

"I found a photo in my mother's memory book," I say. "It's old, from the Great War. But it looks exactly like you. That green army coat, everything."

His hand stops on the doorknob.

"The photo has the name 'Edward Gainsbury' written beneath it. That mean anything to you?"

He still doesn't answer, but his chest moves faster. He starts to shake his head.

"There's a record." I'm babbling. But I have to make him listen. He's the only one who can help me, I'm sure of it. "It's a recording of a girl telling a story—a story with Edward Gainsbury in it, but it all happened in 1918. And I've seen these handprints—faces in windows —music coming from nowhere—"

He glances at me over his shoulder. "I thought I heard music the other day," he says quietly. "Coming from the woods."

"*Yes*. There's something strange going on. That's why I'm here." I laugh I'm so relieved. I'm not the only one who's heard it.

"You know that name, don't you," I say. "Edward Gainsbury. Is that your last name, too? Gainsbury?"

His eyes go dark, like shutters closing over a window. His hand makes a fist around the top of my pack. "Why do you even care who I am?"

I feel a surge of indignation. "Oh, no. You can't blame this on me. All of this started when *you* came sniffing around the boardinghouse." Without stopping to think, I jump up and poke him hard on the shoulder. Like I would've done if he were my brother, and Nate was being completely impossible.

"*Ouch*." He grabs his shoulder. He's scowling. But at least it's a real emotion. Not the distant, now-I-want-to-be-alone bunk he's been feeding me.

He sets down my pack, wiping a hand across his mouth. He turns away from me, leaning a hand against the closed door.

I stand there, waiting for him to say something. I'm not leaving until I get answers.

Finally, he sighs. "Fine. You're Dinah, right? Let me finish making the coffee, and I'll try to explain. As much as I can, at least. There's plenty I don't understand, either."

I drag my pack over to a crate and sit down. He goes to the table, picks up the kettle, and pours hot water into the cups. Then there's a few minutes of silence while he watches the coffee grounds settle.

There are dark half-moons beneath his eyes, like he hasn't slept well in a long time. Like he's seen darker things than his years otherwise betray.

As he hands me a mug, the cuff of his sleeve rides up. There's a couple of small, circular scars on the inside of his wrist. But he starts talking before I can ask.

"I got here a few days ago…a week or so. I remember waking up at night, looking out the window. It was snowing hard." He sits on the narrow cot across from me and stares into his cup. "I just woke up, saw the snow, went back to sleep. I was groggy. Tired. When I woke again, the sun was up. But I couldn't remember how I got here."

"You're talking like you just appeared. *Poof.*" I wave my hands like a magician. But even with all the odd things happening, his story doesn't add up. This cabin is well stocked. A couple of his shelves are packed with dog-eared books. He's not some desperate squatter here —that canister of coffee alone would've taken more ration stamps than a single man should have. But he hasn't been going into town. So where'd the supplies come from?

"Of course I didn't just *appear.*"

"Then where were you before?"

The muscle in his jaw works. "It's hard to say."

Like *that's* any clearer. "How about this. Do you know where you are *now?*"

"Powder Ridge, Colorado." There's a flash of that scowl again. I don't mind the scowl. I swear, it's the only real part of him.

"For a long time," he says, "I've had these black outs. I'm never sure how long they last. I'll just wake up in a new place feeling awful. When it's dark, sometimes I forget where I am. Sometimes morning comes, and I still can't remember."

"All right," I say hesitantly. "What about that morning you went to the old bunkhouse? What were you doing then?"

"That was my first morning here. I was...confused. I woke up here and heard something outside. Somebody singing. It sounded strange. Far away."

Music, I think. *Why is it music?*

"But when I went outside," he continues, "I didn't see anybody there. I decided to walk around some, get my bearings. See if I could find anything familiar. I was wandering around when I found that building—the bunkhouse—and I thought I saw somebody up on the third floor. And then a little while later, I saw you climbing the building from the outside. It seemed like an odd thing to do, so—"

"Wait, I saw somebody up on the third floor, too. Before I went up there. That really wasn't you?"

Somehow, I'd still been hoping I could find a sensible explanation for what's been happening to me. That hope is receding further and further away.

"The place looks condemned," he says. "Who'd be mad enough to go inside there?"

I raise one eyebrow. *Except me?*

There's a tense pause. We both sip our coffee. Then I spit mine back into the cup.

It's possibly the most wretched thing I've ever tasted.

I'd wonder if he's trying to poison me, but he makes the same grimace.

"Lord, that's awful," he says. "Ugh. I'm sorry. I don't know what I did."

"How about I make the coffee next time?" I set the mug between my feet. I smile a little bit in spite of myself, and when I look up, I find him almost smiling too.

"I thought I saw someone looking in my window yesterday," he says. "A girl. She was gone when I got outside. And I thought maybe it was *you*. But it wasn't you, was it?"

"I've never been here before in my life. I mean, not till just now."

"Dinah, why is all this happening? What's it supposed to mean?"

He genuinely sounds like he doesn't know. Can I really trust him, when I don't even know his name?

Just the other day, I came after this guy with a rock hammer. When he got it away from me, he threw it as far as he could into the forest. Damn waste of a good rock hammer, I might add. But he didn't try to hurt me. Even when he tackled me, he only did enough to defend himself. He was scared. I know how awful it feels to be afraid and alone.

I scoot forward on my seat, resting an arm on the table. "That's exactly what I'm going to figure out. But first, you have to tell me your name."

He studies me for a long moment.

Then he says, "It's Edward Gainsbury."

18

Millie
1918

The funeral procession begins outside of Gainsbury House. The sky is an unrelenting gray. The hearse departs first. It's driving so slowly that I find myself holding my breath until it turns onto Main Street. The mourners follow, most of them on foot, dressed in their finest black clothes. Each small party kept its distance from the others.

I wait until the end of the long line of people, and then I join the procession beside Mrs. Bishop. I'm wearing black as well. As you might guess, I've *always* got a black dress packed with me. Inevitably, I will need it.

The rest of the Gainsbury family has already gone ahead with the hearse. The mood was solemn in the house this morning, which is to be expected for such an occasion. But I couldn't help feeling that the tension was just as much to do with Mr. Gainsbury's sternness. He made his three children line up in the entryway for his inspection; even Lydia, who is just barely strong enough to be out of bed. He scolded Grace for crying and told Lydia that her hair looked dull.

To Edward he said, "Stop slumping. Stand up tall like a man." I wanted to go offer Mr. Gainsbury my *own* opinions about what makes a man, but I didn't dare come down from the upstairs landing.

I walk down Main Street with the entire procession before me. It's just begun to snow.

I don't even know if I'm invited to the funeral. Perhaps Mr. Gainsbury will think it is inappropriate. But now that Lydia has recovered, I don't even know if I'm still his employee. In any case, I'm determined to go. I didn't know Beth Gainsbury long, but I shared an intimacy with her. I intend to honor her memory today.

I see Briony's black feathered hat before she reaches me. She strides over, nodding politely to people who don't affect to notice she's here. I'm beginning to see how things work in Powder Ridge. The townspeople have put up an invisible, silent wall of defense against Briony, all the while insisting that it doesn't exist.

She falls into step beside me. "Is this where the troublemakers line up?" she whispers.

I smile discretely. Mrs. Bishop harrumphs and walks faster to go ahead of us. Then there's a voice from behind us.

"Miss Boylan, I imagine you won't be staying much longer, now Lydia's better?"

I look back and see Rachel Kohler. She's dressed in simple black like everyone else, yet the careful tailoring of her coat makes her figure as striking as Briony's. White snowflakes settle on Rachel's wide-brimmed hat. I quickly face forward.

"I'm not sure," I say. "Did you get the message I sent, Miss Kohler?" A few days ago, I passed along a note with Mrs. Gainsbury's last words. I wanted to make sure Rachel knew that Beth was thinking of her.

"Edward told me," Rachel says. "We spoke this morning."

Briony's feathers dance as she tosses her head. "Edward doesn't seem ready for Millie to leave Powder Ridge," she says.

116

"Perhaps *you're* not familiar with Edward's preferences, Mrs. Spencer," Rachel says sweetly. "Not the way I am."

"Perhaps *you'd* be surprised, Miss Kohler," Briony quips.

I elbow Briony in the side. My eyes must be as big as the face of the clock on the bank building. I don't like being caught in the middle of this conversation. But Briony is dissolving into silent giggles. She mouths to me, *I'm kidding!* Her giggles turn into a sneeze.

"I hope you're not unwell," Rachel says, in a tone that suggests she means the opposite. "Our town has seen enough illness already," she adds. "Miss Boylan knows that firsthand."

The three of us are quiet for the rest of the walk. Briony doesn't sneeze again.

At the graveyard, townspeople are spread between the tombstones to hear the minister speak. Briony and I stand on a gentle hillside, overlooking the crowd. They have spread out so as to minimize the chance of catching disease. Some of the mourners have faint shadows probing them. Will death come for them next? Or are the shadows simply drawn by death's proximity to this place? These are questions I cannot answer, no matter how it infuriates me.

" 'And yea, though I walk through the valley of the shadow of death...' "

Edward stands near the front with his family. His skin is waxy today, and there are bruise-colored half moons beneath his eyes. Edward is watching the crowd instead of the minister. The graves and the living are dusted with the same coating of white. His eyes find mine, and his gaze is vacant. The shadows are heavy around him today, blanketing his hat and shoulders like a sooty counterpoint to the snow. I remember my own mother's funeral service; the emptiness that I felt. I had stayed with her until the end, keeping those vicious pinprick eyes away from her face, but that knowledge didn't ease the loss. I felt as if my true self had gone away with her, and the girl left standing beside her grave was nothing but an imposter. Is that how Edward is feeling now?

He sways in place. He still hasn't had any morphine since the day before yesterday. His leg must be in terrible pain by now, not to mention the agony of his body's desire for the drug. He had seemed so well yesterday. Should I have offered the morphine to him, even though he didn't ask for it? But that wouldn't have been right, either. I don't know what to do.

The coffin is lowered into the ground. The family members take turns shoveling snow and dirt into the grave. Edward struggles to stoop down when his turn comes, but he refuses any aid.

The shadows drip down over his forehead. They cover his eyes.

I know then that something is terribly wrong.

"Millie?" Briony asks. "What is it?"

I begin to walk forward. Edward is still battling with the shovel. He manages to move a heap of dirt onto the coffin. But then he starts to sag. Grace puts her hand on his arm in concern.

I'm running now. Pushing through the other mourners, who gasp at my brashness. I'm nearly there when Mr. Gainsbury sees me coming. He steps in front of me. He wears a fine wool overcoat, a handsome gold-chain watch. His mustache comes to a severe point on each side.

"What do you think you're doing?" he demands.

"Let me through," I say. "Edward is ill."

Murmurs spread through the crowd, and then the noise turns to shouts. Lydia screams.

There's a terrible thud.

Edward has collapsed into his mother's open grave.

19

Dinah
1943

"Is Edward Gainsbury your dad's name, too?" I ask. We're still sitting by the table in his cabin. He shakes his head. "That's not my father's name."

"But you must be related to the Gainsburys here in Powder Ridge. Grace and Liddy? Jim and Mitchell? You're a cousin from somewhere."

"I don't know any of those people."

"But then what are you doing here? Who *are* you?" I push back from the table and get up. "Because you can't be the *same* Edward Gainsbury from that picture, the soldier who fought in the Great War who wore a coat like that one." I point at the torn army jacket he's still wearing. "That kind of thing isn't possible."

He holds up his hands. "I never said it was. I didn't fight in any war. That's the whole reason I'm hiding up here—*avoiding* the war."

I pace across the tiny room, kicking my pack out of the way as I pass. "And what's so bad about serving your country? That's what my brother's doing right now. He got drafted and he left." Left *me*. Nate left me, and this lousy Edward Gainsbury lookalike is here instead. It's not right. "Are you that much of a coward?"

"I'm not a coward." He stands, slamming his hands on the table. His coffee mug jumps and the liquid sloshes. "I hate being cooped up here, but it's for a reason. It's safer this way. There are things I can't tell you, and if you won't accept that, then you might as well go."

I cross my arms and frown at him. We glare at one another. Finally he flops back onto his seat, sighing. But he doesn't tell me to leave.

"Do you have a nickname?" I ask.

"A what?"

"Something I can call you. There's too many 'Edward Gainsburys' already."

He shakes his head, still scowling.

"What about Eddie?" I suggest.

"I think people used to call me that sometimes when I was a kid. I never liked it."

"Eddie it is."

He rolls his eyes, but I ignore him. I sit back down on the crate.

"So, *Eddie*, you saw me climb up the bunkhouse the other day. And then you decided to follow me? Why was that, exactly?" Because that part still seems odd to me.

He traces his finger around the top of his coffee mug, looking sheepish. "It's been a long time since I had anybody to talk to. Friends. I thought maybe they'd put me here because—"

There's a thud outside.

Eddie looks up sharply. He shoots up to standing, spilling half his coffee down his pants. "Dammit," he whispers, and I don't think he's talking about the mess he just made.

"*Hide*," he tells me.

I grab my pack and squeeze into the corner behind the stove. I'm out of sight from both the window and the door.

They put me here, he said. Who did he mean by *they*?

Eddie goes outside and closes the door behind him. I hear voices—Eddie's deep one, the other indistinct. He's talking to someone out there. I have to know who. I edge out from behind the stove, listening, but they're speaking too low.

Things get quiet outside. My whole body tenses. I take the knife out of my bag and stow it in my pocket, just in case.

The door opens again, and I scurry back behind the stove.

"You need to go," Eddie says. He seems shaken. His eyes are very wide. He's brought a green canvas bag inside with him, and he sets it on the ground. The top falls open; there are groceries inside.

"Wait! You have to tell me—"

But he pushes me out the door and shuts it in my face. There are fresh footprints out here. Large boots. Who do they belong to?

Eddie opens the door just a crack. "Dinah, don't just stand there. *Go.*"

"When are you going to answer my questions?"

He sighs again. "I'll meet you behind the bunkhouse tomorrow afternoon," he says. "Four o'clock. We can talk more then. *Just* you, nobody else."

Eddie tells me how to get back to the mining encampment from his cabin. But instead, I decide to follow the boot prints that the mystery person left outside his door. I go a short ways through the trees, but then I come to a frozen stream. The footprints disappear. No matter how much I search, I can't pick them up again.

The next day—Monday—Jim and I go to work as usual. There's a warm spell today, with temperatures getting up into the fifties. It's a regular heat-wave considering it's November. Even up on Cherry Mountain, the snow is turning to dirty slush.

The waste pile is one big cesspit of muck. Every swing of my hammer sends out a spray of brown water. By the end of our day, Jim and I are drenched up to our thighs. I can feel mud crusted on my cheeks. Jim has swathes of brown clay on his forehead from wiping his sweat. My boots squelch with every step.

I tell Jim that he can go on home, but that I have a few more things to do. "You know the way by now," I say. "You don't need me." I keep my voice cheerful. I don't want him to know how nervous I am about seeing Eddie again.

"But I'm supposed to bring you today," he says. "So Mama can thank you in person. What will I tell her?"

McGrady pokes his head out of the stable door. "You're doing what now, Dinah Weller? There somethin' wrong I need to know about?"

"Mind your business, McGrady. Isn't there an alcohol still you need to tend to before it explodes?"

To Jim I say, "Your mama doesn't need to thank me."

Yesterday I asked Abby to break my twenty from the assay office's till, and then I stopped by Gainsbury House to give Jim a tenner. I wonder if Grace realizes that I've overpaid Jim for his few days of work. What if she's sore about it? She might think it's charity and feel insulted. I guess I might feel the same, in her place. But that doesn't change the fact that I want her family to have that money. They need it just as much as my family.

"But Dinah, she and Aunt Liddy want to *invite* you. To Thanksgiving. Your family, too."

"Oh." I'd forgotten that Thanksgiving is next week. Now, I don't know what to say. "Are you sure? My parents?"

"That's your family, isn't it? Thanksgiving is for families. Except Mitchell, who's in Heaven, and Nate who's in the war somewhere."

McGrady comes all the way out of the stable, fists on his hips. "I don't want you tromping around here after hours, causing trouble like you own the place. I *knew* somebody's been around here when they weren't supposed to. Should've known it was you. This ain't a playground, Dinah Weller. It was one thing when your brother was minding you, but I've never thought a girl should be up here—"

"For crying out loud McGrady, *shut up*." I shake my head. None of this is important right now. It's past four o'clock already, and I'm supposed to meet Eddie behind the boardinghouse. What if he gets sick of waiting and leaves? I certainly don't want to go in those woods alone again. Too many bizarre things have been going on.

Cursing under his breath, McGrady goes back inside the stable. I finally get Jim off on his way toward town. When he's gone, I run for the boardinghouse and skirt around to the back.

Edward isn't there.

"Shit," I mutter. "Shit, shit."

"Psst," someone whispers. "Hey."

I scan the trees and see Edward crouched behind one of them. He's wearing his same army jacket again.

"I was afraid you weren't coming," he says, standing up. "You're a mess."

"Thank you."

"Don't mention it. C'mon, I need to show you something." He turns toward the woods.

Immediately I have a million questions. But instead of asking them, I decide—for once—to just wait and see.

Eddie leads me to the old, falling-down cabin that I've now passed several times. Here, the snow has softened, but hasn't yet melted.

"So these are my tracks here from earlier today," he says, pointing. "But look at these." He gestures to another set of footprints that seem to be coming from the ruined cabin's front door. It's one of the few parts of the place that're still standing. The unknown tracks definitely aren't mine from yesterday. I wasn't walking in this spot.

"That's odd enough," Eddie says. "But now, see where they go?"

We follow the footsteps to the clearing—the same place where I first spoke to him, and the same place where I heard that music and saw footsteps appear out of nowhere just yesterday. Eddie stops at the edge of the trees, bracing his hand against an aspen trunk. The snow here is sheltered from the sun, so it's barely melted. I can see the footprints continuing, going around in a sort of ring.

"Remember what I said yesterday?" Eddie asks. "I told you I thought there was somebody looking in at my window. I wanted to figure out who it was. But when I was out looking around this morning, these were the only tracks I found."

"There *was* somebody other than me at your cabin," I remind him. "You talked to him. Or her. You wouldn't tell me who it was. You made me hide."

"I mean, *before* that," he says tensely. "Before you got there."

I glare at him, waiting for him to fess up about what he's hiding. Once again, he doesn't.

"Please Dinah, just look at the direction of these footprints," he says. "That's why I brought you here. They don't make any sense."

I try to see what he's seeing. Carefully, I shift my weight, following the footsteps with my eyes. The tracks circle round and around the clearing in a spiral, ending in the center.

There, they vanish.

My next question is going to sound bizarre, so I don't bother trying to prepare him for it. I just ask it.

"Do you believe in ghosts?"

He lifts an eyebrow. "Maybe. Is that what we're dealing with, here? A ghost?"

I don't answer. I really don't know *how* to answer.

I keep expecting to hear that music again. My ears are straining. My nerves are on edge, and my heart is beating fast in anticipation. I find myself humming the tune, just so I can stop worrying about hearing it. I won't let it scare me anymore.

Eddie tilts his head, listening. "I know that song. 'When Irish Eyes Are Smiling.' I remember…" His eyes get a faraway look. He shivers and crosses his arms over his body. "Someone used to sing it."

"Exactly! It was playing yesterday outside your cabin."

"I didn't hear it yesterday. I haven't heard that in ages."

Dammit. I can't stand this feeling—like I'm treading on brittle ice and the whole world keeps shifting beneath me. I want someone to grab hold of me and pull me back to solid ground.

"Say, I still believe you," Eddie says when he sees my frustration. "That's why you asked about ghosts? You think all this…" He waves at the clearing. "The footsteps.

The music. The faces in the windows. It's all because a ghost is haunting us? That's what led me to you? And you to me?"

With a single word, I feel like Eddie has thrown me a life preserver. *Us.*

"Possibly," I say. "Probably."

"The ghost of…who?"

That's the essential question.

"Remember the record I mentioned yesterday?" I ask. "It played that song: 'When Irish Eyes Are Smiling.' I'd play it for you, but…you'd have to come into town with me."

I hold my breath. He's going to say no. He's going to be angry that I even suggested it.

But instead, he nods. "You think you can get me into town without anyone spotting me?"

"Sure," I say. "You'd actually want to go? You seemed a little paranoid before about getting too far from your cabin."

Who is bringing you supplies, Eddie? What are you so afraid of?

"I'm not supposed to leave. I told you, it's safer. But if it's just for a little while…" He gives the clearing a last glance over his shoulder. "Take me into Powder Ridge. I need to hear that record."

20

Millie
1918

Three men help carry Edward upstairs into the sickroom. "Get some linens onto that bed!" Dr. Durham shouts. Mrs. Bishop and I rush to find fresh sheets. The place has been cleaned since Mrs. Gainsbury's death, but we haven't had any chance to prepare it for more patients. With Lydia downstairs, there was no need. But Mr. Gainsbury has insisted that his son be treated here, even though this is the place where Edward's mother died just days before. That won't weigh easily on Edward's mind.

We stretch a sheet over the bed—I choose the cot that was Lydia's, not Beth's—and the men lay down Edward's insensible form. The doctor already confirmed that Edward is breathing. But his heart is weak. His skin is on fire with fever.

"Everyone out," Dr. Durham says.

I raise my hand to protest. "Doctor, I—"

"Miss Boylan, you may stay. I'll need an assistant. Remove his coat and prosthesis."

"But Doctor, please. You must listen to me." The man bristles at the way I'm speaking to him, but I have to tell him everything I know. Even if that means angering the doctor. Even if it means betraying Edward's confidence.

I explain about the morphine. How I think Edward is in withdrawal. The doctor stares at me for a long second, and then he's in motion. Together, we remove

Edward's coat. The doctor opens Edward's eyelids. Tugs up Edward's sleeves.

Scabs mark the fresh injection sites on his arms.

"This can't be," I say. "I have his supply locked away in my room. I checked it this morning—he hasn't touched it." A terrible realization is spreading through me, despite my denials. Edward has been lying to me.

"Miss Boylan, you may be a nurse of a sort. But you're still a young girl. You are dangerously naive." The doctor opens his medical bag and begins laying out various instruments. "I doubt Edward's sudden illness has been caused by an overdose of morphine—he's been in full view of his family for the entire funeral, so it's likely been over an hour since his last injection."

"Then what's causing this? Could it be the flu?" Was I wrong to think he wouldn't contract the illness again?

"I can't yet say. But regardless, his morphinomania has made matters worse. I fear your choice to keep Edward's secret may have cost him his life."

The next hours are pure hell.

Dr. Durham gives Edward an injection to stimulate his heart. But he won't revive. The doctor barks his orders at me. For endless minutes, the doctor massages Edward's chest. His pulse is too slow. His breathing is too shallow.

We remove the prosthesis only to find that the stump of Edward's leg has broken down. It's bleeding and festering. There is presence of infection. If it gets worse, another amputation could be necessary, farther up the leg. I clean the wound, apply antiseptic ointments, and re-wrap the bandages. His skin is burning with fever.

Edward may have lied to me about his supply of morphine, but the terrible urge inside of him was driving the act, not his will. The doctor is right. The real fault is mine. I thought that the small power I possess in my hands would be enough to hold back the anguish Edward is facing. That I had the *faintest* idea of how to treat a wounded soldier with a morphine addiction who's just lost his mother.

I'm a fool. I don't know how to save Edward—how to save *anybody*. I only know how to watch people die.

I smooth the hair back from Edward's forehead. He looks so vulnerable. We're both old enough to be grown now, and we've seen far too much of the world. Yet we have both faltered so drastically. I want nothing right now so much as my mother. I need her to tell me things will be all right.

Finally, the doctor announces that the worst danger is over. Edward's heartbeat is more steady, and the fever has begun to drop. He is not going to die just yet.

"The infection hasn't progressed too far. I'm hopeful." He smooths his beard and pushes his spectacles onto his nose. "But Miss Boylan, I must clear Edward's system of the morphine. This is absolutely essential. You should have seen that from the beginning."

I want to protest that I told Edward the same already, but I sit quietly and take my scolding. Just yesterday, I was laughing with Edward as we sledded down that hill, and I hadn't the slightest suspicion that he was so near his breaking point. I have far more to learn than I ever wanted to admit.

The doctor stands. "I'd appreciate if you would clean and pack my instruments. I need to find an assistant of stouter constitution for the task ahead. This will not be easy, and it certainly won't be pleasant."

"Stouter constitution?" I ask. "Do you mean someone with more experience, or someone who is male?"

The doctor begins cleaning his spectacles, probably so he need not look at me.

"Forgive me doctor, but I assure you I'm more than competent. I want to help." I *need* to help. I must redeem myself, not only in the eyes of Dr. Durham but to Edward.

"That will be impossible. You won't be able to stand it, and I'm sure that Edward would prefer that any young lady, even a nurse, not see him like—"

"No, Doctor." I put steel into my voice, though inside I am trembling. You'd think the man had never heard of Florence Nightingale or Clara Barton. Or Marie Curie, for that matter. I'd thought such prejudices were left behind in the last century. "Edward would choose me. If he could speak now, he'd tell you that he doesn't want another soul to know about his morphia addiction." Too many would judge it as a moral failing on his part. If the world is going to know, then I want Edward to make the choice. Not anyone else.

Dr. Durham purses his lips together and regards me skeptically. "And what do you propose we tell Edward's family, Miss Boylan? How will we explain the days of pure torment that Edward is about to endure? This agony that he might not even survive?"

"Influenza," I tell him. "The sickness has already been rampant in this house. Everyone will believe it."

I don't think anyone knows that Edward already had the flu in the army. But even if they do, they won't question the doctor's diagnosis.

He turns to study our patient again. For the moment, Edward is peaceful. How long he will remain that way, I do not know.

"Very well," the doctor says. "Influenza. But you'd better resume wearing your gauze mask. And not just for verisimilitude. You must tell me now. Are you absolutely sure you can bear this?"

I nod, even though I'm not sure. I'm not sure of *anything* anymore.

21

Dinah
1943

That night, we sneak through alleys and side streets to reach the assay office. Abby lets us in through the back door.

"I was afraid you weren't coming," she says. "My mom thinks I'm auditing the books for the mining company, but she won't buy that excuse all night. She'll plotz if she finds out we brought a fella here."

Abby and Eddie say awkward hellos. She gawks at him. "Wild. So you're Edward Gainsbury. You're not addicted to morphine, are you?"

Eddie opens his mouth, but no sound comes out. His look is incredulous.

"Abby's kidding." I laugh, nudging him ahead of me in case he's thinking about turning tail. It was hard enough to get him here. At one point on our walk down the mountain, Eddie stopped altogether and threatened to go back to his cabin. He said he was afraid to get into trouble. I promised that no one but Abby knew he was here. The draft board certainly wasn't patrolling the streets of Powder Ridge. He just shook his head. He eventually calmed down enough to come with me, but I got the sense that it's not the draft board that's making him so skittish.

"Sorry," Abby says. "Welcome to the Powder Ridge Assay Office, such as it currently is. Make yourself at home. Can I get you something? Club soda, cigarette, whiskey? Milk?"

"Um...I'm not sure. I don't get out too much to be honest." Eddie's eyes are moving all about the room. "This is a swell place. I haven't seen anything like it." He walks over to a set of scales. He gently touches one of the balances and makes it rock back and forth. Then he turns around, a tentative grin on his face. He looks younger suddenly, not so burdened by dark things.

"Actually, I'd love an Italian soda, if you can make one. Do people still drink those?"

Abby shoots me a bemused glance. "Sure," she says. "If you don't mind canned seltzer. What's your favorite flavor?"

"I...don't know."

"Listen to me, talking like this is a soda fountain." Abby laughs. "I know I've got some raspberry syrup around here. My father's favorite." She digs a mostly-empty bottle out of a cabinet and starts making the sodas.

When Eddie sips his drink, he closes his eyes and sighs. "Just as good I as remember. At least I think I remember. Maybe this is even better."

Eddie keeps going around the assay's back room looking at rocks and old equipment. He peers into the huge mouth of the iron furnace, which has been cold now for years. Eddie asks all kinds of questions—about what we do here, how the mine used to work, what Main Street is like. His face lights up when he sees the radio set.

"Can I turn it on?" he asks. "I used to listen to shows all day long. I miss that—made me not feel so alone."

Abby finds a news broadcast. Eddie sips his raspberry soda and listens raptly, as if he hasn't heard anything about the outside world in months.

"Why don't you have a radio anymore?" I ask him.

"Hmm?" He looks up from his soda. "Oh, well, it got taken away. Sort of a punishment I guess." He shrugs one shoulder.

"A punishment? For what?"

"That's probably the wrong word," Eddie says. "Sounds worse than it is. I just wish I could follow what's happening with the war." He fiddles with the dial, turning to a different station. As if he's said something normal, not completely awful.

It's wrong. So wrong that the raspberry soda starts to turn cloying in my stomach. Eddie said that he has to hide. He insisted that it's for his own protection. But it seems to me like Eddie is a prisoner.

"Are you going to spend Christmas with your family?" Abby asks. "I mean, I assume you're a goy."

Eddie slurps the last of his soda. His eyes have gotten furtive. "I might. Some of them."

"What are they like?" I ask. "What are their names?"

Abby shakes her head lightly at me. *Too many questions, Dinah.*

Eddie keeps playing with the radio dial. "I haven't seen most of my family in a long time. We used to be close. But something changed, and I had to leave, and... How about we listen to your mysterious record now?"

I want to press him further, but he's antsy enough as it is. "Sure," I say. Maybe Millie's story about the other Edward Gainsbury will jog something loose in Eddie's mind. Get him to open up.

Abby's already got the record player switched on. Another moment, and it's starting to play. The three of us sit and listen. Millie Boylan begins to speak. But it's not the same recording as before.

"Whether it is death itself, or some creature that keeps death's vigil, I cannot say. But I felt its malevolence. And now, it knows my name."

22

Millie
1918

Edward has been tossing this way and that, halfway between sleep and waking. Moaning and crying out like he's not just in terrible pain—he's actually terrified. What sort of feverish dreams are plaguing him?

There are wisps of shadow clinging to his temples. I sense that there are more of those cursed shadow-things nearby, too, just waiting for me to drop my guard. This is a battle, and I am Edward's only defender. Yet I'm so anxious that I can barely sit still. All of the uncertainty is driving me mad.

I sit back in my chair and place a hand over my chest. My heart is beating so hard that my entire body shakes with it. It's still been only hours since Beth Gainsbury's funeral, yet it feels like days. The clock insists it is nearly three o'clock in the morning. Dr. Durham left only a short while ago to get some sleep. On the way out, he spoke to someone on the landing—was it Mrs. Bishop? Grace? Whoever it was, I heard her crying. They think Edward has Spanish flu, the same flu that killed Edward's mother. Already, I regret the lie. It's so cruel. I want to go find Lydia and Grace and tell them something else. Promise that Edward will be all right. But I *can't*. I don't know how this will end.

The doctor said that Edward might not survive this ordeal.

Edward's arms lay exposed over the blanket, and the circular marks I see there are a constant reminder of what's at stake. Where did he get the morphine, if not from me? Did he hide additional vials among his things? Or did someone else in Powder Ridge provide them? I'm furious at that possibility. In fact, I'm having trouble checking my emotions.

It isn't wise, the way that I feel for him. He's like no other man that I've met—so courageous and intelligent, so kind. My attraction to him is undeniable. But Edward's truly my patient now. He needs the clear thinking and the cold focus of a professional. Except for Dr. Durham, all he's got is me. I'm terrified that I won't be enough. How will I live with myself if I fail?

Oh Millie, buck up girl. I brush a tear away from my eye.

There's a knock at the door. It starts so low that I'm not sure what it is at first. But then the knocks get louder.

"Millie?" a small voice asks. "Please let me in?"

I debate for a brief moment. But the pleas continue, and I can't just let her stand out on the landing and cry. I tuck Edward's arms inside the blanket, switch off the light by his bedside, and go to the door.

When I open it, Lydia peers at me through the crack. "You must let me in."

"I can't," I say, blocking her. "You heard the doctor."

"You said Edward wouldn't get sick!" Tears streak down Lydia's face. "You promised me he wasn't in danger."

"I'm terribly sorry, Miss Gainsbury, but—"

Lydia pushes her way into the room. I just don't have it in me to stop her. Should I slam the door in the face of this poor lass, who's already lost her mother, nearly died herself, and now fears for her brother? I haven't the strength. It's barely been one day with Edward sick, and already, I'm faltering.

Lydia kneels by Edward's bed like she's praying. I go to her side. "Your brother wouldn't want you to see him like this," I say.

"What do you know about my brother?" she asks matter-of-factly.

"But you're still too weak, Lydia. You only just recovered. You have to rest."

"Then I'll rest here. I'll take turns with you. Or don't you sleep, Millie?"

My eyes sting, I'm so tired. I consider letting her stay. I can't tell Edward's sister the truth about his morphine addiction. It would be a betrayal. But his symptoms— from Dr. Durham's description and my own experience at my mother's clinic, the withdrawals will be similar to a severe flu. Lydia might not know the difference.

But she'll see the scars on his arms. If she guesses, will I insist on the lie? And what if her own health weakens again from the stress?

Edward moans like he's in agony. His hands claw at the sheets.

Lydia stands and faces me. "I won't leave my brother. He needs me, Millie. Please."

She's got all the determination that I wish I had in this moment. That settles it. I know I shouldn't. But I relent.

Only later will I realize what a fatal mistake I've made.

23

Dinah
1943

Abby lifts the needle from the record. We've just heard Millie say that she's going to assist Dr. Durham with the detoxification. The story makes odd jumps. It's that damned scratch down the side. But I've gathered enough to know that Millie's Edward is—or I should say *was*—ill, both from infection and from withdrawals. Grace and Liddy Gainsbury think that he died from influenza, and Millie's story explains why—they only *thought* he had the flu because Millie and Dr. Durham were protecting Edward's secret.

What else did Millie lie to them about?

Eddie stands. The color has drained from his cheeks. For a brief moment, his gray eyes look solid black. As if a shadow has just passed across them.

"This is going to seem really strange," he says. "But…can you look at something?"

He's rolling up the sleeves of his shirt.

Eddie holds his arms out, showing the insides of his wrists and elbows. There's the scar I saw before on his wrist. But his arms are riddled with more of them: raised, circular marks; reddened vertical lines. Actually, they look the way that Millie described Edward's injection scars.

Instinctively, I cringe away. I don't want to see what I'm seeing. Abby inhales sharply.

"I'm *not* a drug addict," Eddie says nervously.

"Then where'd they come from?" I ask. "Were you in the hospital?"

Eddie shakes his head. "I used to get sick a lot, I think. There are things I'm not allowed to ask about. They told me it's better not to know. To keep me safe."

His chin trembles like he's barely holding his composure. I feel like I might spit back up that raspberry soda.

"They" again. Who, Eddie? I want to shout. *Who?*

Abby doesn't say anything. She's still staring at the scars.

"There's more." Edward goes to the table and sits. "Don't scream, all right?" He bends forward, takes off his shoe, and starts rolling up his trouser leg.

Abby shoots me a panicked glance. What on earth is he showing us?

Eddie pulls his trouser up over his knee, and I see it —the scar. There's a ring of scarred tissue a few inches above his knee. Abby and I both stare at it. I can hardly believe what I'm looking at. I slowly reach out and touch the scar with one finger. It's smooth, and the skin feels thin. The rest of his leg extends below the scar tissue, seemingly intact.

"What is going on?" Abby asks. "How did you get that scar?"

"I. Don't. Know." It takes Eddie a long time to say these words. Each one is like a plea—he's begging to know what happened to him, but also begging not to remember.

Tears have flooded my eyes. This is wrong, all of it. I can't wrap my mind around these things.

"I shouldn't have come here," he says. "This is all a mistake." He starts for the door. I run after him and grab his elbow.

"Eddie wait, please."

He shakes me off. "*Don't touch me.* Leave me alone." His voice is shrill. Suddenly he grasps his head. He's gasping for air, hyperventilating. Eddie knocks into the wall and then slides down to the floor. He puts his head between his knees.

"I didn't mean to upset you," I say. "I just want to understand all this."

"I know," he replies. The words sound like a moan.

"Do you really want to leave?"

He shakes his head.

I'm not sure what else to do, so I wait. I get myself together, because whatever Eddie's been through, it's much worse than what I'm feeling. I can't help him if I fall apart.

After a long time, he looks up at me. "There are dark places in my memory. Time that's missing. I told you that. But I've been having these dreams. I see images when I'm awake, too—people, places. Ever since I got to Powder Ridge. And it's worse every time I see you. I don't know what it means."

Abby crouches beside him. "Maybe we can help you find out. Let us try."

His gaze is steady now. He whispers, "I'm afraid to remember."

24

Millie
1918

Over the next days, I lose all sense of time. I barely notice whether the sun is up or down; the meals delivered to us blend together. For much of it, Lydia stays by my side. She follows my instructions, serving as an extra set of hands.

Dr. Durham is angry when he sees Lydia, but I let her handle the arguments. Edward's symptoms are far more terrible than the doctor's wrath could ever be.

He has long since vomited up anything resembling food. Yet still his body retches. He writhes and scratches his skin and begs for relief from the pain, all the while remaining insensible to the world. His skin burns with fever. Sweat drenches his clothing and the bedsheets time and again. There's a tempest of need inside of him, and it never lets him rest. And all the while, the shadows hover around him. They are always darkest during his half-waking fever dreams.

"Doctor, do something," Lydia demands. "He seems to be suffering more than my mother ever did. Are you sure this is the same flu?"

Dr. Durham doesn't risk a glance at me. "Edward is a soldier. He's fighting the illness as a man would, that's all."

Lydia rolls her eyes at the doctor. But she seems to accept his answer. She doesn't remark about the scars on Edward's arms. Instead, she becomes an expert at changing the bandages on his stump. She bathes him and tends to him without needing any more advice from me. Every time I venture into the hall, Grace is there waiting. Dr. Durham has banned her from the sickroom for her own wellbeing. But she always begs me to know what's happening, how Edward is doing. "Save him, Millie, please," she says. "I nearly lost him once already. I can't live without my brother." Whenever I feel tired, I think of Grace waiting for news. I can't let her down.

About a week after Beth Gainsbury's funeral, Edward is still unchanged. He's looking more gaunt by the day. Barely able to keep down broth, much less any substantial food. Yet the shadows around his head have faded to mere wisps. It would seem a hopeful sign, but I'm still ill at ease. The air in the room is oppressive. I feel anxious. Watched by something unseen.

I'm trickling water into Edward's mouth when Lydia stays my trembling hand. "Rest," she says. "You won't do him any good if you fall ill yourself."

I stumble out into the hall, grateful that neither Grace nor Mr. Gainsbury are there to pepper me with questions I can't answer.

Even as I plunge headlong into sleep, I still think of the wisps of shadow that hover around Edward's sickroom. From the first moment I saw Gainsbury House, there's been a darkness hanging here. I know that I haven't yet seen the last of it.

When I wake, it's still dark. The house is quiet. I have no idea how long I've slept. Stretching, I get up.

After a quick visit to the bathroom, I return to the sickroom.

But I stop in the doorway. The room is dark.

"Lydia?" I ask. Where could she have gone?

Slowly, I walk into the room. My hands reach out in front of me, fumbling for a lamp. But I can't find one. Lydia must have taken the lantern by Edward's bedside and left in a hurry. Now I'm getting anxious. Is Lydia all right?

"Millie?"

The voice is faint. I go farther into the room. "Lydia?"

"Help."

The word comes out as a low rasp. But it doesn't sound like Lydia's voice. Could that be Edward? Is he finally conscious? My eyes are adjusting to the low light. Yet when I look toward Edward's bed, another shock meets me. He's gone. I see his blankets all in a tumble, but the rest of the bed is dark. He couldn't be well enough yet to stand. He must've fallen.

"Millie?" he says again, more plaintively this time. "I'm...frightened."

I rush to the bed, looking around the sides for his crumpled form. But then a weak hand grasps my wrist. I almost cry out. I realize that Edward *is* still in the bed, and my breath turns to a sob.

He is cocooned in darkness. The shadows have knit themselves around him completely. It can only mean one thing.

He doesn't have long to live.

25

Dinah
1943

The three of us stare at each other. I'm the one who finally asks the question, even though we all must be thinking it. "What if the Edward Gainsbury from 1918 never died at all?"

Right away, Eddie says, "I can't be him."

"Then explain that scar." Abby speaks sadly, apologetically. "Explain the marks on your arms."

"But I *know* I can't be him." Eddie pushes down his pant leg, and then rests his head in his hands. "People can't just reattach lost limbs."

The very idea is grotesque, a real life version of Mary Shelley's *Frankenstein*. Not to mention impossible. But it's like Abby said—why should it matter whether you "believe" in it or not? You shouldn't ignore what you see before your eyes.

"What about Millie?" Abby asks him. "Do you remember her at all?"

"No."

"But the song," I remind Eddie. "You remember that song, something about 'Irish Eyes Are Smiling.' You remembered someone singing it to you. Who was it?"

When Eddie meets my gaze, his eyes are red and bleary. "*I don't know.* It was just a feeling, and now it's gone."

Abby sits atop the mail counter. The three of us are quiet for several minutes, thinking. As I pace, I watch Eddie surreptitiously from the corner of my eye. He hasn't answered any of my questions, not fully. All I can do is forge ahead and hope that he'll decide to talk. And maybe, he'll start to remember enough that we can understand what's happening.

Abby slaps her thigh. "Wait. Millie is around our parents' age. Right? She doesn't live in Powder Ridge now, but what if somebody around here remembers her? They might even know where we could find her."

"I thought of that," I say. "My mother might know her. But I'm not welcome at home right now."

"Then we could ask around," Abby suggests. "See who can tell us anything about Millie Boylan." Eddie looks up sharply, and Abby adds, "We wouldn't let anything slip about you, obviously. I know how to be discrete."

Besides, if we told anybody our current theory—that the Edward Gainsbury sitting with us could be the same Edward Gainsbury who supposedly died in 1918—who the heck would believe it?

"Let's just listen to the rest of the record," Eddie says. "I need to get back soon." He sounds defeated. No, that's not it—he sounds like somebody who has too much weighing on his mind, and he doesn't want to share it. Does he not trust Abby? Does he not trust *me*?

Should we trust *him*?

Abby starts playing the record from where we left off. But it's changed yet again. This time, it's a girl's voice humming "When Irish Eyes Are Smiling" instead of a piano playing. She doesn't sound happy though. The humming is slow. Mournful.

There's a subtle shift in the room. A stale scent in the air, like the inside of an old icebox. Like that third floor room in the bunkhouse. The humming sends chills down my back, as if fingertips are tracing the outside of my jacket, and instinctively I look over my shoulder.

"I know," Abby whispers. "Feels like someone else is here, doesn't it?"

Eddie is biting down hard on his lower lip.

Then, the humming stops. Millie begins to speak. Her voice is laced with static. The merest whisper.

"*I'm in the dark.*"

26

Millie
1918

I can't see Edward's face. The shadows are too thick. Immediately, I reach out for him, trying to wave the darkness away. But the darkness is everywhere. Permeating this entire room. It is night outside the window and night within, and there is no longer even a trace of light for relief.

And where has Lydia gone?

"Edward?" I ask. "I'm here."

I touch his chest. The shadows swarm onto my arms, scorching me like acid. But I grit my teeth against them and keep trying to push them away. I can hear Edward breathing raggedly. He's groping for me in the dark. His hands find my shoulders, and the weak, desperate way he tries to hold onto me breaks my heart.

"Millie, help me. I can't...I can't see."

I cannot see him either. I find his face and press my hands to each side of his head. But the shadows won't dissipate. I feel them climbing up my arms. I bite back a scream of pain. My skin is boiling.

"No," I moan, but they keep coming. Somehow the darkness around me grows even blacker. Oh Lord, they're everywhere. Roiling in hideous waves across my skin.

I open my mouth to scream, and the darkness rushes in. I can feel it burning my throat, filling my lungs. There's a painful impact against my side as I fall to the floor.

Then my mind goes blank.

I try to call out, but there's nothing. No sound to make, no mouth to speak. I'm in utter darkness. I can't breathe.

But I'm not alone.

Out of the dimness, there are two pinprick eyes staring at me.

27

Dinah
1943

"I'm in the dark."

Abby's hand flies to her mouth. The record keeps playing.

"Everyone's gone," Millie whispers. In the background, the recording crackles and hisses. *"Except the eyes. They're watching me. And I keep coming back. I can't escape."*

Tingles race along my skin.

"It's here with me," she says. *"Edward, I'm afraid."*

There's a pause in the recording. Static plays.

Eddie says quietly, "Please, turn it off."

"There's a cabin. A door scratched with the shape of a cross. I want to go to you, Edward, but I can't. Help me."

We hear Millie crying. My hand reaches for Eddie's. His skin is cold.

"The cabin. The scratched door. The cross."

Eddie stands up. His chair tips backward and crashes to the floor.

"Please, Edward. Find me. I'm in the dark. Find me."

"Turn it off," Eddie says. He goes toward the player. "Turn it off!"

Abby runs to the record player and lifts the needle. Eddie has rushed out the back door. I follow him.

He's vomiting onto the snow.

He wipes his mouth, stands, backs away until he bumps against the assay building. "Dinah, do you think Millie Boylan was talking to *me* on that recording? Am *I* the Edward that she needs to find her?"

I don't have the answers. He's looking up at the sky, his eyes unfocused.

"The door," he says. "The cross. I know what she's talking about. I know where it is."

We plan to set out at dawn. Abby goes home to sleep, but I stay at the assay office with Eddie. We find an old bedroll for him in the storage room. He stays quiet, seemingly occupied with his own thoughts.

In the morning, Abby brings fresh clothes, including a heavy coat that belongs to her father. Eddie can finally take off that military one. He pulls a navy-colored knit cap down over his head, hiding his overgrown hair. He's far less recognizable now.

We leave the assay office at first light. Just in case, I go ahead to scout. Eddie is going to follow ten minutes behind, and then Abby will come last. But our precautions are unnecessary. I don't see a soul on the way up to Cherry Mountain.

We meet up on the far side of the boardinghouse. It's windy this morning, and I pull up my scarf to hide my face from the chill.

"This way," Eddie says.

He's told us where we're heading: the ruined cabin by the clearing. The same place that so many strange things have already happened. But still, my pulse gives a jolt when we see it.

The wooden boards have turned a mottled gray with age. Only one wall is still fully standing. The others have either slumped or collapsed into a pile of splintered boards. The door hangs at a sharp angle by a single, rusted hinge.

We stop a few yards back, as if there's some invisible barrier keeping us away. None of us makes a move to go any closer.

"It's there," Eddie says in a low voice, pointing.

There is a small, rudimentary cross scratched into the lower half of the door.

Abby takes an audible breath. She walks slowly over to the door and bends to look. "The wood is pretty weathered where it's carved. Seems like it's been here a long time."

I kneel beside Abby and run my fingers over the indentations in the wood. They're smooth and cold. "What are we supposed to be looking for?" I ask.

Eddie crowds in between us. Using his gloved hands, he brushes the snow and ice away from the ground under the doorway. He tries to dig into the dirt. But he doesn't get far. The ground is too frozen. Quickly, he gives up.

Eddie stands and grabs hold of the tilting door. He pulls, and its remaining hinge gives way with a meager popping sound. He sets the door over to one side of the cabin.

When he steps inside, Abby and I are right behind him. I switch on my flash light and shine it into the space.

It's like a cave. The walls have fallen against one another, leaving a hollow underneath. There's a few pieces of black metal that might've been a stove. Rusty metal springs that probably belonged to a bed.

Stooping, Eddie crawls forward into the room. I use the flash light to illuminate the space in front of him. Planks cover the floor, but they've shifted over the years. The gaps between the wood don't show earth beneath. Only darkness.

"Under the floor," I say. My voice sounds strange in the cramped space. Muffled. "There's something down there."

Eddie lifts a plank easily. The nails must have rusted away into nothing. He moves it aside. There's definitely a cavity of some kind under the floor, and not very deep.

"What's that?" Abby asks, leaning forward.

Eddie takes my flash light and shines it into the hole he's made. There's something like ragged fabric, maybe leather. I can't tell what it is. Eddie moves another plank, revealing more of the object.

"It's a suitcase." He tugs gently on the handle, sliding it free of the hole. He tries to lift it, and the top clasp breaks. The contents spill everywhere.

"Dammit," he says. But he makes no move to touch any of it. Just shines the light onto each item one by one:

A black piece of clothing, folded so long it looks more like paper than fabric.

A hairbrush, a few glass pots of cosmetics, an ancient jar of Colgate dental powder.

A couple of novels with yellowed pages.

A small drawstring pouch that looks like a coin purse.

A white nurse's cap.

Abby crawls onto the ground beside Eddie. Carefully, she picks up each item and places it back in the suitcase. Eddie sits back against his heels and watches her. He's breathing so hard you'd think he'd just run a mile.

"Blood," Abby whispers. She's holding up the nurse's cap. There are dark brown stains along its edge. There's a long hair stuck to the fabric. It glows in the flash light beam. A long, red hair. My stomach starts to twist.

"I think I need some air." Eddie pushes himself up and nearly knocks me over as he gropes for the doorway.

I'm not feeling too well myself. But I pick up the flash light that Eddie dropped, and I kneel beside Abby. She's still got the cap in her hand. Her fingers are going pale, starting to shake. I take the cap out of her grip. I drop it in the suitcase.

"We should get out of here," Abby says.

I want to go, too. There's not enough air in here. Those collapsed walls tilting toward us; the rotting smell of the wood. But instinct compels me to stay. We aren't finished yet.

Something worse is coming. Much, much worse.

I push the suitcase to one side. I try to lift another plank from the floor. But it won't come. Abby grabs hold of its edge. Together we pry it up. There's a loud snap and the board flies upward, revealing another section of the cavity that was hidden beneath the cabin floor.

I'm not prepared for what we see.

Abby screams and turns away. "Oh, no. No. It can't be."

Stomach acid is rising in my throat. It burns. I'm going to throw up. But somehow I keep my mouth closed. Tears are pooling in my eyes.

A skeletal hand stretches toward us, palm up and fingers splayed, as if it's reaching out for help.

We remove more of the boards. There's a body lying in the ground, curled into a fetal position. A cape or jacket of some kind covers most of it. Mercifully, the person's face is turned away. But long wisps of bright red hair still cling to the skull.

Neither one of us speaks. Abby exhales slowly, her whole body shuddering.

I think we're looking at the last remains of Millie Boylan.

28

Millie
1918

I dream I am in darkness. I'm *of* darkness. I can't breathe. Why won't they let me go? Why do they just watch me with their cold eyes? Not two eyes, no—there are hundreds of them. Thousands. Legions. Each one glints like the faceted eye of an insect.

Their voices are needles slipping underneath my skin. *Millie. Millie. Wake up.*

"Millie, can you hear me? Can you wake up?"

I gasp as my eyes open. Light pours in. Assaults me. I squeeze my eyelids shut again. The darkness closes back over me.

"Millie? Are you awake?"

Awareness slowly returns. I feel the air moving through my nose. My chest moves and my lungs fill gratefully. Something touches my cheek. It's warm. Kind. The voice speaks again, and this time I recognize it.

"I think she's awake," Lydia says. "Her breathing changed. See her eyelids fluttering?"

Another voice speaks. "Millie, can you hear me?"

It's Edward. Is he really here? Am I truly free? I want to see him. I blink my eyes, adjusting to the light. The memories begin to return: the sick room; how the shadows covered Edward. How they tricked me. Lunged for me the moment I was close enough.

Edward and Lydia are standing over me. I'm lying in a bed. I go to sit up, but my arms are too weak to hold me. I try to speak but my mouth is so dry.

"Careful, now. Don't try to move just yet." Edward sits beside me, and his arm slides beneath my shoulders for support. It's a lovely feeling.

There are several minutes of fussing. Lydia fetches a glass of water. Edward helps me sit upright against a wall of pillows. He looks surprisingly well considering the ordeal he's just been through. His hair is combed. Indeed, it's been trimmed. His face is clean shaven, and his eyes have lost the sunken, dull cast that they had during his withdrawals.

I swallow and say, "I don't understand. How are you already so well? Just last night…Good gravy, Edward, I thought…"

I thought you were dying.

He and Lydia exchange a glance. "Millie," he says, "you've been asleep for five days."

"*Five days?*" That just can't be. It isn't possible. "But Lydia, I was only just looking for you. It was dark, you'd taken the lamp from Edward's room." I'm still trying to piece together those last moments that I was conscious.

"Grace had disappeared, and my father insisted I find her," Lydia says. "I was so upset when I got back and you were sick. But Millie, that was five days ago. There's no mistake."

"Can you tell us anything about what happened?" Edward asks. "Why you were unconscious so long? Dr. Durham was here, but he's had no answers."

I'm so dismayed that I can't reply. I can only remember the shadows that covered him—how they lured me closer—but nothing afterward. Does this mean that Edward didn't see the darkness attack me that night?

I try to get out of bed and practically collapse onto Edward's chair. He catches me, and the obvious strength of his arms fills me with relief. He's really better. He isn't going to die. The shadows are finally, *finally*, gone from around his head. I put a hand to his cheek, and I'm amazed at how cool and dry his skin feels.

Lydia clears her throat.

I draw back my hand from Edward's face. "I'm sorry," I say, not sure if I'm speaking to Edward or his sister or both of them.

You've been a burden, a voice rasps in my head, unbidden. *You're not wanted here.* I shake off a chill.

"It's quite all right," Edward murmurs, his gray eyes locked with mine. Then his expression changes. Something is wrong.

"What is it?" I ask.

He blinks and shakes his head. "Nothing, I'm sorry. I thought I saw something. Trick of the light."

"You must be starved," Lydia says. Her manner is stiff. I can never quite tell with Lydia what she's thinking. She gets up and leaves. The door remains open to the hall.

"We need to talk," Edward whispers to me. "I have some business with my father to see to today, but we can take a walk later, if you're up to it. Away from prying eyes or ears. Promise you'll stay here? You'll go nowhere else?"

I nod, though I'm only more confused. Why is he worried that someone is listening?

After a few minutes, Lydia returns with a dish of oatmeal, which I devour. Then she helps me to the bathroom to clean up. I thank her; she certainly needn't have helped me so much. Lydia must have been changing my bedclothes, feeding me water and broth all this time. It's humbling. I can't imagine how I'll repay this debt.

But Lydia brushes off my thanks and my apologies.

"My family owes you far more than money could account for," she says.

She politely faces the door while I strip and then climb into the clawfoot bathtub, which is full of steaming water. I sigh and slide down until the water reaches my chin. It's almost too hot, but it feels blissful. The knots in my back and shoulders begin to unwind.

"You must've worked yourself too hard," Lydia says. "My brother thinks something strange is behind your collapse and unconsciousness, but I'm sure you just needed a long rest."

I hope, rather than believe, that she's right. I work a bar of soap into a lather. "What have I missed these past few days?" I ask.

"Oh, too much has happened." Lydia leans against the vanity. She chews her lower lip for several seconds before saying more. "We found out that Grace has been spending time with Briony Spencer against our father's wishes. He was furious."

I groan. "Oh, no. The poor dear. Is Grace very upset?"

"She hasn't come out of her room. It's just as well. Every time I go in to check on her, she's bawling her eyes out like a child. My father forbade her from coming to look after you, otherwise she'd probably be here right now, making a scene. It's disgraceful."

The severity of her tone surprises me. "I take it you don't approve of Grace's emotion?" I ask carefully. "Or is it Briony Spencer you don't approve of?"

"I don't know Briony Spencer. I only know what I've heard about her, and I don't think she's the kind of woman who should befriend my thirteen-year-old sister." Lydia's fist comes down on the marble top of the vanity, making me jump. Water splashes from the tub. "But what shocks me even more, Millie, is that *you* know Mrs. Spencer so well. You've known her for years, haven't you? Yet you hid that fact from my father and my family. And you have even encouraged Grace to continue her association with the Spencers! Isn't that true?"

"I—" How can I defend myself without speaking of Edward behind his back? I don't want to cause even more family discord. "It's true that Briony is a dear friend of mine. But I didn't hide anything from you or your family with ill intent, Lydia, I swear to you."

"But you didn't volunteer the information, either."

She's right. You're a liar. You put Edward in danger, nearly killed him. You don't deserve to be here. It's that rasping voice again—like a multitude of voices laid over top of one another, speaking in unison. I don't like it. The thoughts reflect my own doubts, yet they feel foreign. Cruel.

Soap is drying on my shoulders. I try to rinse it away. Suspicions are building in my mind, and I know I shouldn't give in them, but I can't help myself. "And who did volunteer this so-called information? Was it Rachel Kohler?"

"So what if it was?"

I knew it. No doubt it'll sound dramatic, even paranoid, but Rachel has been plotting against me since the day she saw Edward almost kiss me. The very same day that we'd been to visit Grace at Briony's mansion.

Lydia rubs a hand over her face. "Please, don't misunderstand me. I'm not ungrateful for all you've done for us. I've stood up to my father on your behalf, and that's no easy thing. If he had his way, he'd have put you on the first train out of Powder Ridge, conscious or not. I couldn't allow that. Edward wouldn't either. You can stay until you're feeling well enough to travel."

As long as it's not too long, her tone implies.

I should have expected this. I would never have imposed on the Gainsburys if I'd had the choice. But to hear this from Lydia—a lass I've come to think of as my friend—the sting is vicious indeed. And here I am, sitting exposed in this tub of rapidly cooling water.

I can barely lift my eyes from the rug on the floor. "I'd like to get out now, please."

She holds out a towel, turning her face away. I cover myself, water dripping from my hair down my shoulders.

"You're right," I say. "I'll pack my things. I'd like to say goodbye to Grace before I go, if that's all right."

Her posture relaxes. She's relieved. "Of course."

I expect Lydia to leave the bathroom, but she lingers, staring stonily at the tile. "Millie, is there anything else you've been keeping from me?" she asks. "Anything at all?"

I weigh my words carefully. Could she know about the true cause of Edward's illness? But if she already knows, there is no reason to tell her. And if she doesn't, I'm not the one she should be asking.

"There's nothing," I say.

She leaves the bathroom, and the door closes with a firm click.

I glance up at my reflection in the mirror. I'm shocked by how gaunt I look. My skin is translucent, traced with garish blue veins. My lips are chapped and beginning to crack.

As I stare, a dark shape passes behind me across the tile wall. I gasp and turn, but there's nothing there. At least, nothing that I can see.

I dress hurriedly, avoiding any more glances in the mirror.

I pack my few belongings in my small suitcase. I make the bed in Edward's old room. I brush strands of my red hair from the pillow, smoothing away every small trace that I've been here. There isn't much to do.

I find Grace inconsolable in her bedroom. She's already so upset about losing Briony's friendship. Her eyes lighten with hope when she sees me, as if I'm bringing some possibility of good news. But I've done all I can for this family. Mr. Gainsbury and Lydia have made their wishes clear.

When I tell her I'm leaving, she hardly seems to understand. "But where will you go?" she asks. She sniffles through a stuffed-up nose.

"Denver," I say. "Home." But is it home, really? I don't know what home means anymore. No one is waiting for me there. I don't even know if I can continue my work as a private care nurse. Nothing is certain for me now.

Lydia is waiting for me by the front door. She has my suitcase and the check signed by Mr. Gainsbury. Neither of us mentions Edward, who is still away from the house. It will be easier leaving this way, without him trying to talk me out of it or reminding me of the bond that we share. There's so much to say to Edward that I don't know how to say anything at all.

He's safe and well, which means my work in this house is done. Whatever those shadows did to me five nights ago, it's beyond anything that either Edward or I can fathom. We'll both be safer if I move on.

I button my coat, take my suitcase in hand, and walk out into the cold, watery light of midday.

29

Dinah
1943

Millie is dead. Somebody hid her body and her suitcase beneath the floor of that cabin, erasing her from the world. Somebody killed her.

Murdered her.

The girl we heard on that recording was kind and compassionate. If there's any justice in this world, then how can such a loss go unnoticed, much less unpunished?

My brother's usually the one to consider such existential questions. I thought I was the cynic, the one who didn't worry about big ideas like *justice* and *faith*. Between the two of us, Nate is the one who's always been searching for more.

We have no synagogue in Powder Ridge, and the number of Jewish families has dwindled since the mine closed. But for years now, David Spivak—Abby's father—has held High Holy Day services at the assay office for those still here. My mother was born Orthodox but she isn't religious, and my father was raised a Baptist but hated the strictness of his parents. So my family never went to services—neither Jewish nor Christian—until Nate was twelve. He'd learned from the Spivaks that Mother's Jewishness passed down to us, and Nate latched onto the idea. He even took Hebrew lessons with Mr. Spivak. Nate tried teaching me, but I wasn't too keen. The words wouldn't stick in my head.

On Yom Kippur last year, Nate helped Mr. Spivak read from the mahzor. I closed my eyes, just listening, and I could almost understand why Nate wanted to be there. I willed my heart to atone for being jealous. For not wanting to share my brother with anyone or anything else. I did feel something, though it wasn't exactly relief.

After Mr. Spivak blew his grandfather's shofar, Mrs. Spivak served cheese blintzes, smoked trout, and mountains of scrambled eggs to break the fast. Well, Nate's the only one of us who fasts. But it was the best meal I've had in ages. Even my parents had a good time. Mother actually giggled as she licked the last bits of cream cheese from her fingers.

I remember that walk home. It was a perfect early fall day, crisp enough to make my nose cold, but not so chilly that I needed a sweater yet. The smell of woodsmoke was in the air. Leaves crunched underfoot. It was the kind of day when the war seemed impossibly far away. So far it could never touch us.

Nate was pushing Papa's wheelchair fast enough to make the metal scream, both of them laughing. You have no idea how rare it is to hear my father laugh. It's a strange sound, like a car engine that's trying to start but not quite making it. Only Nate can coax it out of him.

My mother was hugging me to her side. "I'm glad Nate talked us into going. Maybe next year I'll bring my apple kuchen." There was no bitterness in her voice. No slur of liquor.

I put my arm around Mother's waist and hugged her back. I was feeling hopeful. Nate and Papa were far ahead of us. They'd already turned a corner, gone out of sight.

It was almost dark. The silhouette of Cherry Mountain loomed ahead. The wind picked up as the street fell into shadow.

164

"Do you hear that?" Mother said. There was a sudden edge to her tone. A warning. Her mood was changing just as quickly as night was falling. "It sounds like moaning."

"It's just wind."

She pulled away from me. "Don't tell me it's just wind. I know what wind sounds like. Nate shouldn't have left us behind." We kept walking, now several feet apart. Mother crossed her arms over her middle. "I just don't like being out at night alone. I've complained a million times about getting more streetlights, but nobody listens."

I didn't point out that she wasn't alone, she was with me. Besides, there's no crime in Powder Ridge. Nobody's been murdered here since the turn of the century at least. Not since its Old West days, when it was a town full of treasure hunters and gunslingers.

"What are you afraid of, Mother? Monsters? Ghosts?"

She walked faster. Her heels clomped on the sidewalk. It was getting darker, and I could barely make out her shape.

"You can scoff, Dinah," she said. "Laugh all you want. But if you'd been through the things that I have, maybe you'd have a little more sympathy for me."

She hurried toward home. I was sorry for upsetting her, but she could be so impossible. I strolled awhile, kicking leaves. Night closed in, and there was no moon that night. It was dark. So dark I must have missed a turn, and suddenly I couldn't recognize the houses in front of me. They all looked the same—boarded up and abandoned. I couldn't find a street sign. It's stupid, but my heart started tapping a rapid beat.

Then, I saw something. There was movement in the shadows. As if the shadows themselves were shifting, gathering together into some shape.

I turned to run and smacked into a solid form.

"Dinah, what are you doing? Where've you been?"

It was Nate. I grabbed my brother's shirt and hid my face against his chest. He walked me home, laughing at me for imagining monsters. He said our mother's paranoia had gotten to me. But I was just glad he was there. With Nate by my side, I wasn't scared of anything. I believed in *him*, and that was enough.

There's one thing that I do know: I had no idea until now how bad things really could be. I never imagined that there were such dark secrets buried in our town.

All this time, Millie's been waiting to be found.

Abby and I stagger out of the ruined cabin. I've already replaced the boards over Millie's remains.

Eddie is bent over, one hand against a tree, dry heaving. He looks up at us.

"She's in there, isn't she?" he asks. "Her...body, I mean."

Abby nods, wiping her eyes with the back of her hand. "Eddie, can we go to your place?" she asks. "I don't think I can be here anymore. It's just too much."

It's how I feel exactly. Eddie nods and leads us away from the ruined cabin. The sky is getting lighter by the minute, and I can almost pretend that the past night was a horrific, vivid dream. If only that were true.

When we're inside his small house, Abby and I sit on the floor beside his bed. She takes my hand and squeezes it. Eddie starts heating the kettle and puts his can of ground coffee on the counter. We all stay quiet until he passes out mugs of his terrible coffee. I take a sip, ignoring the bitterness, welcoming the jolt from the caffeine.

Eddie sits on his bed, his mug in his fist. He brushes tears from his eyes with his sleeve.

"Do you remember her?" Abby asks him.

"I don't know what I remember," he says thickly. "I don't want to talk about it."

Murdered, I think to myself again.

This isn't just some ghost story anymore, or a strange mystery about a fella who shouldn't be here. It's bigger than the three of us can handle.

I stare into the muddy surface of the coffee. "We have to call the county sheriff," I say.

Eddie stands and leans against the counter. He sets his coffee aside. He hasn't taken a sip. "We will. But I need some time. If the sheriff's people come out here, they'll find me, and they'll start asking all kinds of questions."

I wave my hand at the front door. "But there's a girl's dead body about five minutes away from here. This isn't about the draft board anymore."

"You think I don't know that?" Eddie asks. "Do have have any idea…" He cringes and covers his eyes with his hand.

"What're we supposed to tell the sheriff?" Abby asks me. "That a magic recording led us to that cabin and made us pull up the floor?"

I shake my head. I don't know what I'm going to tell them. I haven't thought that far ahead. But does that really matter? Can't we just play the weird record for the police so they'll hear Millie's voice for themselves?

Unless the record changes again. Just plays "When Irish Eyes Are Smiling." Or doesn't play at all.

"It's been decades since...whatever happened," Abby says. "Dinah, would it really hurt if she waits a few more days?"

Rots a few more days under the ground? I want to shout this out loud. Not at Abby though. I don't want to shout at her; I want to shout at the world to protest the injustice of it. It's so obvious now: Millie is the ghost who's been haunting us. It must've been her in the boardinghouse, her footprints in the clearing, maybe even her face looking in at Eddie's window. She's been trying so hard to get our attention so we'd find her. How many other people has she tried to contact? How long has she already been waiting? Listen to me, thinking about this ghost like she's not only real, but a conscious person. Yet there's no use denying it anymore. I guess I believe in something after all.

I open my mouth, but I don't know what to say. As much as I don't like it, I guess Abby's right.

"OK," I say. "We'll wait a few days. But we have to tell someone soon."

Abby stands up, brushing off her wool skirt. "Eddie, how much time do you need?"

He looks around the cramped cabin like he's already saying goodbye. Is that what this means? Goodbye? Eddie is going to be sent off to some other place, and we're never going to see him again. We might never find out who he really is.

"A week," he finally says. "Just give me a week, and then you can call the sheriff. You can call whoever you want."

"What're you going to do?" I ask him.

Eddie doesn't look at me. He pours his coffee into the waste bin.

"I'll be fine," he says. "Don't worry about me."

A few minutes later, Abby and I head back toward town. We're both too shaken and too exhausted to speak. Fog lies heavily on the mountain. It swallows the tops of the trees. I can't shake the feeling that somebody's out there, just out of sight, watching us as we pass.

Millie
1918

It's not until I'm in Briony's living room, wrapped in a warm quilt and sipping red wine, that I let myself cry.

"Let it out," my friend says, snuggling against me. She draws my head down onto her shoulder, the same way that my mother used to do, and I cry even harder. "It'll all be OK. I promise. This'll sort itself out before you know it."

If only my problems were so simple. But Briony doesn't know the whole truth of what's been going on. Only Edward Gainsbury does. And that's a big part of the trouble.

After leaving Gainsbury House, I almost went straight to the train station. But I couldn't leave without saying goodbye to Briony. And of course, after one look at me, she pulled me into the house and has been mothering me ever since. Apparently, she's been asking about me for the past several days, demanding to know what happened. She was relieved to find me standing upright and in one piece.

"Courtland is already spreading the word that you're looking for new clients," Briony adds. "In no time, you'll have a new patient in some other town and those awful Gainsburys will be long forgotten. And I'll be the only one who's sad because I'm missing you."

I heave a stuttering sigh. "Oh Briony, I don't know. I'm not sure I can keep up with this line of work. I've seen so much death." And death has seen me. I keep having that feeling that I did in the bathroom—like there's a shadow passing behind me, cast by someone I can't see. But every time I go to look, it's gone.

You have seen nothing of the truth, I hear inside my head. *But you will.*

I shiver, despite the warmth of the quilt around my shoulders.

"Then you'll find a different job," Briony says. "And until you decide, you can stay here in Powder Ridge with Courtland and me. As long as you like."

"So close to the Gainsburys?" And though I don't want to be petty, I can't help adding, "Rachel Kohler won't like it. She's already tried her best to get rid of me."

Briony cocks her head, her eyebrow arching. "Is that so?"

I set down my glass of wine. "She's the one who told Mr. Gainsbury that you and I are friends. Rachel must've seen me visit you that day. And I suspect she's also the reason that Mr. Gainsbury knows about Grace's art lessons here."

Briony purses her lips. "I did hear a salacious rumor. I should've realized it was Rachel who started it. She's a snake, that one. She's grasping for some way to hold onto Edward. But it isn't going to work."

There's noise in the hallway. Briony's housekeeper opens the door and pokes her head in. "Ma'am? Edward Gainsbury is at the door. He's asking for Miss Boylan."

Briony and her housekeeper both stare at me. Briony's grinning, but I have a funny, sick sort of feeling in my chest. How did he find me? Well, perhaps it was no great mystery. There aren't many places in town I could have gone.

"I can bring him here, if you want," Briony offers, gesturing to the comfortable living room around us. "Just for a chat. See what he has to say."

I can imagine Edward sitting in the wingback chair across from me, drinking his own glass of wine. It would all be so civilized, so simple. As if we were just two friends. But it would also be a lie. In some ways, I've never been closer to anyone than I am to Edward. Since the day we met, I've felt powerfully drawn to him. Yet those hopes have only grown more impossible by the day.

I don't regret leaving Gainsbury House this morning. The same reasoning still applies—it's better if Edward and I stay apart. It's *safer*.

"Tell him I'm sorry," I say, "but I can't see him again. Not ever."

Briony looks disappointed, but she nods. She and the housekeeper go out of the room. They shut the door behind them, and I hear their footsteps moving down the hall. I'm alone in the room. There's a sudden draft, and I draw the quilt around my shoulders. Is Briony at the door now? I wonder how Edward looks, how his expression changes as she gives him my message.

A dark shape flits across the lamp. I look up quickly, but see nothing there. The chill in the room deepens.

Oh, damn it all. I don't know if I'm imagining things or not, but I don't want to stay in this room another minute. I steal out of the door and head for the front of the house. As I reach the end of the hall, I hear low voices. Briony is in the foyer with Edward.

"I just can't understand how all this happened," Briony is saying quietly. "One day Millie is taking care of you, and the next she's ill herself. Yet she treated all those other patients and has never been sick once. Nobody will give me a straight answer, and Millie certainly doesn't know. And then Lydia practically throws her out on her ear, as if she's some unwanted houseguest. It isn't right."

This isn't what I told Briony, but I'm grateful to my friend for defending me.

"Lydia threw her out?" Edward asks. "Are you sure? My sister told me it was Millie's idea. That she wanted to go right away."

The sound of his voice makes my heart race. There's a mirror hanging on the wall, and I can see Edward's face in the reflection. Despite the lingering traces of exhaustion, he is still so very handsome. His jawline is prominent along his profile. His broad shoulders cut an appealing figure. I wonder how he has faired since his recovery. Does he still feel the call of the morphine?

"Of course she wanted to go!" Briony says. "Rachel Kohler has been spreading stories about Millie to everybody who'll listen, your father especially. Just yesterday, I tried to quash a rumor that's circulating. I never thought that Lydia would believe it, though. I'd thought better of her."

His eyes are unfocused, moving about the entryway, and he seems upset. I draw back into the hallway so that he won't see me.

"What rumor?" he asks.

"It's related to me." Briony huffs. I can imagine her touching her hair. She does it when she's feeling self-conscious. "I've never tried to hide my past. I was young and desperate, and my brother and I would've starved if I hadn't been working in Denver. But for Rachel to imply that *Millie* engaged in that profession?"

I take a sharp inhale and cover my mouth to hide the sound. I step forward so I can see Edward's reaction. His cheeks are now vividly pink. "I—well, I'm sure Lydia didn't really believe—"

"Oh, yes she did. Why else would she turn on Millie this way?"

I want to melt into the hall floor, I'm so mortified. Briony didn't mention this rumor to me, no doubt to spare my feelings. I can't believe Rachel would be so vicious. What else might she be capable of doing? It's good I'm leaving town soon. I don't want to find out.

Edward's cane taps on the floor as he shifts his weight. "I will speak to Rachel. I'm going to make this right."

"Good. I suggest you go right away."

Briony starts moving toward the door, but Edward holds up his hand. "There's more going on than false rumors, though," he says. "Much more. That's why I need to speak to Millie. I'm afraid she's in danger."

"Danger?" Briony's voice raises in pitch. "What danger?"

"It's hard to explain. I just need to speak with her."

"Edward Gainsbury, I demand to know what you mean. Why is Millie in danger? Tell me right now."

He sighs. "Have you seen anything…odd about Millie's eyes?"

My eyes? My fingers come up to touch my eyelids, but of course I feel nothing unusual. What is Edward talking about?

He knows, the devious voice giggles in my ear. *He sees what you can't.*

I shake my head, wishing I could rid myself of these unwelcome thoughts.

Briony is pacing around the entryway. "I don't know what you're talking about. You're frightening me."

"That's not my intention. *Please*, Briony. I'm begging you. Let me see Millie."

I'm at the very edge of the hallway. One more step, and I'd be in clear view. I could talk to Edward right now. And I do want to be nearer to him. Especially now that he's no longer my patient. But is it the right choice?

"I'm sorry," Briony begins to say, "but I just—"

I walk into the entryway. "What's wrong with my eyes?" I ask him. "What did you see in them?"

31

Dinah
1943

When I'm woken in the morning, part of my brain thinks I'm still dreaming—I was in a dark place, trapped, running out of air. I almost scream when I feel hands on my shoulders. The sun is barely even up, and the assay office is still so dark that I can only see outlines. Shadows lie over everything. It makes me think of Millie's voice on the recording. I try to tug my sleeping bag over me, but it's pulled away again. Cold air rushes in. Then the overhead lights flip on, and I squint.

"Dinah, wake up," Mrs. Spivak says. She's wearing denim Levis beneath her wool jacket.

It's a good thing that Eddie didn't come back with me. He's still up at his cabin since yesterday morning, when we found…what we found. I don't like to think about it.

"Your mother came to see me last night," Abby's mother says. "Tomorrow's Thanksgiving. She wants you to come home."

That makes me sit up. I shake off the fog of sleep. My mother wants me to come home? And she's gone to Mrs. Spivak about it?

"Where's Abby?" I ask. She went back to her house last night. But why isn't she here, instead of her mother? Except for the one-week deadline, we've left everything up in the air.

"Abby's cleaning up. Her aunt arrives today for the holiday. Now get moving, Dinah. Enough of this. *Go home.*"

She throws my pants at my head and tells me to get dressed. But at least she gives me a cup of coffee and a slice of babka before I leave. She's brought me breakfast from her own kitchen. Mrs. Spivak always thinks of things like that.

I walk home and pause before my front door, ready to face a mother who sees me as just one more burden, and a father who probably doesn't think of me much at all. I blame Thanksgiving.

Aren't holidays grand?

I raise my hand to knock, but the door flies open.

My mother stands there, her eyes wide, her mouth set in a flat line. She's already dressed and has her grocery basket tucked beneath her arm.

Mother clucks her tongue and says, "Oh, Dinah." Then she's hugging me. The grocery basket is digging into my side. She smells like primrose toilet water. "I've missed you," she says. "I shouldn't have said those things. You know I didn't mean it. I've been so worried about you."

"I'm sorry I took your photo album," I hear myself saying. My voice cracks. "I'm really, really sorry." Why do I always do this? She shows me the slightest kindness, and all I can feel is hope that I'll be a good enough daughter this time. That she won't blow up at me again.

"Let's not talk about that, shall we? It's all forgotten." Mother closes the door and ushers me down the sidewalk. "We have preparations to make. Grace and Lydia Gainsbury invited us for dinner tomorrow. I'm making kugel. My grandmother's recipe."

My mother is rarely so chipper. I can't remember the last time she visited, or even mentioned, Grace Gainsbury. "You're friends with *Lydia*?" I ask. What happened to not even mentioning that family's name?

Mother fusses with her basket. We pass a lone neighbor, who nods in greeting.

"Lydia and I were friends, once," my mother says wistfully. "It's been too long."

I'm surprised, but I don't want to question this change of attitude. I might be able to make use of it. I'm picturing Eddie's face and the matching photo of Edward Gainsbury from 1918. What happened back then between my mother, Millie, Edward and Lydia? Could my mother know something about Millie's fate?

I think about this as we walk through the market, picking up dried noodles, eggs, cream and sugar. I can't figure out how to ask her. I know from the recording that Millie and my mother didn't get along. I don't want to set my mother off; her good moods are so fleeting as it is.

At the register, Mother digs her ration book from her bag and tears out her stamps. She drops a few coins onto the counter. Then she glances at me. "Dinah?"

Grumbling, I take out my money and pay the rest of what she owes.

As we walk home, I decide to test the waters.

"Say, are there pictures of you and Lydia together in your photo book?" I ask. I'm carrying the basket, and it thumps heavily against my leg.

Mother's back stiffens. "Didn't you look already?"

"Yes. A little. I mean..." I grasp for a better response. "There were lots of people I didn't know. I'm not sure what she looked like when she was younger."

"It's ancient history to a girl like you. Why are you suddenly so curious about all this?"

I keep my eyes forward on the street. Why's she scrutinizing me so closely? Is she hiding something? Or is it just her usual skepticism showing through?

"I'm bored without Nate," I say. "And the news about Mitchell Gainsbury, then meeting Lydia...It just made me curious about how things were during the Great War."

Mother chuckles without humor. "I'm a living relic, am I? A mother can always count on her daughter to make her feel old. Why can't you let me enjoy my few decent memories in peace?"

I drop the subject.

When we open the front door, I hear the radio blaring. My father's in the living room. I put the groceries on the kitchen counter, and Mother takes each item out slowly, not looking at me. I'm getting the silent treatment. Which is better than yelling, I guess.

All in all, things are back to normal.

I stop by the living room and sit on the divan beside my father. His head is tilted to the side, listening to one of those dramas sponsored by dish detergent. He doesn't acknowledge me. I wait until the announcer starts on the advertisement.

"Papa? I'm sorry about the other day. The record I was playing?"

He grunts, which from my father could mean *yes* or *no* or just *I don't give a damn.*

"What was that, anyhow?" he asks. "That strange song? I just...didn't like it." He hasn't looked over at me. His fingers clutch the blanket in his lap.

My father's tone is odd. For him, it's almost apologetic. "Just a record I found in Nate's room," I say.

"You got rid of it? I don't want that in this house. That music."

I pause. His hands are shaking. There's a bead of sweat at his temple. He's always railing against things he doesn't like—jazz music, Congress, women wearing pants—but he rarely gets physically agitated.

I didn't bring the record home, of course. Abby is keeping it safe until we can meet again. I don't know if it's finished telling Millie's story, or if there's still more to come. *One week*, I keep thinking, and then I realize—it's only six days now. By then, we'd better have a coherent story to tell the sheriff.

Either way, I have no intention of bringing the record back to my house. My mother already put that scratch on it. I'm not going to give her the chance to finish it off.

"Yes, I got rid of it," I say to my father.

Only then does he relax. "Thank you, Dinah," he mutters, reaching to turn up the volume on his radio show. "You're a good girl."

I don't know what's gotten into him.

I head down the hall to my bedroom. I feel a chill in the air as I near the door. The doorknob is ice cold. But this morning has already been strange. I don't think to stop or turn around. This is my home. I've felt plenty of bad feelings here, but never fear.

There's a surreal moment when I watch myself turn the knob and push open the door. It creaks on its hinges.

The room is frigid. The curtains are fluttering. A gust of air blows in through the open window. I take a step inside, and my socked foot lands on something hard. It crunches.

Glass. There's glass everywhere—the floor, my narrow bed, my nightstand. It glitters in the sunlight. On my blankets, the glass is frosted lightly with snow.

I hear a noise behind me and whirl around. My mother is standing in the doorway, staring at the mess in my bedroom. "What happened here?" she asks in a monotone.

"My window's broken," I say. "You didn't notice? Didn't you or Papa hear something while I was gone?"

She just looks around the room. Her eyes shine like they're made of the same broken glass that's scattered everywhere. I bend down and start picking up the shards, placing them carefully on my flattened palm. What a mess. I'll have to get out the giant canister Hoover that Mother keeps in the cellar.

I hiss with pain. One of the glass slivers has pricked my palm. I pull it out, and a bead of red wells up.

"You should be careful," my mother says.

"Thanks," I snap. "Never would've known if you hadn't told me."

She leaves the room, closing the door behind her. I feel a surge of anger so furious that it makes my head swim. I have to close my eyes and squeeze my fists and breathe for a few moments. It's either that or scream.

Slowly I clean up the mess, shard by shard. When I reach beneath my nightstand, I find the rock. It's about the size of my hand. A river stone, probably worn smooth in one of the local creeks. There's a scrap of newsprint tied around the rock with a piece of twine. My fingers are numb from the cold, and it takes several seconds for me to pull the paper free and unfold it.

It's a few columns from a newspaper article. There's no headline. I can't tell where or when it was printed; it's torn from a larger sheet. But there are words underlined in pencil. *Are. Else. What. Doing.*

I study them for a little while, and then the order becomes clear.

Quit what you are doing, or else.

I crumple the paper and throw it against the wall. I just want to get it away from me. Cold air blows into the room and the ball of newspaper dances along the floor.

Somebody tied that paper around a rock and threw it through my window. But who? I don't even know when exactly this happened. It could've been this morning. It could've been two days ago.

I know one thing for sure; it wasn't any ghost who threw that rock.

I thought I was just imagining it before. But somebody has been watching me.

32

Millie
1918

Briony takes Edward and me to the cozy living room. She picks up the empty wine glasses.

"I'll be in the front parlor if anyone needs me," she says.

Edward waits patiently for her to leave, holding his cap in his hand. As soon as the door closes, he takes a step toward me, and my heart leaps straight into my throat. I walk over to the fireplace instead. The flames are intense, the heat giving me an excuse for the glow that's no doubt rising on my cheeks. I'm afraid of what might be wrong with me—what did he mean about my eyes? But somehow I'm even more nervous about the other things he might say.

"I'm sorry I left the way I did this morning," I tell him. "How are you feeling?"

He walks over to the fireplace and stands beside me. We both look into the dancing flames. "I'm much better, all thanks to you. The past five days…it's been unbearable. Not knowing if you'd wake up. Not knowing if I was the cause."

I think of how the shadows covered him in a deathly caul. How they leapt at me when I came near. It wasn't his fault. But will he see it that way? He's always too quick to blame himself.

"And the morphine cravings?" I ask. "Are they gone?"

He hesitates, and I glance over at him. He's turning over his cap in his hands, squeezing the brim. "The craving may not ever be gone entirely. That what Dr. Durham tells me. But I'm doing my best. I like to think that you need me. That's given me strength."

And then I left today without a word to him. I thought a quick exit would be best for all of us. I've done everything wrong. At so many turns.

I don't want to ask this next question, but I must. His health, and indeed his life, could depend on it.

"Edward, you told me the day your mother passed that you'd given me all of your morphine. But clearly you had access to more. The doctor and I—" He turns his face away in shame, but I press on. "We saw the fresh injections after you collapsed at the funeral. I'm not asking this to judge you. Far from it. But I have to know. Where did you get the additional doses?"

Because if he got more then, he could get more now.

"I'm sorry, Millie." His voice breaks when he says my name. He sits on the sofa, covering his eyes with his hand. "I hated the position I put you in the night my mother died. I swore to myself I'd stop on my own. I wanted to show you I was strong enough. But I couldn't. I *had* given you my entire supply, but…there are unfortunately certain unsavory people in Powder Ridge who cater to needs like mine."

"Who?" I demand.

He shakes his head. "I'm going to handle that on my own. But I promise you, it won't be a problem again. I'm finished with all that."

"Edward, please—"

"I don't want you to worry about me. That isn't why I came. I'm here for *you*, Millie. Look at me. I need to see if it's there."

"You mean my eyes? If *what's* there?"

"Something…dark. A shadow."

Unnerved, I edge closer. He stands, leaving his cap on the sofa, and takes hold of my chin. He gazes intently at me, turning my face this way and that. The flames reflect in his eyes, but the heat is no longer comforting. Sweat is running down my sides.

Suddenly, he jerks backward. "My God. It's there. Look. *Look.*"

He spins me around so I'm facing the mirror that hangs over the mantle. Edward stands directly behind me, his arm looped protectively around my waist. At first, I can only look at Edward in the mirror. His face is too pale. He's blinking too fast. He inhales sharply at what he sees.

I meet my own gaze in the reflection.

For a moment, I stare at my haggard face. There are strands of gray hair at my temples, ones I hadn't noticed before. Fine lines at the corners of my eyes. Shocking on a lass who's not even twenty-two. What have I done to myself?

Then, something swims across the white of my left eye.

Do you see us now, Millie? Do you?

I cry out, leaning back against Edward for support. He sways slightly, and I remember his leg. How the stump was breaking down and infected not too long ago.

"We should sit down," I say. My fingers are shaking as I take his hand and move toward the sofa. I'm afraid that if I keep standing, staring into that grotesque reflection, my knees might buckle and I'll make both of us fall to the floor.

We sit, and I start talking.

I tell him everything—how I first noticed the shadows around the dying at my mother's clinic, how their behavior began to change since I came to Gainsbury House. And finally, I confess what really happened the other night: how the shadows attacked me. How I felt them flooding into me. The nightmares that I endured during my long sleep.

"When you woke up yesterday," he says, "I thought I saw something dark move across your eye. Like a tiny fish gliding through water. It was there, then gone. I didn't know if I'd just imagined it. Lydia said she didn't see a thing. I thought...I don't know what I thought. It seemed so hard to believe. But when you left suddenly, I worried why exactly you were running."

"I don't know what's happening to me. What if the shadows are *inside* me?" That malevolent thing, that legion of evil voices. Has it found its way beneath my skin, feeding upon and amplifying every negative thought?

"Then we'll find a way to purge them. You're one of the purest, kindest people I've ever met. That's why the shadows ran from you before. They've found a way to strike out at you, but they can't change who you are."

But who am I, if I'm not a nurse who helps people through death? "What if these shadow-things make me cause harm to the patients I try to help?"

"Touch me," he says. "See if you do me any harm. I'm betting you won't."

"But—"

He takes my hands and places them on either side of his face. His eyebrows lift. I hold my breath. Nothing happens. His skin is soft, burred with just a hint of fine whiskers.

"Millie, you don't have to face this alone," Edward says. To my surprise, tears gather at the corners of his eyes. "Believe me, I know what a terrible burden that can be."

A tear slips and trails down along his nose. I wipe it away with my thumb. My touch lingers on the curve of his cheekbone. I can't help but glance at his slightly-open lips.

And then, drawn together by a single mutual thought, we kiss.

I've kissed a few men before, mostly young interns who I've met through my work. But no one has ever kissed me the way Edward Gainsbury is kissing me. Slowly, deliberately, attuned to my every breath and movement. I wonder briefly how many other girls he kissed while overseas. How many women he's held. But soon enough I'm not thinking at all. There's only his taste—herbal, a mix of licorice and peppermint—and the sensation of his hands grazing my arms.

I pull away to catch my breath. "Not a bad experiment," I joke. "At least we're sure you're safe from me."

"I'm so far from safe," he says. "My heart isn't safe with you. Not by a mile."

I look down at my lap, where our hands are now entwined. I want to give him a chance to change his mind. And could there be a worse time? I have some sort of monster inside of me, and he chooses now to profess how he feels?

"You're still recovering."

"I'm entirely well," Edward says, "and I feel more a man than I have in some time." He touches my waist. His hand trails along my skirt to my thigh, squeezing gently through the fabric. "I'm desperate for you. You don't know how many times I've imagined how your skin would feel against mine."

My body sings with desire. But those hateful rumors return to my mind—the lies about me that Rachel's spread.

Edward must see the hesitation on my face, because he says, "Millie Boylan, I am in love with you."

I grab his shirt by the collar and tug him closer. Our mouths meet again, and I don't kiss nearly as politely as I did before.

He loves me. And I'm sure I love him. Such wonderful words. I'd almost forgotten the sound of them. And there's no one I'd rather hear them from. But there's so much standing in our way.

"What about your father?" I ask. "And Lydia? They don't approve of me." *Nor will the town,* that insidious voice says to me. *Those rumors that Rachel is spreading. Just think of the names they'll call you.*

"My family will come around," he says, "or they won't. Either way, I don't care as long as I'm with you."

I lick my lips, savoring the herbal flavor that's lingering there. *You can't believe him,* the voice says. *He will leave you behind, heartbroken and alone.* I press hard against my temples to banish the thoughts.

It's been so long since I've felt such a deep connection to anyone. I can't let it pass me by out of fear.

"I *do* love you." It sounds like I'm arguing. Trying to prove that it's true, or single-handedly overcome the odds against us. But he doesn't seem to notice the strangeness of my phrasing. He grins and pulls me into his arms.

"I have some things to take care of," he says. "A conversation with Rachel, to start. One with my father. And a few other matters. But I'll be back later, and I swear Millie, we are never going to spend another day apart if I can help it."

I smile, and it's such a relief that I can't hold myself back from asking, "What about the nights?"

I mostly meant to tease. But his look has as much heat as the flames dancing in the fireplace. "You can guess my preference. But I'll leave the nights up to you."

He puts on his cap, and with a wink, leaves the room.

When he's gone, I wait a moment to see if Briony will return. But I hear her speaking with Edward in the hallway, their voices growing smaller as they near the entryway.

Slowly, I walk over to the mantle. The mirror shows me a tarnished reflection of the room: Briony's silk curtains, her lovely damask chairs, the plush sofa where Edward just kissed me. Lovely, dear Edward. The space feels smaller and colder without him in it.

There's a shift in the light, a sense of something moving behind me. But nothing appears in the mirror.

Finally, I dare to look directly at my own face in the glass.

An amorphous shape flickers at the edge of my eye, almost out of view. There's a hissing whisper in my head.

Millie, it says, drawing out my name. *You belong to us now.*

"No! I won't listen to you. I refuse."

I squeeze my eyes shut, and when I open them, the dark shape is gone from my eye. But those whispers still vibrate along my spine, like the hum of the final note of a song.

33

Dinah
1943

Gainsbury House has been transformed for the holiday. The chandeliers are shining, candles glow on the windowsills, and fresh boughs of evergreen decorate the dining table. Delicious smells waft from the kitchen: braising meat, rosemary, butter, and yeasty dough.

"Rachel, how has it been so long?" Lydia asks. My mother holds out her hand to shake, but Lydia sweeps her into a hug.

"Oh," my mother says in surprise. She tucks her hair back into place. She styled it today, but it's so thin that it's escaping from the pins.

Jim has rolled Papa's wheelchair into the dining room. "I remember you," Papa says to Lydia. "From the mine? When those fellows were sick?"

"Of course. How could I forget?" Lydia shakes his hand. "I'm so glad we're all here. It feels like a fresh start. Never too late to renew old friendships, is it?"

My father lifts an eyebrow at me. *What does this Gainsbury woman think she's doing?* his expressions says. But his cheeks are beginning to glow from the warmth of the room. I'm starting to defrost, too, despite my anxieties.

I've been more distracted than usual the last couple of days. I've hardly slept. I covered up the hole in my window with some pieces of wood, but it doesn't do much to keep out the drafts. And that rock, it's warning…I shiver just thinking about it. Whoever's responsible, they might know about Eddie Gainsbury. Maybe they even know about Millie's body in that cabin.

They know that *I* know. And whatever it is they're hiding, they don't want anybody else to find out.

In just a few minutes we're seated around the table, and more food than I've seen in a month is arrayed around us. Mashed potatoes, buttered carrots, rolls and a boat of gravy. The centerpiece is a roasted leg of lamb. I can't imagine how Liddy and Grace got enough ration stamps for such a feast, but I'm not in a mood to question. I pile my plate with food. My shoulders are starting to relax.

For a while, everything is fine. Nice, even. I don't even cringe while my mother drones on about Nate and how swell he looked in his army uniform. The Gainsburys listen politely, but I'm sure they must be thinking about Mitchell. No one has even mentioned him yet tonight. Grace has been especially quiet so far.

My mother takes a long pull of wine, emptying her glass. "Could you pass that, please?" she asks Grace, gesturing at the bottle.

Lydia picks up the bottle and holds it out to my mother. "We're so glad that Jim's working at the mine, now," Lydia says. "Grace was so nervous at first. But you love it, don't you Jim?"

"Sure I do," he says. "I think I'd like to be a real miner at one of those big outfits, blasting away rock or working in the mill."

"Really?" I ask encouragingly. From the corner of my eye, I see my mother take another gulp of wine.

"It'd be exciting," Jim continues. "And I'd make even more money to help my mama."

Grace beams at him, though her eyes water. "You're a peach."

Lydia dabs her mouth with her napkin. "But Jim, you'd have to move to another town to get a real mining job. There's nothing like that here. You have to be realistic about your limitations."

Jim frowns. "I wanted to be a soldier like Mitchell. I could've protected him. But they wouldn't let me."

"Life isn't always fair," Lydia says. "I can tell you that from experience."

Jim looks crestfallen. Grace puts her hand over his. "If Jim wants to be a proper miner, we'll find a way," Grace says quietly. "We could move somewhere new. Leadville, maybe."

"I think that sounds swell," I cut in. "I'd miss you, though."

Jim hasn't mentioned anything like this to me. But he does seem to enjoy the work up at the mine; he's strong and works harder than McGrady or even Terrance. It's a shame, actually, that Jim didn't start working with Mitchell at the mine last year. He could've gotten a position somewhere else by now, in a town that's still kicking. Wasn't that the best any of us in Powder Ridge could hope for? A way out?

Lydia scoffs. "Leave Gainsbury House for Jim's wild ideas? Gracie, you're not being serious."

"Why not?" Grace looks to my parents. She's sitting straighter, seeming to gather her energy. "We all need a little help sometimes, don't we? What's wrong with that? Don't you agree, Mr. Weller?"

My father stares at her impassively. If Grace hopes he'll pipe up in support, then she's in for a long wait. My mother just tips back her wine glass again.

I open my mouth to change the subject, but Lydia is determined to have her say. "You *can't* leave Gainsbury House. I've given up my practice, my life, all to come back here. We've been waiting all this time to be together again, and now that we're finally about to have the chance, you're talking about—"

Grace stands up so quickly that she knocks over her glass of wine. "Liddy, you don't even know what you're…" Her chest moves up and down. "How can you, of all people, talk about being together? After what we've both lost?"

A purple stain is spreading across the tablecloth. Grace picks up her fallen wine glass and her still-full plate, and then excuses herself for the kitchen. Jim follows her a moment later. There are muffled sounds of crying. Then the shattering of glass. We all jump in our seats.

I start to get up, but my mother grips my wrist and pulls me back down into my seat. "Dinah, stay out of it," she murmurs, her words slurring.

I glare at Lydia, who stabs a carrot with her fork.

Lydia says, "Of course she's grieving. But my sister can't abandon Gainsbury House just to run away from her sadness."

"Isn't that what you did?" I ask before I can stop myself. My mother's right. I should stay out of it. But Lydia is being self-righteous and unfair. "You said you left Powder Ridge for medical school after Edward supposedly died. Wasn't that running away?"

Be careful, I warn myself. I've already said more than I should.

Lydia sits back and regards me calmly. My mother, though, fixes me with a furious gaze. "You don't know what it was like to lose Edward," my mother snaps. "Don't you dare presume to judge Lydia or Grace. Or *me*."

She sounds drunk. She's getting upset over the photo book again. That's what this is about. Her memories of Edward. Her *secrets.*

"I'm not judging anybody," I say. "I'm just trying to understand what happened back then."

Grace has come out of the kitchen. She leans against the wall, listening. Her face is tear-streaked. I wonder how much she's heard.

"What do you mean, Dinah?" Grace asks. "What do you think happened?"

They're all staring at me.

"I just..." I push my plate away. I'm so tired of dancing around the truth. I keep hearing that Edward Gainsbury died, yet there's somebody who shares that name—and far too many other similarities, besides— who's up in a cabin on Cherry Mountain right now. Both things cannot be true. If Grace, Lydia and Jim are really his family, then Eddie should be here with them, not all alone.

And there's a girl who died, who was probably murdered and buried and whose ghost is still crying out for answers. Crying out to *me.* All four of the adults in this dining room were in Powder Ridge back then.

Does one of them know what really happened here in 1918?

"There was a nurse who came to Gainsbury House that year," I say. "Millie Boylan. Do any of you remember her?"

Grace inhales, her eyes growing slightly larger. My mother and Lydia exchange a glance.

"That nurse?" my father asks. "Red hair, wasn't it? Why do you care about her?"

My mother finishes her glass. "That's a good question."

They're waiting for my answer. "I overheard her name at the market. They were talking about the last war. Remember, Mom? I told you I was curious about the Great War. Because Nate's a soldier now, too."

My mother's lips twist skeptically. She doesn't say anything.

"Millie was hired by our father," Grace says. "It was a long time ago. She left and never came back. Never even wrote."

"Nothing but a whore," my father mutters. "That was the rumor."

Grace looks horrified, but Lydia holds her hands aloft as if to stem the tide of this conversation. "Those rumors most likely weren't true," she says. "But not everything from the past is worth dredging up, Dinah. Perhaps we should have some dessert now?"

I go into the kitchen with Grace. Jim is there, wearing a pair of crocheted mitts, staring at the stove. "Is everything jake?" he asks warily.

"Of course," Grace says. "Jim, Rachel's kugel should be warmed up by now. Why don't you take it out to the dining room? Dinah and I will get plates."

When Jim is gone, Grace turns to me.

"Why did you really ask about Millie?"

"I told you. I overheard someone at—"

Grace shakes her head. "I doubt that. Some things aren't talked about in this town, and Millie Boylan is one of them."

"Why?"

She glances over my shoulder at the door. "Ask Briony Jameson," she whispers. "Terrance Jameson's sister. You work with him, right? From the mine? If you want to know more about Millie, you should ask her."

34

Millie
1918

Not long after Edward leaves, Grace appears at Briony's house. But she doesn't dare use the front door. The neighbors might see and report back to her father. No, Grace approaches from the rear of the property and knocks briskly at the delivery door.

Briony and I are sitting at the kitchen table, eating Hershey's Kisses. The silver wrappers crinkle as I open them. I've always thought that there's nothing that chocolate can't fix, and today's events are certainly putting that theory to the test. It's been so upsetting, bizarre, and yet so incredibly wonderful that I can barely think.

Then there's the knock. We both look toward the door. Grace's pretty face is staring through the glass.

"My goodness!" Briony says. She jumps up and opens the door. A gust of cold wind follows behind Grace. She comes inside, shrugging off her scarf and coat.

"Millie," Grace says, breathless. "I'm so relieved to see you. I was worried you'd already taken the afternoon train to Denver."

I stand up from the table. "What's wrong?"

"Mrs. Bishop—our housekeeper, remember?—her husband works up at Cherry Mountain Mine. And she just told me he's sick! It seems like the influenza. He's been ill since yesterday and already he's bleeding and his skin is blue. And two other men at the mine have fallen ill with fevers just this afternoon. Everyone at the mine is in a panic."

"Oh, no," Briony murmurs. "This is terrible. And Courtland hasn't even heard!" She dashed off toward her husband's study.

But Grace didn't come here to warn Courtland Spencer—she came here for me. And I know why.

She's selfish, that hateful voice says to me. *Grace is like her father and sister, plotting against you.* I tell the voice to stop spouting lies. Every time it speaks, I feel a wave of weakness afterward. I steady myself with a hand on the back of the kitchen chair.

"You want me to go up to the mine?" I ask.

"Please, Millie. My father is too proud to ask you. He's gone for Dr. Durham. But that doctor didn't help Lydia get better—*you* did. If anyone can manage this, it's you."

"I didn't cure Lydia. She was strong, that's all."

But Grace won't be dissuaded. "You can help. My father will be grateful. The whole town will be grateful."

I know what she's trying to do, and God help me, it's working. I'd like to help the men at the mine if I'm able. And if I can win Mr. Gainsbury back to my side in the meantime, so much the better. But can I trust myself with that shadow-thing inside of me? I didn't hurt Edward today, but can I be sure that I won't harm another just with the contact of my skin?

"*Please* Millie," Grace begs. "I want to go tell Mrs. Bishop that we're doing all we can."

I'll wear cotton gloves at all times. That'll have to be enough. "All right," I say. "I have to explain to Briony and pack my things. I imagine I'll be staying on Cherry Mountain for a few days, at the least. But Grace, will you tell Edward where I've gone?"

She agrees and rushes back home. I sigh, glancing at the plate of forgotten chocolates. I grab a couple and tuck them in a napkin for later. This day's trials are far from over.

Courtland Spencer himself escorts me up to the mine. We ride in a cart pulled by a couple of donkeys. I've changed into my white nurse's uniform, which is currently hidden beneath my winter layers. The suitcase with the rest of my belongings lays beneath my feet. The sun is sinking behind the mountain peaks to the west, and an icy wind blows mercilessly against my face.

"I apologize for the rustic means of transport," Courtland says. His long mustaches glisten with frost. He clutches his hat against his head. "The rest of Powder Ridge is grand, but up at the mine we're all business."

"I'd expect nothing less," I say, my teeth chattering. We reach a high valley, nestled into the saddle of the mountain. The mining encampment appears, lit up bright as day with lights strung along high wires. It's a small town in its own right, complete with multiple saloons, stables, and stores. I'm amazed that every doorway blazes with electric bulbs. It's not nearly as rustic as Courtland suggested. But I suppose that light is a necessity here, since the mine apparently runs twenty-four hours, seven days a week.

A rhythmic banging echoes across the basin. I ask about it, and Courtland says it's the stamp presses at the mill. They're crushing ore so it can be processed.

We keep following the path as it winds through the buildings, and finally we arrive at a massive, three-story structure. Its countless windows are each lit up against the night.

"The boardinghouse," Courtland announces. "I called ahead to arrange a room for you. It won't be fancy, I'm afraid, but I'll bet you'll have your hands full in any case. Be aware that the electric lights cut off at ten for the men's curfew. I'll return first thing in the morning."

I step out, and he hands me my case. "I'm grateful you're doin' this, Miss Boylan. Don't send that skinflint Gainsbury your bill. Send it to me. I intend to pay ya double your usual rate."

I insist that isn't necessary, but I don't have time to stand in the cold arguing. I thank Courtland, ask him to give my best to Briony, and head into the boardinghouse.

35

Dinah
1943

Terrance lives on the outskirts of town beside the mining company's livery. The stables themselves sprawl over the property, with enough space to board over a dozen animals. Once, this side spur of road would've been bustling with activity at every time of day. But now, BT's the only creature living here. I spy BT's lumpy nose peeking out from his stall.

The only other house on the street is Sean McGrady's. There are rusty car parts and old mining equipment strewn across his yard. All his windows are blacked with shoe polish. The county sheriff and everybody else knows that he's making cheap moonshine, but nobody cares these days. Except his buyers, of course, like my mother. McGrady's alcohol still is probably bubbling away right now.

It's the Friday after Thanksgiving. All us rock scroungers are taking the day off. I reach Terrance's postage stamp of a porch and pull back my hood, dusting off my coat.

My knock is too loud, like the wood is cracking. But after several seconds, nobody has answered.

I'm about to knock again when I see movement in the window. The curtain pulls back just enough for a pale face to look out. I see wisps of blond hair. Large, heavy-lidded eyes.

I wave at her, trying to smile in a friendly way. The curtain falls. Then the door squeaks open. Briony has a black shawl wrapped around her and a long, old-fashioned black skirt. She's so tall I have to look up at her.

"I'm afraid Terrance isn't home," she says.

"Actually, I'm here to see you. You're Miss Jameson, right?"

Her eyes brighten. "Last they told me. And you're Dinah Weller." A smile plays on her lips. She seems to enjoy the surprise on my face.

"You know me?"

"I know all of you," Briony says. "Terrance tells me his stories every night when he gets home, and it's just like a radio show. You, your brother—how's he doing overseas, by the way?—grumpy old McGrady. Poor BT, always working too hard and never complaining. BT's the hero as far as I can see. No offense meant."

She laughs at my confused expression. "I don't get out too much," she explains. "A girl has to find her entertainment where she can, right? Well come on in, sugar. Make yourself at home."

She opens the door wider so I can come inside. The front room is stacked full of account books and winter gear. I follow her down a hallway toward the rear of the house. We walk into a tiny sitting room. But I stop short in the doorway.

The room is crammed full of fancy furniture. Brightly-colored paintings adorn the walls. There's a thick rug on the floor, a velvet divan, curtains made of lush material. But when I look closer, it's obvious that it's all a bit worn out. Threads are fraying, holes haven't been mended.

"This used to be my parlor furniture when I was a married woman," Briony says, grinning. She plops down onto an overstuffed armchair, tucking her legs beneath her. Her hair, while threaded with pale gray, is still long and lustrous. Her blue eyes are large, full of humor and intelligence. She's like a gemstone that fell from its setting and got lost; maybe it's been neglected, but the shine still comes through.

"My old house was much grander," Briony says. "It's the schoolhouse now. Can you believe that? They spoiled all my decor after Courtland died."

"I didn't realize," I stammer.

When I heard about Briony Spencer in Millie's recording, I didn't come close to making the connection to Terrance's sister. I never even wondered about her until recently. I've never seen her in town, never heard her name mentioned except by Terrance in passing. Was I really so closed off from the world around me all this time?

"Oh, it's no matter. Nobody's fault, really, except Fate. I'd just rather not leave the house, so I don't. It's not the best way to make friends, but the truth is, I don't think most people in Powder Ridge have missed me after all that happened. They probably think I slunk back to Denver. *C'est la vie.*" She jumps up, a look of horror suddenly on her face. "You probably want something to drink, don't you? I should get you a drink. Lord, I've forgotten how to do this."

I rush to sit down. "No, no, I'm fine really. I'm sorry about your loss. When did your husband die?"

She sits slowly, eyes moving over the room. She tugs her black shawl around her. "Oh, it's been a long time now. Back in '18, when the flu swept through town. We thought it was over, and then it hit the mine. But that's not why you're here, I'm sure. You're young, you don't need to hear about my troubles. What can I do for you?"

I cross and uncross my legs, trying to get comfortable. The chair creaks beneath me. "Actually, I'm here to ask you about that year. Nineteen eighteen. My mother—Rachel Weller, I mean back then she was Rachel Kohler—she has this photo album, and there are pictures in it. Of people here in Powder Ridge. It made me curious."

I pause, watching her reaction. But Briony is sitting very still, just looking at me.

"I was wondering about a nurse who came to help with the flu outbreak," I say. "Millie Boylan? You knew her, I think?"

Briony takes in a long breath, then seems to hold it. Thoughts and emotions pass across her expressive face. Hints of nostalgia, anger, confusion and sadness.

Eventually she says, "Of course I knew Millie. She was my best friend. My only real friend, except Courtland, and…" She shakes her head, wiping at her eye. "I'll tell you. But I think I should get us a drink after all. This is going to take some time."

In the kitchen, she makes us each a mug of hot cocoa. She spikes hers with a glug of whiskey. We sit at the table, and she begins to tell me a story.

Some of it, I've already learned from Millie's recording. How she came to Powder Ridge to help the Gainsbury family. How Mrs. Gainsbury died from the flu, how Lydia managed to recover. Briony doesn't seem to know anything about the strange shadows that Millie saw, the portents of death. And she's judicious when she mentions my mother, although I can tell there's still dislike after all these years.

"Millie gave so much to the Gainsburys. Nursing them through all that. And then she fell ill herself, and what do they do? Kick her into the street. It was awful.

Not that I was surprised, given the other things that Samuel Gainsbury was capable of. Thank goodness Courtland and I were able to take her in. Edward came here—I mean not here, my old house, you understand—to beg Millie's forgiveness. She loved him. That's the really unfair part of it. His family was trying to keep them apart."

"And he loved her back?"

I remember Eddie's anguish as he listened to Millie's recording. *Find me Edward. I'm in the dark.*

"I thought so. I suppose he did." Briony tips back the last of her cocoa. "Here's the really hard thing about growing up, Dinah. You learn that love doesn't save you. Didn't save Courtland. And it didn't save Edward, either."

She closes her eyes and slumps in her chair, as if she's too tired to go on. Frost has covered the kitchen window. It's so dark in the room you'd think it was dusk and not midday.

"What happened?" I ask quietly.

She sighs, gathering herself up. She stands, picks up our empty mugs, and begins washing them out in the sink along with the rest of the waiting dishes. "We got word that the flu had appeared up at the mine. It's odd how such things spread. Riding along like a stowaway on a train, on someone's breath or hands or clothes, biding its time before it strikes. We know it's a virus now, which we didn't understand then. But still, who can say why a demonic little virus attacks some, and leaves others alone? Anyway, several men were sick at the mine. That's how Courtland caught it. I got sick, too, but I survived and he didn't. His children contested his will and they won. Got everything. Left me with nothing, except my memories and some things from our house. Terrance took care of me once he got home from fighting in the war, God bless him. But my few friends had abandoned me, even Grace Gainsbury, who I'd thought cared for me."

Briony turns off the water. Spins to lean against the counter.

"Listen to me, going so far afield. That was all after Millie was gone."

"That's all right," I say. She's been through a lot. No wonder she doesn't leave her house. This town has treated her like dirt. Yet she stayed here to be with her brother—that much, I can understand.

"Where had Millie gone?" I ask.

Briony's gaze traces the ceiling as she remembers. "She went to help take care of the men at the mine, right when they first got sick up there. Millie packed her belongings and left my house, dressed in her nurse's uniform—and that was the last time I ever saw my friend."

I think of Millie's body curled up beneath those floorboards. The strands of red hair on her nurse's cap, the blood on its corner. There's a twisting sensation in my chest. For a moment, I can't speak.

"Do you know what happened to her?" I ask when I'm able.

"They said she ran off. You see, Edward Gainsbury died up there at the mine—I never *did* get a straight answer about that, it didn't make sense—and there was some cockamamie story about it being *her fault*. It's ridiculous what they claimed. But even assuming she was distraught, why did Millie run? Without a word to me, not even saying goodbye? It's—"

There's shouting outside the house. We both stop to listen. But the words are indistinct.

"It's Terrance," Briony says. "I hope everything's OK."

She tries to see out the kitchen window, but either the snow is too thick here or the angle is bad, because she rushes off toward the front of the house. I'm a few steps behind her. In the front room, Briony pulls back a threadbare curtain, and we both look out.

Terrance and McGrady are standing in front of the stables. They're yelling at each other. Briony cracks the window, and their voices leap into the room.

"Hell no," Terrance is saying. "Not in this snow. It'll be dark on your way back, and BT's gettin' too old. He's going to get hurt."

"He's a goddam donkey," McGrady says.

Terrance gets into McGrady's face. "That damn donkey is my livelihood! Why's this so important, anyway? I had the makings of a straight in that hand you interrupted. You know that poker game only happens once a month and you've spoiled it for me."

McGrady pulls a greasy wallet from his pants pocket. He takes out several bills. "I'll pay you double the usual."

Terrance glares at him a moment. Then he grabs the money. "Fine. But this is the last time." Grumbling, he goes to BT's stall.

McGrady waits, shifting his ample weight nervously from boot to boot. He's got several green canvas bags at his feet, all stuffed to the brim.

There's something long and narrow poking out from one of the bags. It looks like an awful lot like the butt of a shotgun.

"Do you know what this is about?" I ask Briony.

"Sean McGrady's always got some scheme, that's what," she says. "He's been taking BT up to the mine at odd times lately. Even in the middle of the night!

Whatever black market enterprise he's got going now, it must pay well."

"Black market?" I ask. "What do you mean?"

Briony lifts an eyebrow at me. "Don't you know about your hometown yet, sugar? Powder Ridge is too small for many things to stay completely hidden. There's an unofficial market for meat, gasoline—anything your ration stamps can't afford. McGrady's got his fingers in that, and near everybody knows it. Just like everybody knows that McGrady is really a Gainsbury. They just don't talk about it."

My eyes widen. "A *Gainsbury*? Sean McGrady?" This can't be right.

"Oh, it's true. Not his fault he was born out of wedlock, or that the town was complicit in hiding old Samuel Gainsbury's sins. Sean was the half-brother of Grace, Lydia and Edward, but he grew up in poverty at the mine instead of that grand house. I've always thought that wasn't right. But Terrance and I had things hard as kids, too, and we've managed to live honestly."

Briony moves away from the window. "I'm sorry, McGrady always puts me in a foul mood. Terrance will come in when he's done, and we can ask him for the scoop. More hot cocoa while we wait?"

She heads into the kitchen.

I'm still staring out the window. I'm trying to find some resemblance in McGrady's weathered face—some hint of Grace or Liddy or Edward—but I can't.

I spot the green canvas bags at McGrady's feet, and I get a funny feeling. I've seen bags like those many times before. At the assay office. At the market. The bags have *Cherry Mountain Mine* stamped on them, so they're all over town. I think there's even one or two in our house.

But I'm sure I saw one of those bags in Eddie's cabin. A green canvas bag filled with groceries—delivered by some mysterious person that Eddie didn't want me to see.

McGrady's been going up to the mine at odd hours.

McGrady is Edward Gainsbury's *half-brother.*

BT's saddle bags are packed, and McGrady is leading the donkey down the snowy road. They're headed toward the trail up to the mine.

I run to the kitchen. "I'm sorry Briony, but I gotta go. I forgot my mother wants me home."

"But Terrance will be in any minute. And the cocoa!"

"Sorry," I say again, running to grab my coat and my boots. I spy a pair of heavy leather mittens hanging from a peg; I borrow them, along with a pair of snowshoes that are sitting in the corner. I need to get out there before McGrady gets too far ahead.

I'm going to follow him. But I think I already know where he's going to go.

36

Millie
1918

"You're the nurse?"

A slender fellow in a felt hat jumps up from the wooden crate he's sitting on. We're just inside the entrance to the boardinghouse. A cacophony of sounds come from further in the building: men's voices, doors slamming.

"Yes, that's me. Millie Boylan. You are?"

"Joe Weller."

"Nice to meet you, Mr. Weller. Mr. Spencer said you've a room ready for me?"

His eyes slide up and down my body, pausing at my waist. "Yeah, think so. I could give you a private tour, if you're interested."

Go with him, that devious voice says. *Get him alone and drive a scalpel into his heart.*

Damn these thoughts. They aren't mine. The fellow's a cad but he's not worth a second thought, much less violence.

I walk past Joe Weller. "Show me whoever's in charge here," I say over my shoulder. "Obviously it isn't you."

"Dr. Durham *did* leave me in charge." Joe's tone has turned surly, but he leads me through the long corridor. "And the foremen ain't here, neither. You think they want to get sick? Half the miners have already run off, and hell, I've half a mind to head off after them."

A few men lean out of a room to watch me pass, tipping their heads in respectful greeting. They're wearing bandannas or kerchiefs over their faces, but I can tell how young they are. I was expecting old timers.

"Why weren't these men drafted?" I ask.

Joe turns around, walking backwards. "'Cause the mine's essential to the war effort. Gotta have metal for bullets." He takes off his cap and holds it to his heart, miming patriotism. I roll my eyes.

The stairwell is deserted. Electric lights buzz overhead. We reach the third floor, which has been designated the sick ward. As soon as we step out into the corridor, we're assailed by cries of suffering and the sharp smells of blood and vomit.

"They don't pay me enough for this." Joe covers his nose with his sleeve and tries to bolt down the stairs. But I grab him firmly by the arm. He looks surprised by my strength.

"You're not going anywhere," I say. "You said you're in charge, didn't you? Unless you want Courtland Spencer and every other mine operator in this state to hear about your dereliction, then lead the way."

Joe pulls his arm away from me. Reluctantly, he shows me the sick rooms. We glance from doorway to doorway, surveying the situation. Five men have fallen ill already—two more since I first got word this afternoon. Mrs. Bishop's husband is faring especially poorly. Will more follow? I've never worked in a real hospital ward. Never treated more than a couple of patients at a time.

You'll probably fail. You're no nurse, just a small, scared girl.

"I can do it," I say aloud. "You'll see."

"What's that?" Joe asks.

"Never you mind. Here," I say, stopping to pull supplies from my suitcase. I hand him a gauze mask. "Put this on. You'll need it."

I don my apron, mask and gloves, and I get right to work.

"Clear the way," someone yells on the stairs. Another man is being carried upstairs by his fellows. He's feverish, coughing, weak. Can the disease really be spreading so quickly? Beth and Lydia Gainsbury had the same flu, yet their illness seemed so manageable by comparison. Perhaps it's the way these men live in such close quarters, breathing the unwholesome air of the mine. I bark orders at Joe Weller, who grudgingly follows them.

Just two hours later—so unbearably soon—the first of my patients dies. Mr. Bishop, the husband of the Gainsburys' housekeeper.

Through his final moments, I try to help clear his airways. But it's no use. The poor man is choking on his own fluids. His face turns progressively bluer. I can tell that the end is near. There are still a few strands of web-like shadow knitting around him, but they are weak. The vast hoard of darkness that usually appears when death is immediate—it's not here. The pinprick eyes haven't opened.

And then, I feel them—the eyes. They are opening *inside me*. Looking out from within my own mind.

The shadows surge forward like a wave cresting toward shore. They want to get out. They want *him*, Mr. Bishop. To feed on his last agonized thoughts.

Give him to us. You can't stop it.

Suddenly, I understand. They intend to use me. They would force me into serving as their vessel, instead of fighting them as I've done all these years.

But I will not let them control me.

Though I continue to speak calming words, I back away from the dying miner. I close my eyes, calling on the strength within me to keep them in. I won't let this monstrous Legion out. And I sense the shadows' confusion—at being held at bay, thwarted by the very girl they thought they'd conquered.

Then a familiar voice—a far more welcome one—breaks through.

"Have you any extra masks?" Lydia asks. "I was hoping I could—My goodness, Millie, are you all right?"

My eyes fly open. I gasp and grab onto the windowsill for support. Lydia is standing in the corridor, hesitating at the doorway.

"I am," I say. "It's just—"

I gesture at the bed. Mr. Bishop appears to be dead. Quickly, I check for his pulse and, confirming there's none, I pull the sheet over his face.

"Oh, the poor, dear man," Lydia says. "Mrs. Bishop will be heartbroken."

"I'm sorry," I say. It's tragic, though inside I'm relieved. I kept that monster from Mr. Bishop. The evil voice—that voice made from countless echoing tones—is shouting obscenities in my head. But they're ebbing away. Coiling up like a snake, plotting how they might next choose to strike. I'm sweating. What will I do? I cannot live with this inside of me, trying to break me into submission.

Lydia is still looking at me strangely. At the moment, I don't care about any disagreements we may have had earlier today. I need her help. I can't manage this alone.

"You're the answer to my prayers." I wash my hands and find fresh linens for Lydia to wear. Soon we're making rounds side by side. I introduce her to Joe Weller, who grunts a greeting. At least he's hard at work.

"I regret what I said earlier," Lydia tells me. We're changing the soiled sheets of a man who's sleeping. "I didn't give you a chance to refute the rumors. I jumped to the worst conclusions."

"That I'm a prostitute?" I ask. "Or did you think I'm just loose? I don't judge any woman for her choices. Or for what's forced upon her. But if I'm going to be criticized, it had better be for my own actions and no others."

She flinches. "I can tell neither thing is true. But Millie, my brother is obviously fond of you. Can you blame me for being protective? He's been through so much. And after what I found in your room at Gainsbury House—"

"What?" I drop the corner of the sheet I'm holding. "You were going through my room?"

"I was tidying up while you were ill. I found a locked box, and I admit, I was curious."

The locked box. The morphine vials I took from Edward. *Oh.*

"I saw those marks on Edward's arms," Lydia adds. Her voice is so low I can barely hear her. "They're injection scars, aren't they? If those vials were simply medical supplies, why would you hide them away? I began to suspect...well, that he didn't really have the flu. That you had lied to me."

I sigh, tucking in the sheet. "If I lied, it was only because Edward asked me. You'll have to talk to your brother. It isn't my place."

"If that's how it is, so be it." Roughly, Lydia shoves the sheet beneath the sleeping man. He shifts, moaning. She doesn't say anything else to me.

As soon as there's a lull, I excuse myself for a break. Joe's left my suitcase outside a bedroom at the opposite end of the hall. Lydia's things are here as well. And her gramophone box is here too, its lid fastened. She must have lugged the player all the way up from home. Perhaps she has a mind to provide some entertainment for the sick men tomorrow. It's a thoughtful gesture. I'd smile if I weren't so completely exhausted.

Next door, there's a large common room, the very last room in the corridor. I poke my head in the open doorway. Someone has left the lamp on, but the place is deserted. Embers glow in the fireplace, leftover from an earlier blaze. All the healthy men have been relegated downstairs. I can imagine this room on typical nights, men playing cards at the tables, lounging on the sofas in front of the fire. There's a bookcase full of dime novels. This evening, the room is eerily lifeless.

I find the lamp switch and turn off the light. But I keep standing there, staring into the dimness.

There's a crawling sort of feeling within me. I feel trapped. I want to escape from this building, even from my own skin. If only that were possible. With a shudder, I turn away.

I carry my suitcase inside my bedroom next door. There are two bunks here, and I sit down on one of them. I only need a few minutes' quiet. Just so that I can gather my strength. The coal stove is dark, so I light it. Warmth slowly trickles into the room.

I see movement beside me and stifle a scream. It's merely my reflection in the darkening window. But my God, for that split second I didn't recognize myself.

I startle awake. It's pitch black outside. I didn't mean to fall asleep.

I can't tell how long I've been out. Lydia has been here. Her bag is on the other bunk, and her gramophone is set up on a small table. "When Irish Eyes Are Smiling" is already on the turner. I switch on the machine and listen for a minute to the music, hoping it will calm me. But the music sends chills along my skin. It's out of place here. Too much a reminder of Gainsbury House. I pick up the needle to stop the song.

Lydia must still be working. I get up and head down the hall. She'll be needing a break.

I check on the sick men, one by one. All seems to be quiet, thank goodness. A wall clock says it's half past nine o'clock. I find Joe Weller in one of the rooms, mopping the floor and looking disgusted. But Lydia isn't here anywhere, and Joe says he hasn't seen her.

"Lights out at ten, though," Joe says. "Wherever she is, she'd better be headin' back. Nobody's supposed to be wanderin' around at night—either they're asleep or on-shift, and that's that."

I hear noise coming from below. Maybe she's gone down there.

I take the stairwell. The wood creaks as I descend. I reach the bottom floor and walk aimlessly, trying to figure out where Lydia might've gone. Most of the doors are closed, men readying themselves for bed. I hear muffled voices. Maybe she went to the kitchen in the hopes of a late dinner, but I can't find it. I start to feel dizzy. The hallways blend together, and the walls seem to undulate in the harsh electric light.

Finally, I'm nearing the front door of the building when I hear the distinctive sound of skirts swishing. I rush around the corner and nearly collide with a young woman in a blue wool cape. But it isn't Lydia.

It's Rachel Kohler.

"Millie!" She takes off her cloche and brushes away the snow. "Have you seen Edward?" she asks.

I shush her, glancing around at all the closed doors where miners are surely sleeping. "What would Edward be doing here?" I ask.

"We argued. He was so angry. He said he was going to…" Rachel presses her gloved hands to her face. "Look, I know that you and I haven't gotten along."

A surge of anger pushes away my exhaustion. Who does she think she is? "That's an understatement. You've got nerve, spreading those lies about me."

"I didn't say anything outright! People gossip in this town. They don't like outsiders. Trust me, I know. It's taken me half my life to be welcomed here. Then you just waltz in, thinking you can have whatever you want? *Whom*ever you want?"

I take Rachel back into the entryway, where we're less likely to be overheard. Snow lies in clumps beneath the front door.

"Edward is a grown man," I whisper. It's so cold here that my breath is visible. "He can make his own decisions. You have no right to interfere."

"No *right?*" Rachel's skin is pale, and two spots of red are blooming on her cheeks. "I gave up everything for him. After Edward enlisted, I waited for him. I wrote him every week. I cared for his mother and sister when they got sick. And I've been Edward's confidante even since he returned. I helped him get what he needed when he couldn't go to *you.*"

I grab her arm. "What do you mean? *What* did you get for him?"

"Would you just listen? I came here tonight because I'm worried. Edward demanded to know where I got the…"

"The morphine?"

Her eyes widen. "Edward asked for my help not long after his mother died. He said he was in pain, he needed relief. But he was afraid Dr. Durham would say no, and he didn't want you to find out. So I went to the only person who *could* help—Sean McGrady. Everybody knows what he sells. I got what Edward needed. And then he collapsed at the funeral."

She's starting to cry. "I did the wrong thing, didn't I? I thought I could trust Sean because he's got ties to the Gainsbury family. But I shouldn't have gotten the morphine. I shouldn't have told Edward tonight *where* I'd gotten it. I only wanted to help him. I've only ever wanted to earn his love."

I watch as she digs a handkerchief out of a pocket and dabs her eyes. The anger has drained out of me. Rachel has made mistakes, just like I have. So many mistakes.

"You think Edward's coming here to find this McGrady person? *Tonight?*" I don't know why Edward would do such a thing, but any reason I can imagine is far from good.

Rachel nods. "When he found out it was Sean, he got upset. 'Millie's up there,' he said. So you see? You've won. He loves you, not me. But I'm worried about him. I don't know what Edward's going to do."

I look around us at the empty entryway. Muddy footprints are all over the floor. Edward could be here already, and I wouldn't even know how to find him.

I'll have to find this Sean McGrady instead.

37

Dinah
1943

At first, I'm not completely sure where McGrady's going. He's a hulking shape up ahead, a dark outline against the white of the storm. The snow is blowing straight into my face, the wind wailing so shrilly that it drowns out any other sound.

I trail him up the path to the mountain and into the woods. The wind is calmer here, and the sound of my panting is loud inside the hood of my coat. Despite the leather mittens, the tips of my fingers are beginning to go numb.

He pauses, yanking on BT's rope. McGrady starts to look over his shoulder.

I crouch behind a tree and keep still. An endless minute passes. Keeping low to the ground, I peek around a snow-covered bush and see McGrady's back, walking away. I get up and continue to follow, keeping off to a diagonal this time. Again, I begin to doubt where McGrady is really going, but then I see it.

Eddie's cabin.

We've looped around and approached from the back. The window is frosted over. Smoke puffs from the chimney pipe in the roof. McGrady stops outside, ties BT's rope to a post, and unloads the saddle bags. Carrying his load of supplies, he goes around the side of the cabin. I hear the door open. Voices come from inside. I creep closer, slipping off the webs so I can move easier.

"I got your message," McGrady says. "What the hell is this about?"

BT snorts and shuffles his feet. He can smell me. "Hey buddy," I whisper. "Everything's jake. It's just Dinah." But he already knows that. I rub his head and his flank. Then I crouch beside the wall of the cabin. Eddie's voice comes next, and I tilt my head to listen.

"I said for you to pass on the message, not come here yourself. Where is she?"

"Like she wants me hangin' around that house? There's already too much attention. I been trying to put a stop to it and then I get your damn note at the stable, like I'm some con-see-erge at your beck and call. I don't take orders."

"Listen—"

"No, *you* listen. You don't seem to understand your position here."

"Get your hands off me." Eddie's voice is pitched high. There's a thump against the wall, and I jump, almost tipping over. McGrady's *hurting* him. My pulse is racing. I crawl along the base of the cabin and look around the corner.

McGrady's shotgun is leaning just outside the cabin door.

I grab hold of the gun. It feels clumsy in my hands. I've only used Abby's peashooter, not a big weapon like this. I put the butt against my shoulder, fumble with the safety—that much I do know—and I barge over to the door.

I turn the knob. It swings open. McGrady has Eddie pushed up against the cabin's wall, Eddie's collar in his fist.

"Hey," I yell. "Let him go!"

McGrady looks over. Takes in the scene: me, snow blowing in behind me, the gun. He moves a few steps to the side, his hands lifting into the air. His face is turning an unhealthy shade of purple.

"Shut the damn door," he says.

I kick it closed with my foot.

"What the blazes are you doing, Dinah Weller?" McGrady's voice is a low rumble, like thunder from a coming storm. He spits as he talks, and drops of saliva catch in his beard. "You got to be the dumbest kid in existence. Can't leave well enough alone."

I'm having trouble holding the gun steady. "That was you who threw the rock through my window, wasn't it? Some kind of warning?"

"What rock?"

"Dinah, he's got another gun," Eddie says.

McGrady reaches into the back of his pants and pulls out an old-fashioned Colt revolver with a shiny grip. My bladder loosens. I just barely keep from peeing myself. I brace the butt of the shotgun against my armpit, but I can't keep my eyes from drifting to the barrel McGrady is aiming at me.

"Why are you keeping him here?" I ask McGrady. He says nothing. Just stares at me murderously. "What is this all about?" I demand.

McGrady starts walking toward me. I back up against the door.

"Stay away," I say, aiming the gun.

"You have no idea what you're getting in the middle of," he says. "You are going to put that gun down, and maybe, *just* maybe, your house will still be standing tomorrow and your parents will still be alive inside it."

"You can't threaten me. I'll go to the sheriff."

McGrady lunges forward. With his free hand he grabs the shotgun, ripping it from my hands. My finger catches on the trigger loop, wrenching to the side. Then I'm on the ground, screaming, as I feel the cold double barrel press against my neck.

"No," Eddie cries. "No, no!"

"Both of you had better listen," McGrady says. "I am going back to town now to sort out the mess you two have caused me. Gainsbury, the minute this storm passes, you're getting the hell out of here thanks to this idiot girl."

McGrady kicks me in the side. I groan as the air goes out of me. I can't breathe.

"I'll want extra pay for my trouble," he says. "And you, Dinah Weller, you'd better keep your mouth shut. Or I swear I'm gonna kill you. I'm gonna walk you out into these woods and you ain't ever coming out again."

"Like Millie Boylan?" I don't even know why I say it. I can barely get the words out.

The gun barrels press into my neck again. "What did you say? *What did you say?*"

Eddie kneels on the ground beside me. "She didn't say anything. Just go, leave us alone, *please*. We'll do what you asked."

The door opens. Wind and snow surge into the room. Then the door slams shut, and McGrady is gone. Each breath into my lungs is agony. After a few minutes, I manage to sit up.

Eddie sits hunched on his bed. Tears stream down his face.

"I never asked you to come here. I never asked for your help."

"I know, but I thought—"

"*No*. You never think, Dinah. That's the problem. You just react. You act like you deserve all the answers, like this is all about *you*. Just because you miss your brother, you latch onto me. But you don't even know what you've done."

I'm still sitting against the wall, trying to find the strength to stand. The wind is howling outside, screaming through the eaves. Eddie looks up, meeting my gaze. And something dark passes across his eyes, like a shadow moving through the room.

"I've been remembering things," he whispers. He stands and leans a hand against the narrow countertop. "I'm afraid it's all going to happen again. I'm scared."

"Scared of what? Eddie, you can tell me. I want to help you."

"You don't know me." He grabs a coffee mug and smashes it to the floor. "I am not your brother, and I don't want your help!"

I try to stand up, my hand reaching out to him, but he throws another mug to the floor. Then a plate.

"Get out," he yells. "Get out!"

I scramble onto my hands and knees, then manage to stand. The storm pushes back against me as I fly out the door. I run through the woods, not sure if those are Eddie's screams I hear or the wind.

That night I can't sleep. My side aches where McGrady kicked me. I've made sure the doors are locked and that my parents are safely asleep in their bed, but it doesn't help. I stare at the wood covering my broken window. I hear the smashing of Eddie's dishes, rehash the worst of McGrady's threats.

After I left Eddie's cabin, I thought about going after McGrady. Confronting him again and demanding answers. But I'm not quite that stupid, despite what Eddie seems to believe.

I'm not your brother, he said. As if I'm some deluded kid. All I really want is to be his friend. I thought he wanted that too. Maybe I *am* deluded. A real sap.

I'll give Eddie the remainder of his week. It's just a few more days. McGrady will pack him up, and then I'll never see Eddie again. But after that I'm going to the sheriff. I want some kind of resolution for Millie, even if it's only a proper funeral. Briony deserves to know what really happened to her friend. Then this will all be over.

I turn over and shove my head under my pillow, wishing I could unwind this tightness in my chest.

My mother's voice wakes me. She's talking to my father in the hall. I must've slept in. I throw on some clothes, smooth down my spiky hair, and go into the kitchen.

The scene is jarringly normal. My mother's frying a couple of eggs for Papa's breakfast. The radio is blaring in the living room. I find a shriveled end of a wheat loaf in the bread box and shove it into my mouth.

"Work," I mumble, heading for the door. I'm going to get Jim and head up to Cherry Mountain like nothing has changed. I have nothing else to do. The sooner I start acting like normal, the better. Right?

Assuming McGrady lets me.

"In this weather?" Mother asks. "Why don't you go see if they need help at the market? It's about time to find winter work, isn't it?"

"Yeah," I say absently.

When I open the front door, a letter falls. It was wedged against the doorframe. "Letter," I say, brushing off the snow. I carry it back into the kitchen. It's addressed, *Mr. and Mrs. Joseph Weller.* The ink of the return address is smudged. I can't read it. I drop the letter on the kitchen table, wondering how it got here. Usually we pick up mail at the post office.

Did Abby bring the letter here this morning? Did she come here to see *me*? Maybe she knocked and nobody answered. It seems strange, though. She wouldn't come out in this storm, in four feet of snow, just to say "Hi" and hand-deliver a letter.

Unless the letter was just an excuse. Maybe Abby wanted to see me.

Maybe something's wrong.

My fingers shake as I lace my boots. I race to Abby's house, but despite my furious knocking, nobody answers. My lungs are aching from the cold. Wind blows shards of ice in my face, as sharp as tiny needles. All around me, the snow falls relentlessly.

I head to the assay office next. There's light in the window, and Abby's curled hair and beautiful heart-shaped face are right where they should be—behind the counter. I'm so relieved at the sight that I have to stop in the middle of Main Street. McGrady really scared the heck out of me yesterday, put me on edge. But he hasn't done anything to Abby. Everything's OK.

I push through the door and start shedding my sodden coat and gloves.

It's only then that I see the tears on Abby's face.

38

Millie
1918

"Stay here," I say to Rachel.

I race upstairs and find Joe Weller. "Joe, does Sean McGrady live here in the boardinghouse? I need to speak with him."

He squints at me, his lips drawing into a smirk. "Why do you want him?"

"I hear he can help me with certain medical supplies. With so many men sick, I'm afraid I'll run low." I doubt morphine will help men with the flu, but Joe Weller doesn't know that.

He seems to ponder my words for hidden meaning, but doesn't find any. "His room's on the second floor. Four doors down on the left from the stairwell. He ain't real charitable, though. Bring money."

I nod. "I need another favor. There's a young woman downstairs by the front door. Give her an escort back down the mountain." Having Rachel here will just cause more trouble.

Joe's eyebrow arches at the mention of a young woman. "Don't get any ideas," I add. "You take her straight to Courtland Spencer's house, and if there's anything untoward, I'll have your head."

Joe takes off his apron, muttering to himself about how presumptuous I am. Just as he heads down the stairs, Lydia passes him, coming up onto the landing. She's carrying a tray with steaming mugs and a stack of buttermilk biscuits.

"Where's he headed?" Lydia asks. "You didn't tell him he could go to bed, did you? Every five minutes he's been begging off work. We have a long night ahead of us."

I try to quickly explain what's happened, which only sends Lydia into a panic. "Edward's here?" she asks. "What do you mean? Why?"

I've been intentionally vague. I haven't mentioned Sean McGrady, alleged purveyor of illicit morphine. "We'll sort this all out. Let's check on our patients, and then we can look for Edward. We'll have to hurry, though. Lights out is in twenty minutes."

I take the tray from her hands and set it on a console table in the hallway. I'm afraid that neither of us is going to be eating anytime soon.

I go straight to Sean McGrady's door and knock.

There's no answer.

I press my ear to the door. I hear muffled voices, but I can't make them out. Perhaps they're coming from another room.

I continue my search, wandering the halls and hoping to find my way to either Mr. McGrady or Edward. But all is quiet. Did Rachel get her petticoats in a tangle for no reason?

After about ten minutes, I give up and go back upstairs to tend to my nursing duties. Soon, Lydia joins me. She hasn't found any sign of Edward either. And right at the stroke of ten o'clock, the electric lights in the hallway go dark. Someone will have locked the front door now, too.

Wherever Edward is, I don't believe he's here.

We settle into our work. Comforting, cleaning, changing sheets and trying to raise spirits. Earlier Joe set up carbide lamps in each room, and they burn with an unearthly light. The hallway is pitch black, and I rush from room to room, uneasy about wandering too far in that dark.

After midnight, our sick ward is quieting again. Most of the men have returned to their fitful sleep. I tell Lydia that she should go to our room for a nap. Her eyes are red and only half-open as it is. She agrees, and takes one of the carbide lamps down the hall. I watch as the door opens, and then Lydia disappears inside.

I continue to make my rounds, hurrying from room to room. Darkness engulfs me whenever I pass into the hallway. It's as thick as a solid wall, but I keep imagining pale hands reaching out of it. Like some undersea creature appearing out of the deep. But even worse? That darkness also calls to me. As if the shadow-things in my mind are taking hold, trying to control me. They long for the dark. That's where they'll bind me and never let go.

I'm exhausted. I begin to feel as though I'm in a trance, my body going through its motions while my mind sits back, observing.

In one of the rooms I pause and close my eyes, trying to steady myself.

"Nurse?" The man in the bed calls out for me. "I'm thirsty somethin' terrible."

I go to his side, helping him drink. The minutes pass slowly. By the time he finally slips into unconsciousness, I'm half asleep myself.

Then I hear noises out in the hall. Men's voices. Instantly, I'm pulled back to alertness. I tiptoe to the closed door and put my ear against it.

There are footsteps, growing louder. Coming up the stairs.

"You're bein' stupid," someone says. "We could make a deal that benefits us both."

"I don't want a deal. I want all of it gone."

I gasp, covering my mouth. It's Edward's voice. He's here. But how? The outside doors are locked.

But Mr. Gainsbury is the Assistant Superintendent here. Wouldn't he have a key to all the buildings? Wouldn't it be easy for Edward to pocket his father's key ring? I curse myself for not realizing it before.

Their footsteps pass by. I can't imagine what they're doing on this floor, with all these sick men. I keep absolutely still, listening.

"Nobody else is going to suffer like I have," Edward says.

The other man laughs. "You talk big with that gun in your hand. *Gainsbury.* Like that name buys you the right to rule this town. You don't know suffering. But maybe you will."

Their footsteps recede. There's the sound of a door opening, hinges moving. Then the hall goes quiet. Slowly, I open my door and look out into the dark. There's a thin rectangle of light at the very end of the hall. The common room. That's where they've gone.

I don't like this. Not at all.

I take a tentative step out into the darkness. The vicious whispers immediately assail me. *He doesn't love you. He doesn't want you here.* Every false word makes me cringe. But that's what they want, isn't it? To make me doubt myself. To feed on my fear.

I begin to walk down the corridor. I hold my arms in front of me. All I can see is the outline of the common room door. It feels like I'll never reach it. Like the darkness is pressing in on me, crushing me with its weight.

But then my fingers touch solid wood. The door moves inward by a fraction. It isn't latched. I bring my eye to the crack.

The man I assume to be Sean McGrady is bent over the fireplace. He's around twenty years old—close to Edward's age—with the beginnings of a beard and his skin tanned by the sun. He's stoking the embers with a poker, reawakening the flames. His eyes glint with cunning. Edward stands behind him, aiming a Colt revolver at McGrady's back. I recognize the gun—it's the one that was hanging on the wall of Edward's old bedroom at Gainsbury House.

"You're gonna regret this, little brother." McGrady says in a conversational tone. "You know that your daddy is my daddy too, right? You have any idea what your family owes me?"

"I know who you are. It's nothing to do with me."

"You're wrong there. Samuel Gainsbury might've been willing to accept his only son, even a bastard one— except he had two sons. He had you, didn't he?"

Edward flinches. The gun begins to sag in his grip. "You think I don't hate him too? I...I suppose I could try talking to him for you. I might be able to get money, but only if you do what I'm asking."

"I don't know, maybe money's not enough for me anymore." McGrady keeps poking at the fire. The flames glow red against his face. "I like that Rachel Kohler. She's pretty devoted to you. Or what about that red-headed nurse I've seen you with? Ain't she up here right now, taking care of those sick men? She might enjoy getting acquainted."

Edward takes an unsteady step forward. "Shut your mouth. Just burn the vials and be done with it."

"Yes, sir." McGrady says in a mocking tone. Holding his hands up as if in surrender, he walks over and kneels beside a chair. He pries up a wooden panel from the floor and removes a small box. Glass tinkles inside. He takes off the lid, holding it aloft. Edward is leaning forward, eyes fixed on the vials inside the box.

"Like what you see?" McGrady asks.

"Throw them in the fire," Edward says. But his voice is weak. Cracking. "Do it."

Moving fluidly, absolutely calm, McGrady removes a small leather case from the box. He flips open the case, revealing a syringe. "I could give you one last taste. As a favor from one Gainsbury son to another."

39

Dinah
1943

"What's wrong?" I ask.

Abby stubs out the cigarette she was smoking. Without a word, she turns and heads into the back of the office. She waves a hand, beckoning me to follow.

I stop mid-step, appalled at the mess.

There's broken glass on the floor. The window in the back door must've shattered—there's a canvas tarp fixed over the hole to keep out the snow. Papers and equipment are scattered all over the floor.

Abby takes a stuttering breath. "I found it like this when I got here this morning. My mother helped with the tarp, but she had to go—she's on the shovel crew and they're out dealing with this storm. I've been here alone…trying to clean up and figure out what's missing, and…"

She starts to sob, and I don't even think. I just go to her and wrap her in a hug. Abby puts her face against my neck, hugging me back. She smells like cinnamon babka and Chesterfields. A surprisingly pleasant combination. There's a warm, spinny feeling in my belly.

I don't think I've ever held anybody this way. Not even my brother. *Definitely* not my brother. But with Abby it feels right. We're the same height, and my arms fit perfectly around her waist. I don't ever want to let go.

"I'll help," I say. "Did they take anything?"

"I can't tell."

"Money from the till?"

She shakes her head. "Not that there was much money inside. Why would someone do this?"

"What did they break the window with?" I'm still holding Abby, but now my eyes are scanning the floor. I'm looking for a river rock wrapped in newspaper.

"Don't know," she says. "But they broke the window and then reached in and unlocked the door."

"But there was no message?"

"Message?" She lets go and takes a step back, wiping her eyes. "What are you talking about?"

Now I'm afraid this will upset her more. But Abby insists on knowing. I tell her about the broken window in my bedroom, the rock.

I tell her about following McGrady yesterday. How he threatened me and my family.

She stares at me in disbelief. "All this happened and you didn't tell me?"

"I didn't think McGrady knew you were involved. I'm so sorry."

"That isn't it—besides, we don't know if it was him. But I want to know when you're in trouble. I thought you trusted me."

"You were with your mom and your aunt for Thanksgiving. I wasn't going to intrude." I thought Mrs. Spivak was probably sick of seeing me. She basically forced me to go home the other day, and Abby didn't seem to have a problem with that. I wasn't sure if Abby wanted me around at all. Maybe she just wanted to forget the last several days. After finding Millie's body in that cabin, who would blame her?

"I've been missing you," Abby says, "and you didn't even think of me?"

"I…" She missed me?

There's a tremendous boom outside. It's so strong that I feel the ground shaking under my feet.

We run out the front door. Several other people have come out of storefronts and are looking around, their faces frightened.

"Smoke!" someone shouts.

There's a column of smoke rising in the sky several blocks away. It's making a garish streak against the snowy sky.

Then the fire bell starts to ring.

Abby and I go back for our coats. We head toward the smoke, wading through the ever-deepening snow. Other people are doing the same thing, but nobody knows yet exactly what happened.

A plow truck goes by, clearing snow from the road. Mrs. Spivak is driving it. The fire truck follows.

"How could something be burning in this weather?" Abby asks.

We walk past several streets, nearing the far edge of town. I'm starting to get worried. We're almost to Terrance's house and the stable. But then we get closer and I see the Jamesons' little cottage. I see the stable, looking just the way it did yesterday. Briony and Terrance are standing outside, arms around each other's shoulders. Both look stricken.

The fire truck has pulled up to the only other place nearby—Sean McGrady's house.

But the house isn't there anymore.

The volunteer Rescue Brigade members are swarming, pulling rubble away from the smoking, charred mess that used to be McGrady's house. Snow is falling over the scene like ash.

I nearly trip over something. There are bricks in the road. Pieces of siding. A splintered length of wood that looks like it might've been a table leg.

Mrs. Spivak jumps out of the truck and comes over to head off the crowd. She spots Abby and me and frowns. "Everybody, stay back," she says. "It's not safe here. There's been an explosion."

Briony runs over when she sees me. I introduce her to Abby, but Briony's eyes are glazed. She doesn't seem to hear.

"Dinah, have you seen BT anywhere? Maybe on Main Street?"

"No, I haven't seen him anywhere." I look over at the stables. Terrance has gone to talk to the Rescue Brigade. "Didn't McGrady bring him back yesterday?"

"He did, that's the trouble. Terrance woke up this morning and BT was gone. Sometimes he pulls his rope loose from the tie, but..." Briony gestures at the wreckage of McGrady's house. "Then this happened. Terrance is beside himself with worry."

I promise her that if I see any sign of BT, I'll let her know. Better yet I'll grab his reins and bring him back.

"You don't think he was hurt in the explosion, do you?" Abby asks.

"Lord, I hope not." Briony heads back toward her brother.

The crowd has continued to grow. We all stand there in the snow, waiting for news. But if McGrady—or anybody else—was inside that house when it blew, there's no way he could've survived.

40

Millie
1918

Sean McGrady takes out the syringe. The metal dances in the firelight.

"Stop," Edward whispers. His eyes are fixed on the needle.

I watch from the crack in the doorway, knowing I should intervene. But I'm afraid of startling Edward—his knuckles are white around the gun. I don't make a sound.

"The way I figure it, you're not gonna shoot me. Not your own brother." McGrady selects a small jar of liquid with a rubber cover. He sticks the needle through the rubber. Draws back the plunger.

"Rachel said you were desperate for morphine, and believe me, this is the good stuff. I can only imagine how much you want it right now. I've never been to war. Lost a limb. Who could blame you?"

"*The fire.*"

"Suit yourself." McGrady stands, placing the syringe in the box. He goes toward the fire. Edward relaxes.

But then McGrady spins toward Edward instead. His arm strikes out. With a swift, sudden movement, McGrady jabs the syringe into Edward's neck.

"No!" I cry, pushing the door inward. But it's too late. The gun in Edward's hand clatters to the floor. His body goes limp.

I trip over my skirts and fall to the floor. I'm vaguely aware of McGrady shuffling back in shock when he sees me. Edward is just feet away. I don't think of anything else, not even the shadow-things inside of me that are rejoicing at my agony—only him. I have to reach him.

I crawl forward and pull the syringe from his neck, flinging it to the ground. Edward is face up, his entire body trembling. I don't know how much McGrady gave him. Was it just enough of the opiate to incapacitate him? Or is Edward in immediate danger?

I don't have the chance to find out. I feel a stab of pain near my shoulder. A burning sensation floods through me, followed by a strange numbness. And within moments I don't feel anything at all.

41

Dinah
1943

We stand in the snow, watching the Rescue Brigade sift through the smoking wreckage of McGrady's house. Word starts to travel fast—it was his alcohol still that blew. The alcohol vapor is explosive, and such accidents are known to happen. But the Rescue Brigade is all volunteers, no experts; they're waiting on the county sheriff to arrive from the next town over. But with this storm? That could be until tomorrow.

Abby and I go back to the assay office, where I help her clean up the mess. "I don't get it," she says, sweeping up glass. "You think McGrady broke in here sometime during the night. As a warning to me. And then he blew up his own house? A diversion?"

"That wouldn't make much sense."

I'm scouring the floor, still looking for newspaper messages. Some evidence that it really was McGrady who vandalized the assay office. But I can't find anything. I scoop up fallen envelopes and stack them on the counter.

Could the explosion be a coincidence? Perhaps McGrady has been spending too much time away from home and wasn't keeping an eye on his still. Or did someone else set the fire on purpose?

Last we heard, they hadn't yet found a body in the wreckage. That means McGrady could still be out there somewhere.

Abby stops sweeping, leaning against the broom handle. "Do you think somebody was actually trying to *kill* McGrady?"

I laugh. "They're welcome to try. I'm not going to cry at his funeral."

I thought pretty hard about shooting McGrady myself yesterday. Maybe he has enemies all over Powder Ridge that I don't know about.

People who owe him dough?

My mother.

But I dismiss that thought with a shake of my head. She was home all night. Besides, she'd never sabotage that alcohol still. She's going to panic when she finds out her favorite source of cheap gin has gone up in flames.

No, if McGrady's still alive, then it's more important to know who McGrady might *blame*.

We finish stacking the last of the scattered papers. The storm is blowing at the tarp over the back door, making it puff in and out.

"I wish I could figure out what's missing," Abby says. "There's no warning message, nothing to explain why somebody did this."

"I know. McGrady doesn't seem that subtle. But if it wasn't him, then who was it?"

We sit at the table. Abby rests her head in her hands. Then she snaps up.

"The record," she says.

She runs to a cabinet and flings it open. Paws through the contents. "It can't be gone," she says. "*No.*"

"I thought it was at your house?"

"I left it here so my mother wouldn't listen to it."

I get up to help her look. We scour every shelf, every corner of that office. But the record with Millie's voice is gone. The whole time we search, a sick feeling is growing in my stomach. I keep remembering McGrady's reaction yesterday when I said Millie Boylan's name. He sounded shocked. *Scared.* Why would that be, unless...

Unless he knows that Millie's body is hidden in that ruined cabin?

"I'm so sorry, Dinah," Abby says. "I thought the record would be safe here. How would anybody even know about it?"

I'm not even thinking about the record. If it's gone, it's gone. I'm thinking about Cherry Mountain.

If McGrady realized that we know about Millie's body—and if he had something to hide—he'd try to get rid of the evidence. He might come after us.

He might go after Eddie, regardless of whether Eddie shares his blood. Or maybe he'd go after Eddie *because* they share blood. Briony said that Samuel Gainsbury refused to acknowledge him. McGrady's spent his entire life in the shadow of the Gainsburys.

And Eddie is all alone up there on the mountain.

"We should wait for the sheriff," Abby says.

She's running after me through the snow. The storm has only gotten worse. "We can't wait that long," I say. "We have to get help."

If Abby and I are right—if Eddie is really, somehow, the same young man as the Edward Gainsbury from 1918—then it's past time to tell his sisters the truth.

We're going to Gainsbury House.

It's only about ten in the morning, but the sky is dark gray. At Gainsbury House, there's light showing through the crack in the curtains.

We march up the steps. I knock firmly on the door. Almost immediately, Lydia answers. She has thick gloves on, and her overcoat is damp with melting snowflakes.

"Dinah? What are you doing here in this weather?" Lydia looks past us, as if to check if there's anyone else behind us. "Is everything all right at home?"

Maybe rumors have spread about my troubles with Mother. "Nothing's wrong at home. Can we come in?"

She invites us inside, and we take off our wet coats. Abby introduces herself.

"It's lovely to meet you, Miss Spivak," Lydia says, laying her gloves on a table. "Your parents moved to Powder Ridge after my time. I'm sorry I haven't had the chance to get to know them."

There's a suitcase here in the foyer. "Are you going somewhere?" I ask.

"I'll have to wait until the storm passes, but yes. Just a short trip to take care of a few matters I left open at my previous address. Did you hear that loud noise earlier? I was going to investigate, but haven't had the chance."

"It was an explosion," Abby says. "Sean McGrady's house. They think his alcohol still blew up."

Lydia's hand flies to her mouth. "My Lord. How terrible. Do they need a doctor?"

I shake my head. "They don't think anyone was inside."

Lydia glances to the side, seeming to think. "Then why are you girls here?"

Abby looks at me nervously. I don't even know where to begin. "Is Grace around?" I ask. "She should hear this, too."

Lydia raises her eyebrows. "I'm afraid Grace hasn't been feeling well since Thanksgiving. She's been in her bed, and Jim's been looking after her. What's this about?"

I guess I should just say it. She's waited long enough to know the truth.

"It's about your brother, Edward. He's…" I clear my throat. Abby nudges my hand encouragingly. But I can't quite get the words out.

"This is going to sound very strange," Abby says. "But we think Edward—your brother—might still be alive."

Lydia's reaction is not what I'm expecting. I thought she might laugh at the absurdity of what Abby said. Or get angry, assuming this is a poor attempt at humor. But instead she just stands there, staring at us. I'm not even sure she's breathing.

"We're afraid he could be in danger," I add.

Lydia blinks and inhales, coming back to life. "You'd better come in here," she whispers. She leads us to the small parlor with fleur-de-lis wallpaper, the same room where she showed me Edward's picture on the day we met. Edward's photo is still here, smiling at us from the wall.

Lydia sits on the sofa and gestures for us to take the chairs opposite. "Now tell me what this is all about. From the beginning."

So that's what I do. I start with that day at the boardinghouse when I saw Eddie the first time. Then, following Eddie to his cabin. Getting to know him and suspecting he might be the same Edward Gainsbury who —supposedly—died in 1918. And then finding McGrady at his cabin yesterday.

Lydia's face pales as she listens, but other than that, she seems astonishingly calm.

I haven't mentioned Millie Boylan yet—the handprints, the haunting music, the record. The story is already bizarre enough as it is.

Lydia is not quite looking at me, and after awhile, I realize where her gaze is fixed. She's staring at the picture of Edward on the wall. "And you think Edward is in danger from Sean McGrady?" Lydia asks when I'm finished. "Why is that?" Her thin, white fingers are touching the lace at her collar. "Wait," Abby says. "You believe us? I mean, *I* hardly believe us and I've seen Eddie with my own eyes."

Lydia stands. She walks back and forth a few times across the small space. Like an animal who's been caught and caged. She even sneaks glances at the door, as if she'd like nothing better than to run.

Finally, she turns to face us. She closes her eyes, takes a deep breath.

"I do believe you," she says. "Because I already knew. Edward is alive. I've been helping him hide for the last twenty-five years."

42

Millie
1918

Slowly I blink my eyes. I feel as though I'm floating outside myself. Rocking on the undulating waves of the ocean. I have the sense that something was wrong before, but how can that be? How could anything be wrong in this dreamlike, distant place?

But I start to become aware of the room around me. The crackling sound of the fire. The stifling heat. A figure lying prone beside me.

I see Edward, and I'm pulled back into myself. Nausea hits, making me gag. My skin itches, and my head is aching, heavy. My brain doesn't want to think but it must. It feels like I'm crawling up from the water, but every new wave wants to drag me back down.

Danger. Edward and I are both in danger.

There was a man. Sean McGrady.

I brace my hands against the floor and force my arms to lift me up. McGrady isn't here. But there's a syringe discarded on the carpet. McGrady injected Edward with something. And then me as well? Is that what happened? It must be morphine. Yes. I only see the one syringe. He injected Edward with the bulk of it, then me. But what does that mean? What do I do?

I have to focus. *Buck up, Millie. Think.*

I crawl closer to Edward. His eyes are open. He's making a high-pitched, wheezing sound every time he breathes. But his face is turning as blue as that ocean I was just swimming in. Why? It takes several more seconds before the thought bobs to the surface.

It's the morphine. He's had too much; it's shutting down his body. His lungs can't move enough to take in air. I try to lift his head. His eyes move to meet mine. They plead with me for help. "You'll be all right," I say, my voice slurring. "Edward, listen to me. You've survived worse than this."

Then I feel them—the shadows. Like something dark and monstrous emerging from the deep. Coming up within me. The darkness flows out from my fingers where I'm touching Edward's skin. And I begin to experience the most hideous, unbearable sensation. *Hunger.* They can taste Edward's terror on the air, and they want more. They have tired of trying to control me, and his soul is rich with sorrow. If I let them, they'd flow out of me completely and into this new victim.

Edward's eyes widen. He sees the shadows too.

"Get away from him," I cry.

I let go of Edward, and the shadow-things pause in mid-air. There's a tug deep inside me, like a piece of elastic stretching taut, and I *pull.* I pull the darkness back. The shadows wriggle and writhe like a school of hooked fish. I feel their frustration. This isn't supposed to happen. They don't understand how I've exerted such control.

But my triumph is too brief.

Suddenly I feel weak fingers circle my wrist. It's Edward. His chest is barely moving now, but his gaze is resolute. He nods almost imperceptibly. He would take this darkness from me if I let him.

"I won't," I whisper to him. I will not place this burden upon him.

But the shadows are surging away from me again. I'm losing my hold on them. I don't know if I'm strong enough to keep them in.

43

Dinah
1943

"Edward had followed us up to the mine."

Lydia is standing by the window, staring out into the whiteness of the storm. Abby is clutching my hand.

"I still don't know exactly why he came. Millie Boylan—the nurse who my family hired—she and I were caring for the sick miners. The flu had spread there, to Cherry Mountain. Then Millie heard that Edward was on his way. It was late, past dark. After we couldn't find him, she told me to get some sleep. I didn't think there was anything wrong. I'd been worried about him, of course, after he was ill. I...suspected certain things. But I *trusted* Millie. I never would've thought..."

Lydia blinks, and tears fall onto her cheeks. She presses her hand to her mouth, covering a sob. "I found them together. I found...a syringe of morphine. Both of them had taken it. The shock was almost too much. I didn't want to believe it, that Millie would be involved. That I'd been so wrong about her."

I edge forward on my chair. "Millie Boylan? Are you sure?"

Lydia doesn't seem to hear me. She walks away from the window, wiping at her eyes. "I'm sorry. This isn't the sort of topic you girls should be hearing about."

I'm having trouble sitting still. My feet are tapping against the carpet. Abby puts her hand on my shoulder and asks, "What happened then? Why did everyone think Edward had died?"

"Because he almost did." Lydia sits on the couch again. She wraps her arms around her middle. "Edward wouldn't wake up, but he was breathing. He was alive. And I knew that if I was going to save Edward from that terrible addiction—and from Millie Boylan—then I had to get him away from Powder Ridge. The truth about Edward's weakness was too shameful for anyone to know. My father would've disowned him. I couldn't let that happen."

She takes a deep breath. "You see, we have a half-brother. Sean McGrady."

"I know."

Lydia nods. "Well, Sean was up at the mine that night. He helped me spirit Edward away. I paid Dr. Durham to cover up the lack of a body. There's a marker in the cemetery, but my brother is not in that grave."

Lydia let the rest of her family believe that Edward was dead? The story seems far-fetched. At the very least, it was callous. Yet it does square with some of the things Briony told me.

"What about Millie?" I ask.

Lydia sits up. "What?"

"Millie Boylan. You said you found her with Edward. You and Sean took Edward away after that. But what happened to Millie?"

She holds out her hands, shrugging. "She left town, probably out of shame. That's what Sean told me. Good riddance, I thought. You asked about her at Thanksgiving too. Why?"

I hesitate to answer. Maybe it's the tension that comes into Lydia's voice whenever she speaks of Millie. Or this claim about Millie being a morphine addict. Could Lydia be lying? But why would she do that? It's more likely that she's just mistaken. She thinks Millie left town because *McGrady* told her. McGrady is probably the one who made up this lie about the morphine, too. Then again, why would McGrady do that? I can't make it fit.

Abby is shifting uncomfortably in her chair. "Millie never—"

"Millie never wrote to Briony Jameson afterward," I say, interrupting. "That seemed odd because they were best friends."

Abby glances at me, and I nod, hoping she'll play along. It's better not to get into Millie's death right now. I want to hear Lydia's story.

"I guess I don't really know what went on with Millie," Lydia says. "I was gone myself. I thought that I'd help Edward recover, cure him, and then we could come home. No one in Powder Ridge would know the real truth except for myself and our half-brother. Sean was never treated fairly by our father, and he and I agreed to help one another. Unfortunately, Edward wasn't the same after he woke up. He'd...changed."

"How?" Abby asks.

"There was a darkness in him. I don't mean the morphine. This was something else. Something unnatural. He would rage at anyone who came near. Scream awful things. I had to keep him isolated. But I still had hope that he'd get better. As the years passed, though, I realized that more than just his mind had changed. He didn't age. His leg, the one he'd lost in the war..." She squeezes her eyes shut and shakes her head. "No, you wouldn't believe it. Who could? But I saw it. I know."

The scar on Eddie's leg. So it's true.

"I couldn't bring him back," Lydia says. "It wasn't safe. Not for him, and—whenever that darkness inside him starts to rage again—not safe for anyone else."

I think of the way Eddie smashed the dishes yesterday. The dark looks that sometimes pass across his eyes.

"But Eddie—I mean, Edward," Abby says. "The boy we met was kind. Lonely. We saw the scar on his leg, and that's what made us suspect he might somehow be the same Edward Gainsbury. But isn't there some way for him to come back home now? Be a part of the world again? It's been twenty-five years."

Lydia nods. "Of course that's what I want. He doesn't remember his former life. I've had to lie to him to keep him safe. But I've always hoped that I could bring him back to Gainsbury House, that we'd all finally be together again. When I got the call from Grace that her Mitchell had died—that's when I knew I couldn't wait any longer. I contacted Sean, and he arranged everything. He set up a cabin for Edward, handled the transport and the supplies. It was just supposed to last until I had things settled here. I didn't think I was putting Edward in even greater danger." She drops her face into her hands. "What is it that Sean wants? Is it more money? My share of the inheritance?"

"We're not sure," I say. "We don't even know for certain that Edd—um, Edward's in danger. But McGrady's threatened us, and he held a gun on me yesterday. Edward's all alone up at that cabin. That's why we were worried."

Abby looks over at me. There's confusion in her expression. It's how I feel, too. There's still so much that we don't know. Like the truth about what happened to Millie, and how that fits in with Lydia's story. But maybe we'll never know. I doubt McGrady will tell us.

"Edward's our friend," Abby says. "What can we do to help?"

Lydia stands, putting on a smile despite her tears. "You girls are both very brave. Thank you so much for coming to me. But I don't want you in harm's way. I'm going to contact the sheriff directly—I need to come clean about my brother. Both of my brothers. The sheriff probably won't believe it. But as long as Edward's safe, then I don't care anymore. It's time to bring Edward home."

44

Millie
1918

I will not let this darkness have him.

My clothes are damp with sweat. My jaw aches from gritting my teeth. It seems like an impossible struggle. Like reversing the tide as it's already cresting toward shore. But slowly, bit by bit, the shadows begin to recede back inside of me.

You'll never be with him, the Legion screams. *You'll be trapped. Lost. He'll be dead and gone.*

"We'll be OK," I say. I'm gasping for breath. But I'm winning. The last of the dark wisps fade from Edward's skin. A surge of euphoria passes through me, and I know it's not the morphine. I've done it. I've kept Edward safe.

I smile down at him. Caress his cheek. I can touch him now without any concern. I remember what Edward said to me yesterday—*you're one of the purest, kindest people I've ever met. That's why the shadows ran from you before. They can't change who you are.* It was his faith in me that made the difference.

But his gray eyes bear an unnatural sheen. As if they've turned to glass.

"Edward?" I whisper.

I place my palm against his chest. It's still.

"No. *No.* Edward, please."

I press my hands to his throat, his face. There's no pulse. His lips are blue from the lack of oxygen, cold already to my touch. Tears blur my vision. I cradle him against me. His hair slips between my fingers. The horrible truth rises up within me like dark water, and no matter how hard I swim for the surface, I can't find the light.

"Come back. *Please* come back."

He can't be gone. I love him. I was supposed to save him.

The common room door opens. "Millie?" someone says. "*Edward?*"

The person runs toward us. Pushes me aside. It's Lydia. She's slapping Edward's cheek, tearing his shirt. The buttons pop.

"Edward," she cries. "Wake up, God damn you. Wake up!"

I try to stand, but my legs are too weak. The room is spinning. I have no strength left, and the morphine is still blunting my thoughts.

"Lydia," I say, "he's gone. I'm so sorry. He's gone."

She bats my hand away. Turns toward me with wild hatred in her eyes. "It's not true. He is not dead. He's not!" She watches as I try again to stand, and end up falling to one knee. She sees the syringe on the floor and picks it up. An animal cry comes out of her throat.

"What have you done?" she demands.

I push myself to my feet. But Lydia is advancing on me. She's holding out the syringe like an accusation. "I didn't," I try to say, but the words slur. Lydia grabs at my arm. I stumble backward. My foot slips on slick stone—the fireplace hearth—and I'm falling.

There's an explosion of pressure at my temple. I hear Lydia scream.

At first I'm just confused. My vision goes double, then triple. The world is splitting apart. Disintegrating right in front of me. I can't make sense of it. Something hot and wet is dripping down my face. My lips are moving. "Edward, I love you," I want to say. But then I feel my own body coming apart, too, dissolving. I'm back in that strange, dark ocean, and I'm floating away.

45

Dinah
1943

There's a break in the storm. The sky is still icy white, but the snow has stopped.

Neither Abby nor I want to be alone right now. So we head toward my house. When we come inside, it's quiet. That's what tells me that something is wrong.

My father's radio is turned off.

"Hello?" I say, walking to the kitchen. Abby is a few steps behind me.

There's an overturned bottle of gin. The puddle is still dripping off the table. A shattered old-fashioned glass lies on the floor.

"Mama? Papa?"

I glance into the living room. My father is sitting in his wheelchair. His head is drooping, and at first I think he's asleep. Then I remember McGrady's threat yesterday and panic strikes at my heart. I run toward him.

"Papa? Are you OK?"

He looks up at me. He's crying.

He's holding a piece of paper in his hand.

"Dinah," he says. "Nate's gone. He's gone."

"*What?*"

I grab for the paper. My fingers feel numb; they fumble as they unfold the thin sheet. It's a telegram.

254

Mrs. R. Weller,

The Secretary Of War Desires To Convey His Deep Regret That Your Son Private First Class Nathaniel Weller Was Killed In Action The Eighth Of November In Italy.

The Adjutant General

"Dinah?" Abby asks. "What is it? What's happened?"

The sound of wailing comes from my parents' bedroom. It's my mother. My father is covering his eyes with his hand.

I can't look away from the paper. The words are burning into my head. It isn't true. It simply cannot be true. But I can't escape from these awful words.

Nate is dead. My brother is dead.

Abby pulls the paper out of my hand. "Oh, no. I'm so sorry."

My father's body is shaking as he sobs. I sit on the divan. All the feeling seems to be draining away from my body. Then dark clouds start to close in around me. The room in front of me gets smaller and smaller, as if I'm looking the wrong way through a telescope, until it shrinks away to nothing at all.

Cold water splashes on my face.

"Come on," Abby says. "You have to wake up. Listen, OK?"

But I don't want to open my eyes. I don't want to listen.

Someone shakes me. "You sit up right now, Dinah. This instant." It's my mother.

They push me upright. I'm sitting in the living room. My mother and Abby are beside me. Papa is in his wheelchair. My parents both look haggard, but also somehow electrified. Their eyes are too bright.

"Say it again," Mother begs Abby. "What you said before."

"Listen." Abby's smiling. How can she be smiling? "It's a fake, Dinah. This telegram? It isn't official. It didn't come through our office at all."

"What are you talking about?" I grab the paper away from her and look at it. But it still says the same thing. Those horrible words. Three lines, one sentence. Enough to wipe my every last hope off the face of the earth.

Abby takes the paper gently out of my fist. "I thought it seemed off the moment I saw it. I mean, how'd it get to your house? We haven't had a telegram come through our machine in the past couple days."

I'm shaking my head. I'm scared to believe her. What if I find out she's wrong? How can I bear my heart breaking all over again?

Abby runs into the kitchen and comes back with an envelope. It's torn open at the top. The same envelope that was stuck into our door this morning when I left. She holds it up. "You see this?" she asks. "It's one of our envelopes from the assay office, but I don't recognize this typing. I'm telling you, Dinah. It's a fake!"

My parents are both crying again, but it's from relief this time. I'm starting to believe it myself. It's like a giant boulder is being lifted off of me one inch at a time.

Every time I see the smile on Abby's face, the weight lessens.

"Who would do something like this?" Papa asks. "Who hates us that much?"

My mother's expression darkens. "I can think of plenty. Those Gainsburys, for example. They're jealous we still have Nate, that's what it is."

Abby holds up the telegram again, and there's a flicker in her expression. She sees something in that paper. But she says, "There's no way to know. I'll tell you if I find anything out. But you know what? I bet this envelope and telegram paper were stolen from the assay office last night. If we find out who broke in, we'll know who faked the telegram."

"Thank you, Abigail," my mother says. She's holding tight to my father's hand. I can't remember the last time I saw that.

"Of course," Abby says. She nudges my hand, and her eyebrows raise slightly. There's more that she needs to tell me. But not in front of them.

We get up, leaving my parents quietly talking in the living room, and go to my bedroom. Abby shuts the door behind us. She walks over to me and smoothes the hair back from my face. Her touch almost makes me feel alive again.

"Are you sure you're OK?" she asks gently. "You had a shock back there. You fainted."

"Don't tell Nate, he won't let me live it down." A part of me is still numb. I really thought my brother was gone. And it was worse than I'd even imagined. It was like looking over a cliff into an endless drop, and knowing that was my future.

"Nate is OK. But he's a soldier fighting a war. Anything could happen. There are no guarantees."

"That's supposed to make me feel better?" I tilt my head away so she's not touching me anymore. But she puts a firm hand on my cheek.

"I could lose my father," she says. "And you could lose Nate. But hey, *listen.* No matter what happens, you will live through it. You hear me? You are more than just Nate Weller's sister."

I squeeze my eyes shut. The tears are already rolling. "But I'm not," I say, my voice breaking down the middle just like my heart. "I'm nothing without him. Everybody knows it."

"Not me. It doesn't matter what I think?" Her hand cups the back of my neck. She rests her forehead against mine. I open my eyes, and her gaze is right there, waiting for me.

"I think you're smart," she says. "And brave. And amazing."

I wonder if she could be right. So I do the bravest, craziest thing I can think of.

I kiss her.

I touch my lips to hers, just lightly. So she can pull back if she wants to. But she doesn't. Abby's arms go tight around me. Her mouth presses hard against mine, warm and sweet and eager, and when she takes a breath, it feels hot against my cheek.

We hear my parents' voices in the living room and break apart. Abby bites her lower lip guiltily, then smiles at me. I grin back and then we're both laughing silently. I laugh so much that I lose my balance and sit hard onto the bed. She flops down next to me and we're kissing again, and laughing, and kissing, all without making a sound. Then I just look at her for a while, running my fingers through her curled hair. Her dark eyes with the golden flecks in them. Her lips that're the perfect shade of pink. I didn't know it was possible to feel so broken and so whole all at the same time.

"I noticed something about the telegram," she whispers. "I wasn't sure, so I didn't want to say anything in front of your parents."

"Do you think it could've been McGrady who left it?" I say. I can certainly see him breaking windows. But faking a death telegram?

If it wasn't him, though, does that mean it wasn't McGrady who broke into the assay after all?

Abby glances at my closed bedroom door. "Did you notice how your brother's name was oddly spaced? The letters were almost too close together, like they had to be squeezed in? It seemed really strange. So I held it up to the light, and I thought I could see a different name underneath 'Nathaniel Weller.' The original name was almost washed out, but not quite. It *was* a real telegram, not stolen from the office at all. But somebody must've tampered with it."

"What was the name?"

"Mitchell G. Tate."

"Mitchell?" Jim's brother. "But...how? Why?"

"I don't know. And I can't say for sure who did it. But whoever it was, they must've gotten that telegram from Gainsbury House."

46

Millie
1918

It's dark here. I don't know where I am.

There are things swarming around me. They brush against me as they pass, as filmy and dry as bats' wings.

Let us free let us free let us free

The shadows are outside of me now, yet they're trapped in the same place that I am—wherever that is. They're furious to get away. I feel eyes upon me, and though I can't see them, I am sure that they can see me.

A light appears. I move toward it. A strange scene begins to materialize out of the fog. The light is flickering —it's a fire. A room with tables and chairs and sofas. Two people are bending over something in front of the fireplace.

That's when I realize what I'm seeing. I'm watching myself—my body is lying on the hearth. My forehead has a nasty gash. My blood is seeping onto the hearth stones. My nurse's cap has fallen to the side, and it's stained red along the edge.

Edward lies beside my body. Oh poor, dear Edward.

I reach toward him. My hand passes through an invisible barrier, and I gasp at the odd sensation. A window. I'm looking through a window.

I am outside the boardinghouse common room. I am outside the window *on the third floor.* Yet I seem to be standing on…nothing. Terror envelopes me. This cannot be.

I'm not dead. It can't be true.

The shadow-things fly closer to me, brushing me with their repulsive wing-like appendages. They're drawn to my fear and dismay. They fly in front of my eyes. I force myself to calm, and the monsters drift away. I don't understand what's happening to me, but I can't give in to my fear. Whenever I let my emotions overwhelm me, that's when the shadows close in.

Clearly I'm not dead. I can think and feel and see. This is a mistake. Because if I were dead, Edward would be here with me. Wouldn't he?

I have to find a way to get back.

Peering through the glass, I lean closer. Lydia Gainsbury is in the room with Sean McGrady; they're the ones standing over my body. Lydia is distraught about what she's done. Nearly hysterical. I can read the lass's thoughts and emotions as clearly as if she were speaking directly to me.

It was an accident, she's thinking. *Millie fell and hit her head. Edward can't be gone. There must be some way to undo all this.*

And Sean McGrady—he's reassuring her. He's seen his chance at revenge, and he's taking it.

McGrady panicked after injecting me with the morphine, left the room without a plan. Would I wake up? Should he go back to finish the job? But when Lydia's screams came from this room just minutes later, he moved fast. Half the men in the boardinghouse were woken by the noise, but McGrady made it up here first. Very convenient, that. He locked the rest of the men out, told them to go back downstairs to bed. Blamed the commotion on the influenza that's already running rampant. *Keep away unless you want to be the next in a sick bed.* He appointed himself Lydia's savior to help sort out the mess. When truly, his half-sister is the one who saved *him*.

She made me hit my head. It's Lydia's fault I'm trapped in this strange place. I don't know how to escape.

I blame Lydia and Sean McGrady both—they've taken everything from me.

The shadow-things crowd in around me, blocking out the view.

47

Dinah
1943

We nearly have to break down the door to Gainsbury House. Finally we get an answer. Grace opens the door wearing a housecoat. Her hair sticks up like cotton candy. She has dark circles beneath her eyes.

"What in heaven's name is going on out here?" she asks.

I'm in no mood to be polite. "Where's the telegram that told you Mitchell was killed in action?"

Grace gapes at me like I'm a talking animal. A talking animal whose first words are hateful and offensive.

"Where is the telegram?" I demand.

Grace is about to shut the door. Tears are already welling in her eyes. Abby takes a step forward and rests her hand on the door. "Please, could we just come in? We have a reason for asking. Let us explain."

Reluctantly, she lets us come inside. We make it as far as the foyer, and the first thing I notice is that Lydia's suitcase is gone.

"Where's Lydia?" I ask. "Did she already leave?"

"Leave?" Grace asks. "Of course not. She's just upstairs. Why are you asking about the telegram?"

"We just need to see it," Abby says, far more gently than I would have. "Please."

Grace's entire body sags. She looks infinitely tired. But she goes into the dining room. She opens a drawer in the china cabinet. But what she's looking for isn't there.

"I don't understand," she says. "It was here. I swear it was." Grace starts opening and closing cabinet doors, getting more and more anxious.

"Jim?" she says loudly.

Jim pads in from the kitchen. "Yes Mama?"

"Did you take the telegram about Mitchell?"

He blanches. "No, Mama. I would never." He goes over to help her look. But Abby and I both know that they aren't going to find it.

Abby takes the telegram out of her pocket. She walks into the dining room and holds it up for Grace and Jim to see.

Grace sucks in a breath. "Oh, Dinah! Not Nate, too."

I have to pinch the inside of my elbow. Otherwise I might start to panic again just thinking about Nate dying. Thankfully, Abby is handling the explanations. She holds the telegram to the light, showing them the shadow of a different name underneath. The address line has been altered too. It reads "R. Weller" in those same overlapping letters, but you can just make out "G. Tate" underneath. Grace takes the telegram in her shaking hands. I scrutinize her reactions, but Grace doesn't seem like she's hiding anything.

Jim hugs his mother until she stops crying. I'm still standing in the foyer. I feel terrible for the way I barged in here. But we have to know who did this. And *why*.

"Someone must've stolen it," Grace says. "I've been ill the past couple of days. But maybe my sister saw something." She goes over to the stairs.

"Lydia?" she calls up. "Could you come down here?"

There's no answer from upstairs.

Grace goes up, tightening the sash on her house coat. "Lydia?" she calls again.

Then she comes racing down the steps. "She's gone! All her things are packed, too. I don't understand. Where would she go?"

"Aunt Liddy said she had errands," Jim tells his mother. "She had to go out during the night too."

"During the *night*?" Grace asks. "In the storm?"

Jim nods. "I heard the door before I came down to breakfast. And then Dinah and Abby came here to talk to her—" He nods at us. "And after that, Aunt Liddy took her suitcase and left again."

I find Abby's hand and grasp it. There's a very bad feeling growing in my chest. A crease has appeared between Abby's eyebrows. Grace looks from Jim to us, like she's begging somebody to explain this.

"There's a lot we need to tell you," Abby says.

"Edward is *alive*?" Grace whispers. "You're sure Lydia told you all this?"

We're sitting in the small parlor with the fleur-de-lis wallpaper. We sat here with Lydia just hours ago. Yet the room feels so different. Where the room seemed intimate before, it's now too tight. My lungs can't get enough air.

"I don't like this story, Mama," Jim says. "It sounds like a ghost story."

Grace pats Jim's arm. "That's because it isn't true." She turns back to us, and her expression is a mixture of pity and reproach. "Girls, this is absurd. Lydia couldn't have said all those things, and if she did—well—she's been very nervous lately. I've been worried about her. There are parts of her history that you're not aware of. She's...not been thinking straight."

I want to laugh, though obviously there is nothing funny here. It's just so ridiculous. So many bizarre things have been happening that it all seems surreal. Lydia sat here and told us one thing, and now her sister is calling it madness. But I know what I saw.

"We met Edward," I say. I point at his picture on the wall. "We saw his scars. He's the same person."

Grace jolts up to standing. "That's *impossible!*" she shouts. Then she touches her fingers to her mouth, shocked at the sound that just came out. I've never heard her raise her voice before. Even at Thanksgiving, when she was angry at her sister, she didn't yell so loud.

"It's impossible," Grace says again, quieter this time. She sits and takes Jim's hand. "I saw Edward's body lying in the coffin. I kissed his cheek and said goodbye. I watched them close the lid and carry him to the graveyard. Do you think I'm lying?"

"But..." I look at Abby, and she looks equally dismayed. This can't be.

"Edward died up at Cherry Mountain." Grace closes her eyes, taking a deep breath. "It was an overdose of morphine. That's the truth of it. My father made sure it was hushed up, and we blamed the flu instead. Rumors spread, of course, but most of Powder Ridge accepted our convenient fiction. They were showing mercy—on us, on Edward's memory. Ask your mother. She knows. She blamed herself because she knew about Edward's... problem."

My mother?

"The only part I could never accept was the way that Millie Boylan left," Grace adds. "I know she cared for Edward, and he cared for her. She must've been crushed by his death. But she never would've abandoned us at such a time."

I glance at Abby. "Milly never left Cherry Mountain," Abby says. "We don't know exactly what happened. But she died up there."

Grace covers her mouth with her hands. Abby tells her what we know about Millie's death—what we can explain sensibly, anyway. Meanwhile, I remain quiet, taking the time to think.

If we believe Grace—and what choice do we have, given what she's said?—then the Eddie we met is not her brother. Lydia lied to us for some unfathomable reason, and he's someone else entirely. Yet he looks the same.

And *those scars*.

Once again, I look at Edward Gainsbury's photo on the wall. As if his smiling, carefree face could explain these mysteries.

In my mind, I try to list everything that's happened the past few weeks. How did it start?

It was after Nate left Powder Ridge. That's when I saw the figure in the boardinghouse. The handprints on the glass. I followed Eddie in the woods and heard that unearthly music. Discovered the record in Nate's room and learned about Millie's story. Then Eddie led us to the ruined cabin. We realized Millie was dead.

And after that, everything started to unravel.

Someone—McGrady, I assume—threw that rock through my window, warning me to stop. I learned that McGrady was really a Gainsbury, too. Then I followed him up to Eddie's cabin and confronted him, which possibly was not my smartest moment. Then someone broke into the assay office and stole Millie's record. McGrady's house blew up. BT went missing. And my parents got that fake telegram trying to make them think that Nate was dead. Why?

Why?

All of this speeds through my mind in a matter of minutes. But I can't figure out how these different events are connected. Why does my brother seemed tied into so much of it? What could Nate possibly have to do with Eddie?

"If you're right about Millie," Grace says, "then that's a terrible shame. She meant a lot to me. But I still don't understand why you'd believe that Edward is alive."

"There's a boy in a cabin up at the mine," I explain. "He told us his name is Edward Gainsbury. And Sean McGrady—your half-brother—has been helping him."

Grace frowns and opens her mouth. I hold up a hand.

"I know you don't think Eddie is your brother. But then, who is he?"

For a moment, Grace's eyes trace the ceiling. She's looking for an explanation, too. Then something odd happens to her expression. There's a horrified realization.

Grace jumps up and runs from the room.

"Mama?" Jim hurries after her.

I'm still sitting, staring after them. "Well, c'mon!" Abby says. She grabs my hand and pulls me along with her. We follow Grace and Jim upstairs.

The second floor hallway is dim and cold. Most of the doors are closed. The place has the feeling of a mausoleum. Abby and I pass an open door and glance inside. The room is empty, sheets stripped from the bed. I wonder if this is where Lydia was staying.

It's time to bring Edward home, she said to me just this morning. I accepted every word. But it sure doesn't look like she's coming back. Does Lydia actually believe that Eddie's her brother? Or does she know who he really is?

We find Grace in a room at the end of the hall. She's on her knees, digging through a hatbox that she's pulled out from beneath a four-poster bed. Jim is standing behind her, watching with a confused expression.

"It was here," Grace mutters. She's flipping through a pile of old letters. "I didn't throw it away. I'm sure of it." She pulls out several folded pages and shouts, "There!"

Grace sits on the bed, breathing hard. Jim sits beside her. Abby and I are still in the doorway, and Grace nods at us to come in.

"I got this letter several years ago," Grace says. "I wonder if it might explain some things. But I pray to God that I'm wrong."

She hesitates, chewing the inside of her lip.

"You see," she says, "Lydia had a son."

48

Millie
1918

When the shadow creatures finally dissipate, I find myself standing inside the common room. Sean and Lydia are still here. Lydia is trying to revive Edward, though I know he's beyond help. I'd tear my own heart out if I thought I could save him now, but I can't dwell too much on grief. The shadows are sniffing at me, hungry for dark thoughts.

Finally, Lydia gives up. For several minutes she sobs with Edward's body in her arms. Sean watches it all carefully. He's plotting his next moves.

Lydia gently lays her brother on the carpet and folds his hands over his chest. I walk closer to Sean McGrady, waving my hands in front of his devious face. He doesn't react.

"I know who you are," Lydia says in a monotone. "You're my father's son."

"Not that he ever acknowledged me." Sean picks up the syringe from the floor. "I'm sorry to tell you this, Lydia, but Edward is well known up here at Cherry Mountain. Our brother and the nurse have bought morphine more than a time or two. I tried and failed to put a stop to it—we may not have grown up in the same house, but blood counts for something. Check your brother's arms and you'll see the scars."

"I have seen them," she says weakly. "When he was sick. I thought he got the scars in the army hospital. He spoke during his fever dreams, rambling about some kind of darkness. Shadows that wouldn't leave him alone. But I didn't understand. Oh, I've been so blind."

In a burst of anger, Lydia bends over my defenseless body and yanks roughly at the sleeve of my dress. I try to grab my wrist away from her—so strange these sensations, being outside of my body—but then she cries out and lets go.

"I felt a jolt. Like electricity." Lydia rubs at her hand where I touched her. "Is that normal?"

McGrady only shrugs. "You're upset."

"I'm here," I yell at her. "I'm alive!"

She clearly doesn't hear me. But she gets up and crosses the room, hugging herself around the middle.

"She doesn't have any marks on her arms," Lydia says. "I know Millie, or I thought I did. I'm certain she was hiding things, but a drug addiction? Can you be sure?"

"She must've taken the morphine grains by mouth. It's less potent." He coughs. "That's what they say. Now we got bigger things to worry about, Lydia."

"It's Miss Gainsbury," she says. "I know who you are, but I don't *know* you."

She sits in a chair by one of the card tables, rocking back and forth.

Now McGrady lays his trap. "Our father's an important man around here," he says. "Rumors are one thing, but if this news gets out? Our brother and his— well, *paramour*—overdosing on morphine?" He walks over to my body. Picks up my nurse's cap with its drying crust of blood. The hateful man.

"And then there's the complication of you killing her," McGrady says.

Lydia looks up, blanching.

Killing me. No, that's not right. Lydia made this terrible situation worse, but I'm still here. I'm still alive.

But the blood. There's so much of it on the hearthstones. My body is so still. The horror of it threatens to overwhelm me.

"I didn't kill her!" Lydia cries. "I told you it was an accident."

"Shhh, somebody'll hear. Do you want that? If they do I can't help you. And I'm sure I *can* help you…as long as you help me out in return. We're blood, aren't we?"

Lydia is sobbing again, silently this time. I can't be in this room another second. I walk toward the door and try to open it. But the doorknob slides right through my fingers. I fall forward, and then I actually pass *through* the door. It's the strangest thing I've ever experienced, so odd that I don't even stop to ponder it. I walk onward, this time through the door to the room I'm sharing with Lydia.

My suitcase is lying beneath my bed, and my coat hangs from a hook on the wall. Lydia's gramophone is still there with "When Irish Eyes Are Smiling" cued on the turntable. I try to lift the needle but my fingers find no purchase.

I go to the outside wall and walk straight through.

I'm standing on nothing but air. It should be freezing out here, but I don't feel the cold. Beyond the boardinghouse, the lights of the mining encampment burn in defiance of the night. Yet I'm surrounded by swirling darkness. The shadow-things are watching me, mocking me, drinking in my growing despair. But they are bound to me, as well, unable to break away. My cell mates in this prison.

In the valley below, the fainter streetlights of Main Street twinkle in the town of Powder Ridge. And beyond that, the silhouetted curves of the mountains and the eternal flames of the stars. I can see it all from my perch, but it's never seemed so far away. A world of light that I will never be a part of again.

And that's when I admit the truth.

I am dead. Yet I haven't moved on.

I'm trapped here with these shadows, this Legion of monstrous eyes, and I will never be able to get free of them.

49

Dinah
1943

Grace sits on her bed holding the letter. "Lydia had a son," she says again. "But I should start from the beginning."

She folds her legs beneath her. Abby and I sit cross-legged on the rug. I feel like I'm back in grade school listening to story time. If only this story were fiction and not true. If Lydia had a son…No, I don't even want to think about what this could mean. It's too awful. I picture Eddie in his cabin. His fury and fear the last time I saw him. I hope he's all right.

Please let him be all right.

"After Edward's funeral, Lydia was despondent. For months, she wouldn't get out of bed. I tried to comfort her, and our father screamed and manipulated, but nothing worked. I was scared that if she stayed here, she'd just waste away. Finally I bought her a train ticket. Open-ended. I even packed her bag for her. I told her to go, leave Powder Ridge. And she did. I didn't hear from her again for four years."

Grace takes a stuttering breath. The papers make a rustling sound in her hands. "She called here to say she'd gotten married. She sounded like her old self on the telephone—happy, confident. She said she was in medical school, training to be a doctor, which didn't surprise me as much as you'd think. Lydia had always been driven. I think she needed to make a grand gesture to get past Edward's death. But anyhow, she said she'd fallen in love with one of her instructors, a widower who already had a young daughter. I was sad that I couldn't see the wedding, but I also understood that she had a different life now. She'd gotten away from our father and shed all the sad memories. Like I wished that I could. I suppose I was jealous too. She was pursuing her dreams, when I couldn't because of our father. He made me close myself off from nearly everyone. I suppose that's why I married the first boy who wanted me."

Grace looks toward the window. Outside, wind is blowing snow into the air.

I uncross my legs, unable to keep still. I keep thinking of Eddie in his cabin. "The letter?" I try to prompt. Grace looks down at the papers with dread. She still doesn't read them.

"A year later I got a call that she'd had a son. Lydia named him Edward, after our brother. Everything seemed wonderful for my sister. They were living in Grand Junction, they had a family medical practice. But then, something changed. Maybe it was the stress of having a child—I know how hard that can be—or maybe it was marital troubles. I guess I know about those, too. Anyhow, another five or six years passed, and meanwhile I assumed all was well. Our father had died by then, and my husband had left us, but Jim and Mitchell were growing and they were perfect."

She squeezes her son's hand. "Jimmy, could you make me a cup of tea? My throat is so parched."

"But I want to hear what happened."

"You're sure? Even if it gives you nightmares?"

Jim's eyes widen. But he nods. Grace looks at her son for several moments, and then she starts talking again.

"One day—this would've been the summer of 1930 —Lydia called and said she was afraid. She sounded paranoid. Wasn't making sense. She said that Edward wasn't safe at home, and that for some reason the rest of her family wasn't safe from *Edward*—he would've been only six or so at this time—but she couldn't explain exactly *why*. She said a darkness was following him. Like a demon of some sort. I begged her to come to Powder Ridge. I wanted to help her. But she said she wasn't sure what to do."

Grace unfolds the papers and hands them to me. "Weeks went by with no word. Then I got this letter. It was from Lydia's husband, saying that she and Edward had disappeared. You can read it yourselves. For what it's worth."

Abby and I bend our heads together. Grace whispers with Jim as we read the letter.

Dear Mrs. Grace Gainsbury Tate,

My name is Alfred Sanders. I'm your sister's husband. I'm sorry to introduce myself like this. If I had my way, we would have met long ago, but my wife is a very private person. She's never liked to talk about her past. For years, I didn't even know she was from Powder Ridge. I had to get your address from the papers in her desk. I couldn't find your telephone number, otherwise I'd call immediately. But I want to urge you to respond to me as quickly as possible, preferably by phone. (My information is below). I'm happy to cover the charges. This matter is extremely urgent.

Lydia has disappeared with our son, Edward.

You might think that, as a doctor, I should've seen the signs long ago. But Lydia has been very good at hiding it. And it's progressed so slowly. Recently, after the truth became clear, I had her committed to a hospital briefly for treatment. I was thinking only of her best interests. I'm sure you'll see that. Unfortunately, Lydia was able to talk her way out of treatment. She's a doctor herself. She knows just what to say. And afterward she was very, very angry with me.

It was shortly after she returned home that she and Edward disappeared. I've notified the police, and they're searching. But I thought that perhaps she'd come home to Powder Ridge. She left the car here; I assume she's either taking trains or hitch-hiking. If you hear anything at all of her, contact me right away.

Sincerely,

Alfred Sanders

I look up from the letter. "So you think Eddie is Lydia's son?" I ask. But Grace doesn't answer. Her mouth is trembling.

"The timing fits," Abby says. "Eddie said he's nineteen now, so he would've been six years old in 1930. But he and Lydia couldn't have been missing for that long, could they? Thirteen *years?*"

"And then Lydia turns up in Powder Ridge." I look at Grace. "Or did you hear from her before now?"

Grace nods, clutching at the collar of her house coat. "She called many times. But I didn't see her in person until a few weeks ago."

"You didn't contact this Alfred Sanders? Didn't you wonder about her *son?*"

Grace sighs heavily, wiping her hand over her face. She looks exhausted. "After she left her husband, she took to calling me collect once a year. Always on the anniversary of our brother's death. She was always moving from place to place. I tried to convince her to go home, or at least contact her husband, but she wouldn't listen. And then finally she called and said that Edward had died. This was about ten years ago. She said he died of the flu. Just like we claimed about our brother. The tragic irony was so fitting. The cruel senselessness of it. I never doubted her word. *Never.*"

Grace is pacing the room with her head thrown back, eyes toward the ceiling.

"My sister had been through so much. I thought she was getting better. She settled down over in Silverton about a year ago; that's how I was able to call her when I got the telegram about Mitchell. She didn't even hesitate. She drove here to Powder Ridge the next day. You said Sean McGrady's been helping her?"

I nod. "He's been taking Eddie supplies."

"I didn't know about my father's indiscretions until I was older, and I've never even met Sean McGrady in person. But I haven't heard good things. You think he's dangerous?"

"I know that for a fact. He threatened to kill me."

Grace is bunching her skirt in her fists. "But do you really think that boy in the cabin…"

I picture the day I first saw Eddie. It was right after the season's first big storm. About a week after Nate had left Powder Ridge. That's what stuck in my mind—the fact that Nate was gone. My brother's absence colored everything that I saw. Eddie appeared, a boy Nate's age in a soldier's coat, and somehow I saw a connection to my brother.

But I ignored the *other* thing that had happened shortly before Eddie's appearance at the mine. Mitchell Gainsbury was killed in action, and his family got the telegram that changed their lives.

"When did the telegram arrive about Mitchell?" I ask.

Grace opens her mouth to reply, but Jim beats her to the punch. "November third," he says.

Grace looks surprised. "That's right. I'll never forget that date, not as long as I live. I guess neither of us will." Jim nods sadly.

November third. Just a couple of days after Nate left on the train. But I didn't hear about Mitchell's death until about a week later, when Abby told me at the assay office. That might've been enough time for Lydia to move Eddie into that cabin up by the mine. If she had McGrady's help, of course, and the use of a very efficient donkey named BT.

And that was *exactly* what Lydia told me this morning, wasn't it? That she moved Eddie here after they learned about Mitchell Gainsbury's death. I guess she told the truth about that much. Perhaps she really did want to bring Edward home to Gainsbury House. Only he wasn't her brother. He was her son.

"How could I have known she lied? I *couldn't* have known!" Grace gestures wildly, her hands reaching upward like she's asking for absolution.

"Nobody knew," Jim says. His cheeks are flushed. "Maybe even God didn't know."

"Oh, Jimmy. I think you must be right."

Grace sits down on the bed, deflated. "What's he like?" she asks. "Edward. You said he looks like my brother did?"

"It's uncanny," Abby says.

"I wonder if that's part of it—whatever made things go wrong in Lydia's mind," Grace says. "I can't accept that she'd hide her son away from his family on purpose. There's so much good in her. She needs help. We have to find her."

I have no idea what Lydia might or might not do. I don't really know her at all. But so many things are falling into place now. The picture it's creating is twisted and grotesque.

Grace picks up her teacup, then sets it down again on her dresser. "I'm going to look around one more time for Lydia. I just can't believe she's gone. There has to be some mistake." She goes to the door and waves for Jim to come with her.

Abby and I go out into the hallway. We hear Grace and Jim walking around below, but we don't go down just yet. One look at Abby's worried face, and I'm pulling her to me. We stand there for a few seconds leaning into each other.

"Lydia either lied to us or she's delusional," Abby whispers to me. "But what if she's right about part of it? She said a darkness was following them…Remember what Millie described in her recording? The shadow monsters that attacked her? Could that be what Lydia saw?"

It's possible. I'm remembering what Eddie told me. He described black outs, waking up groggy in a new place. He showed us all those marks on his arms.

Is that what's coming next for Eddie? Another black out, a return to the dark? What if, this time, he doesn't wake up?

Then I think of that ring of scar tissue around Eddie's leg. That came from somewhere, too.

I've seen Millie's ghost. I accept that now. Actually, after what I've gone through these past few days, the idea of a ghost doesn't even faze me. Perhaps there's even something evil at work in Millie's story. But that doesn't mean that a shadow monster—or anything supernatural —is responsible for Eddie's lost memories or his scars. There are more kinds of darkness in the world.

Eddie said he didn't want my help. But I think he needs it.

We meet Grace and Jim downstairs in the foyer. Grace shakes her head. "Lydia really is gone. But Jim found something."

Jim holds up two halves of a broken record, one in each hand. "These were in the trash bin. Do you think it's important?"

"That's the record that went missing from the assay office!" Abby exclaims. Jim hands her the pieces, but they're broken beyond repair.

"Are you saying Lydia *stole* that record?" Grace asks.

"I don't know for sure," Abby says. "But if she did, then she also probably left the fake telegram at Dinah's house."

"My God." Grace closes her eyes, despondent. "Every moment this gets worse."

I'm about to wonder out loud why Lydia would have done these things, gone to such lengths to hurt us. But then I catch sight of the clock on the wall, and the answer is obvious. Time. Lydia wanted to distract us and buy herself time. Yet I came to talk to her about Eddie *after* the break-in, and after my mother already received the letter. That meant Lydia was already plotting her escape by then.

Of course she was—I saw the suitcase in the foyer. The snow on her coat when she answered the door.

And the explosion at McGrady's house? What role might she have played in that? If he really was the only soul who knew the truth, then he'd be a threat to her.

"I'd better call the sheriff, hadn't I?" Grace asks.

"The sheriff is already on his way to Powder Ridge," Abby says. "To investigate the explosion at McGrady's place and the break-in at the assay office. But there's so much snow that he might not make it until tomorrow."

And in the meantime, Lydia has gone after Eddie, planning who knows what. Plus McGrady could still be out there, probably angry as hell.

"We can't wait until tomorrow," I say. "We have to go get Eddie. Right now. Today. Or we might not ever see him again."

50

Millie
1918-1943

Do you know that ghosts sleep?

We may not have bodies, but we do seem to need rest of a sort. I don't know this until I wake up and realize time has passed. And I'm in a different place. It's night again, and the moon is high. I'm outdoors surrounded by trees. In a clearing in the woods. There's a faint glow to the west—the mining encampment. Even here in the woods, I can hear the constant echoes of the stamp presses at the mill.

But there are other sounds, too. The grunts of a man at work, and the sound of metal sliding into earth. I wander for a little while, seeking out the noise. I come to a small cabin. Someone is inside of it, digging. Dirt flies out from the open door. This seems strange until I recognize Sean McGrady's brown canvas jacket and unruly beard. There's a large bundle just outside the cabin, wrapped in black cloth. My suitcase lies next to the bundle.

McGrady is digging my grave.

I suppose this means that only a day or two have passed at most since I died. The shadows are close by, beating their wings, but they leave me be. My sorrow is already fading. I feel very cold, though it isn't the same cold that McGrady probably feels on this winter night. It's a cold that comes from inside of me. I'm turning numb. Like my very soul is a block of ice.

So the anger that I feel toward McGrady is a cold sort of fury. But it's anger still.

I walk over to the cabin. I want to close the door and trap him inside there. In the dark. I want to frighten him. But when I try to touch the wooden door, my fingers slip through. I curse myself. I'm a ghost, aren't I? I should bloody well be able to haunt somebody. But I can't get anything to move. It's like I'm not here at all.

I watch as McGrady buries my body and my suitcase. He places the floorboards back down over the hole. Carries the excess dirt and scatters it, shovel by shovel, between the trees. He's sweating and his face is lined with dirt. He's going to leave. I'm so frustrated I try to stamp my foot, but not so much as a dried twig registers the motion.

Then I remember what happened with Lydia when I touched her hand. I reach toward McGrady and smack him across the face.

McGrady stops. He nearly drops the shovel, though he quickly recovers himself. But he touches his face. *He felt me.*

"You bastard!" I yell at him. "Damn you to hell for what you did!" The shadows sense my rising anger—my coldness beginning to warm—and they immediately flutter around me.

But McGrady is looking back and forth across the clearing. His eyes fill with wonder and dread.

"Hello?" he whispers. "Who's there?"

I'm so amazed that it worked, I could almost laugh.

McGrady goes back over to the cabin. He kneels in front of the door. He uses the sharp edge of the shovel to carve a small cross into the wood. As if marking my grave will buy him forgiveness.

I scream and paw at him until he's running from the clearing in terror. But then the shadows swarm, feeding on my rage, and soon enough I'm swallowed up again by the dark.

The flu takes several more victims. I see the bodies as they're carried out of the boardinghouse, draped in white sheets. But I never see any of these men after they've died. As ghosts, I mean. I'm alone.

The shadows pull me toward the sick rooms, hungry for death and fear. But I do not let them out. Somehow, the shadows are bound to me, trapped in whatever dimension in which I now exist. When we're close to a poor, dying soul, I feel a sort of conduit open—if I choose, I could let the shadows flow out of me and into that other unfortunate individual. I could set the shadows free and let them feast. Perhaps then, I could leave this awful purgatory. But I could never assign such a fate to another person, even to relieve my own burden.

I try to walk down to Powder Ridge. Actually I try to fly, but that doesn't work. I'm nothing like a bird. I don't know how to soar. I'm simply walking high up in the air. But whether I'm in the air or on the ground, I can't get off of Cherry Mountain. Darkness always closes over me, and I wake up in the boardinghouse.

So I stay there on the third floor. I whisper into the dark: *Edward, I'm afraid. I want to go to you, but I can't. I wish you could find me.* I tell the shadows my story. They're eager for every small flicker of emotion. I hate them. But at least they listen.

More and more often, I sleep to escape the darkness. I dream of seeing Edward again.

The epidemic ebbs and eventually passes. Men once again come and go inside the common room. But they all refuse to sleep in the bedroom next door. They say it's haunted. They say that the gramophone in that room— left so carelessly and never recovered—will start to play suddenly in the night. Always the same record, over and over. "When Irish Eyes Are Smiling." Sometimes the men hear it in other places on the mountain.

You see, I've gotten a bit better at making things move. I have the best of luck with the gramophone. I like to hear the music. I haven't got much else to entertain me.

McGrady never ventures up to the third floor of the boardinghouse anymore.

Years begin to pass. I grow ever colder on the inside. I can remember the story, but I'm beginning to forget the feeling of being alive. I wonder if Sean McGrady is still alive, or if even he has passed on to wherever I cannot go.

One day I wake to find the boardinghouse empty. I go outside and walk around the mining encampment. It's deserted.

But then I hear laughter. A boy and a girl are running through the mining encampment, weaving between the now-abandoned buildings. I drink in their laughter like it's water. They go inside the boardinghouse and I follow. I don't want to scare them or get too close. Only to be near them. To hear them giggle and remember some small piece of what I forgot about life. They are so very *alive*.

I watch the pair over the years. I spy as they play in the common room. I see them grow. Eventually, the boy —the older brother Nate—stops coming to the mine. The girl, Dinah, now works alone. She misses her brother desperately. I feel the pull of her sorrow. I'm more awake now than I've felt in years.

But the shadows, too, have reawakened. Their feathery wings brush against my skin and I know they're close. Like me, they're watching Dinah. They're hungry.

In the days afterward, very strange things begin to happen.

I see McGrady passing near the boardinghouse. So he's still here. He looks up at the third floor windows and shivers, and I know he is thinking of me. He's leading the donkey into the woods. I don't bother to follow him.

The next day, I see Edward. *My* Edward.

I run toward him, ecstatic that he's finally here. But that doesn't last long. He can't see or hear me. He isn't dead at all. Though he wears the same army coat that I remember, he looks different when I study him closely. He has different freckles on his chin. A different way of walking and standing. And he has a deep well of despair inside of him. Memories that are so dark he can't let them up to the surface. I start to feel cold again, looking at him. I return to the third floor of the boardinghouse. The shadows come to meet me, supping upon my sadness. The only meal they've had in years. I have to admit—I do feel rather sorry for myself.

But I want to know about the boy who looks like Edward Gainsbury. Like the soldier I loved and couldn't save. I want to help this boy. For the first time in so long, I have a purpose.

Then I see Dinah coming up the path to the mine. So very alone, as alone as me. And I know exactly what to do.

51

Dinah
1943

Jim grabs his gear and is ready in a matter of minutes. But when Grace goes to dig an old pair of snowshoes and a fur-lined parka from a back closet, she finds they're gone.

"Lydia took them," Grace says. She sounds like she still can't believe all this is happening.

"It's all right," I say, handing her my coat. "You can use my gear. My webs are at home, but I'll bring them. I can use Nate's."

We agree to meet up on the path to the mine. Abby and I head out into the snowy street. There's a pensive expression on her face.

Most of the roads and sidewalks are plowed now, which means Mrs. Spivak's crew has been busy. I have no coat, and immediately my skin breaks out in goose pimples. The sun shines in a faint yellow circle behind the clouds, emitting no warmth. It's already the afternoon. Dark will come before we know it.

I'm hoping that all the snow on the path to the mine has slowed Lydia down. But she's got several hours' head start on us. At least.

I tug on Abby's elbow and we run faster, watching for patches of ice.

"You should go get your stuff from your house," I say to Abby. "I'll meet you on the path."

"Dinah." There's something in her voice that makes me stop. I turn to face her, wrapping my arms around my middle. Wind blows down the street, making me shiver, and snowflakes settle on my sweater. Abby's lips and cheeks have turned bright pink in the cold.

"What is it?" I ask.

"I don't think we should go."

"We have to." I'm about to launch into the same arguments I made just a few minutes ago at Gainsbury House—that Lydia might have hurt Eddie in the past, that she might even be responsible for the explosion at McGrady's house this morning—but Abby shakes her head, cutting me off.

"I agree that somebody has to go," Abby says. "I almost tried to talk Grace and Jim out of it—but you saw their faces. Eddie's their family. But if something happens to you and me, our families will never forgive us. Your parents already thought they lost Nate today. Don't give them something real to grieve about."

Like they'd grieve that way for me. But that's beside the point. By sticking my nose into Eddie Gainsbury's business, I might've made things worse for him. I can't back out on him now.

"Let me tell my mother," Abby says. "She'll send up the Rescue Brigade. She'll probably lead it herself. And I bet she can get Terrance Jameson to come, too. He knows the mine better than anybody."

A bunch of housewives and gray-haired men? "It'll take too long to explain what's happening. And then they'll just say it's too dangerous."

"That's because it is! There could be avalanche danger with all this snow. Remember last year? That slide that almost took out the bunkhouse?"

I shake my head. There's a risk, sure, but it's only November. We're hardly into the season yet.

"We'll be OK," I say. "We'll be looking out for each other. Come with me."

"I won't." She means it. She's like me that way; when she decides something, she isn't going to change her mind. "Dinah, please don't do this. I couldn't stand it if anything happens to you."

She puts her hand on my cheek. Her palm is warm, and I close my eyes and turn into it. It's tempting to stay here with her. Let Mrs. Spivak and the Rescue Brigade sort this out.

But somewhere up at Cherry Mountain, Millie is watching. Maybe this is the reason that she haunted me in the first place. So I could help Eddie. So I could *save* him.

I open my eyes. Abby is staring at me. I brush the snow-frosted curls from her face and kiss her, right there in the middle of the street. I don't care if the neighbors see me. I don't give a damn if all of Powder Ridge knows about us.

If this is goodbye, then I'd better do it right.

"I'm going," I say.

Her eyes are glistening, but she blinks the tears away. "You need a weapon. All I've got is my peashooter. It's only a .22. But I can run and get it. Just don't breathe a word to my mother."

I give her hand one last squeeze. "Thank you."

"I'll make sure that the Brigade follows you as soon as possible," Abby says. "OK? I'll be with them if my mother lets me. Don't do anything meshuggah until we get there."

I nod. But we both know it's more than likely that the Rescue Brigade will refuse to go anywhere until enough snow can be cleared. That will take hours. Maybe even until tomorrow.

Eddie can't wait that long.

Grace, Jim and I start up the path in our webs. In my pack, I've got Abby's peashooter and a box of ammunition.

We try to keep to the inner edge of the path, away from the drop-off on the other side. But wind blows in great gusts from the mountain, throwing snow into our faces and making us veer toward the edge. Every step is taxing. I keep scanning for Lydia's tracks, but any traces have been erased by the storm and the wind. It's like some giant hand is trying to keep us back.

We're just rounding a bend when a rumbling sound comes from somewhere up the mountain.

"Look out!" I grab Jim and Grace by their coats and pull them both against the rock wall that edges the path. We land in a tangle of snowshoes and clumsy limbs. My hat flies off. I brace myself for the cascade of snow that could be roaring toward us.

But it doesn't come. The sound dies away. Quiet settles over Cherry Mountain again.

Slowly, we get up and push on.

By the time we reach the basin, Jim is pulling his mother along. My legs are shaking and weak. I'm not sure how long it took us to get up here, but it feels like hours. The sun has sunk lower in the sky.

The path flattens out. We walk through the mining encampment's maze of buildings. The three of us are breathing hard, but none of us says a word. I've got one eye on the slope that leads up to the higher shafts of the mine. It all just looks flat and white, almost the same white as the sky. Abby's warnings have got me worried. That slab of snow could break away from the mountain at any minute. I keep listening for the low *whump* sound that would signal an avalanche. Watching for powder rising into the air.

We pass the overturned mining cart, which is mostly buried in snow. At the boardinghouse, the snowdrift along one of its walls is so deep that it reaches the second floor.

In the woods, everything is eerily quiet. The wind doesn't reach here. Our webs sink into the top layer of powder. The trees look like they've hunkered down, their branches laden.

"Dinah, wait," Grace asks breathlessly.

I walk back toward her. Jim seems unfazed by all the exertion, but Grace is bent over, hands on her knees, trying to catch her breath. Ice crystals have settled onto her eye lashes.

"Are you sure we're going the right way?" Grace asks.

"Yes," I say, though the woods look different under so much snow. I'm fairly sure that the ruined cabin and the clearing are a few minutes ahead.

We keep going about five more minutes. Then ten. It's just trees and more trees. I don't see anything I recognize. We should've found the clearing by now.

I hold up my hand to stop Grace and Jim. Flashing them a smile I definitely don't feel, I turn around in a circle, looking for a landmark. There has to be something. I've been through this way so many times. Even at night! I can't be lost. Not now. My stomach is twisting tighter and tighter. I haven't eaten all day, but last night's dinner is threatening to come up.

"Millie," I whisper. "Help me. Play the music. *Please.*"

But there's only the creaking of the trees.

I walk the same circle again. Grace and Jim watch me with concern. I study every tree. I stare into the sky, begging for some sign.

Then I see smoke. A chimney.

"This way," I say.

We walk for several minutes more. "I smell the smoke," Jim says.

"Me too." I can just make out the streaked wooden sides of Eddie's cabin. I wave at Grace and Jim to be quiet. We cower together behind a large tree.

BT is tied up outside. Poor animal's almost up to his flank in snow. He's nodding his head nervously. There are voices coming from the cabin. They're arguing. I can't hear what they're saying.

"Stay here," I whisper. "I'm going closer."

Grace shakes her head. "No, we stay together. She's my—"

The cabin door opens. Lydia walks out.

"You don't need to understand," she says over her shoulder. "I always take care of things, don't I? You should have more trust in me." She shuts the door firmly behind her.

With a sigh, Lydia lifts a green canvas sack into her arms. She goes to BT and, with effort, tucks her load into the donkey's saddle bag.

Grace steps forward before I can stop her.

"Lydia, what are you doing?"

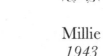

52

Millie
1943

From the third floor of the boardinghouse, I see Dinah, Grace, and the big fellow called Jim. They're wearing snowshoes, and their coats are dusted with white. They're alone.

No. This is all going wrong. All of it.

I already saw Lydia come this way several hours ago, leading the donkey BT. I rushed down to stop her. But when I tried touching her, she didn't even flinch. Her mind was too wrapped up in obsessive thoughts. She tried to kill Sean McGrady, for which I can't exactly blame her. But she can't see what's really ahead of her anymore. She only sees the reality she's created for herself.

Lydia was headed for Edward's cabin. She's probably there now. She could be hurting him, the way she's done so many times before. Dinah has no idea what Lydia is capable of.

Dinah looks up at my window, and I wonder if she senses that I'm here. I'm not sure how much she knows of my story. I tried to put it all on the record. But if she listened, then she'd know about the danger. She would've kept Edward away from the mine. She would have stopped this before it went so far.

The three of them go into the woods. I'm going to follow them. There must be something I can do.

But then I spot movement. There's a figure stepping out from behind the stable. It's Sean McGrady. Half of his face is blistered, red and raw. His hair has been singed away. He's limping and obviously in great pain. His gloved hands are damaged; they can barely hold the revolver he's carrying. And his rage burns even brighter than the fire that nearly killed him.

The shadows swirl around me like a blizzard of blackened ash. They sense McGrady's rage like a starving man smells cooking meat.

It's no use, I tell them.

I've come to understand these shadow-monsters in our years together. They're ancient creatures. Their numbers are countless, and they have existed as long as there has been anguish and pain. Usually, they're like mindless parasites; only when they group together can they look out into the world. A single colony is tied to me now, and they can't feed on any living being so long as we're both trapped. We're prisoners together in this purgatory.

But their greed and hunger is so strong that I'm pulled all the way out of the building and into the open air. I land in front of McGrady and, though the thought of touching him is repulsive, the shadows compel me. I thrust a hand out to his chest.

McGrady stops mid-step. I know he felt the jolt. His eyes are bulging. But his pause is brief. Soon he's limping forward again, casting wary glances at the boardinghouse.

You see? I say to the shadows. *You're as powerless as I.*

I watch as McGrady follows Dinah and her friends into the woods.

53

Dinah
1943

Grace walks toward Lydia. Jim tries to run after his mother, but I somehow manage to keep him hidden with me behind the tree. "Don't you dare go out there," I hiss in his ear. "If Grace needs us, we have to be ready." He stops struggling.

Lydia is staring at her sister in shock. "What are you doing out here, Gracie? You're going to catch your death."

Grace is holding her hands out like she's trying to calm a wild animal. "I know about Edward. Your son. I know he's here."

Moving with infinite slowness, I take off my pack. I pull out Abby's peashooter.

Lydia shakes her head sadly. "He's not my son, Grace. I wanted to tell you. Really, I did. But I had to make sure everything was ready."

I raise the gun barrel so it's trained on Lydia.

"Tell me what?" Grace keeps edging closer. Lydia grabs her sister by the shoulders, and Jim gasps. I cover his mouth with my hand, fumbling to keep hold of the gun.

"That our brother Edward is *alive*."

Lydia hugs Grace. She's laughing. She's lost her mind.

Grace has an arm around her sister. She's turned Lydia so she's facing away from the cabin.

Now's my chance.

I shoulder the peashooter, then unstrap my snowshoes and prop them against the tree. I whisper, "Jim, you have to wait. Don't let Lydia know you're here. Don't leave this spot unless your mother or me calls for you. All right?"

Jim nods. I dash out toward the front of the cabin.

The hinges squeak slightly as I open the door. I cringe, waiting for Lydia to react, but she and Grace are still talking. I go inside, almost tripping over a box of dishes and clothes.

Eddie is sitting on the bed. He's dressed like he's ready to leave—thick layers, boots on, knit cap over his head. But his hands are bound in front of him with rope. He looks up at me with red-rimmed eyes.

"Dinah, what the *hell* are you doing here?" he whispers. "Go. Now."

I lean Abby's peashooter against the door and run over to him. He tries to turn away from me, pulling his hands so I can't reach them. "I told you I didn't want your help," he says.

"I'm not leaving you here. I know, Eddie. I know she's your mother. You love her." The words catch in my throat. I know how it is to love someone and hate them at the same time. "You wanted to protect her. But this has to end."

He squeezes his eyes shut. His hands are clasped together like he's praying. "I thought she was my mother. But I don't even know that much anymore. She told me today that I'm her brother, Dinah. I'm the Edward Gainsbury in that photo you showed me. You were right. But I don't understand it. She said there's something wrong and dark inside me that made me this way."

"No, Eddie. She's wrong, and Abby and I were wrong too. The other Edward Gainsbury was your uncle." I sit next to him on the bed. He still has his eyes closed. It's cold in the cabin, but there are beads of sweat on his forehead. "Grace told us that he died. She saw his body. She saw his burial. He's not you, Eddie. Your mom is very, very confused. I'm so sorry that we made this harder for you."

"But…"

Lydia's voice raises outside. Eddie and I both look to the window. "That isn't true!" Lydia is saying. "I know it's hard to believe. But Gracie, you have to *listen*." Her voice lowers again.

The curtain's partway open, and I tug it shut. "We should go now."

But Eddie makes no move to get up. "I'm starting to remember things," he says, so quietly that I can barely hear him.

Slowly, he extends his hands toward me. He sits still while I untie the knot. His wrists are scraped. He rubs them. Then he rolls up one sleeve, then the other. His scars are garishly vivid in the low light of the cabin. Permanently reddened veins, purple circular marks.

Eddie swallows. "I still don't remember getting any of these. But there was one time, when I was younger— maybe eleven, twelve?—that I woke up in the dead of night and my mother was standing over me. It was too dark to see her, but I could smell the shampoo she liked back then. She took my leg out from beneath the blanket. I felt a sharp pain in my thigh. I went to sleep. When I woke up, my leg had a bandage around it. I was in so much pain. It took months to heal completely."

I think of that ring of scar issue. *His leg*, Lydia said. *The one he lost in the war…No, you wouldn't believe it.*

I don't want to ask. But I think that Eddie needs me to ask.

"What did she do?"

He shakes his head. His face is so pale I can see the vein at his temple. "She said I'd dreamed the whole thing. That I'd always had the scars. It didn't make sense, you know? But today, when she told me I was him, the other Edward, I was so relieved. That meant she didn't… she didn't try to…"

I kneel on the floor in front of him. "Hey, look at me. Your mother is very sick. We're going to get help for her."

His eyes meet mine. "You promise?"

There's a tremendous crack outside, like a firework exploding.

"What's happening?" Eddie cries.

Someone screams. I jump up and pull back the curtain. Lydia and Grace are running toward the cabin. From the other direction, Jim is sprinting out of the trees. There's another shot, and at the same instant Lydia falls. There's a spray of red in the snow.

"No," Eddie screams, watching from over my shoulder. "Mom!"

He goes for the door. But I get there first. I scoop up the peashooter and dash outside. Grace has stopped to help her sister. BT is yanking against his rope. Jim is out in the open.

"Jim, get down!" I yell.

I hear Eddie come out the door behind me. "Untie the donkey," I say to Eddie. He does, and BT races off away from the shooting.

I lean around the corner of the cabin to see what's happening. Grace is trying to pull her sister out of the snow. There's another shot, and the bullet crashes into the wall of the cabin. I jump back. Then, quickly, I peek out again.

I spot the small dark circle of McGrady's Colt revolver, still smoking from his last shot. He's hiding behind a tree not far away. I take aim. I don't remember what kind of range the peashooter has. But I'm just hoping it's enough.

Don't let these gunshots send an avalanche onto us, I think. But the trees are probably muffling the noise.

I aim, crank the lever to move the round into the chamber, and pull the trigger. The gun bucks against my shoulder. It's small pop is a joke compared to the crash that McGrady's revolver made. He ducks back behind the tree. I can't tell if the shot got near him. I haven't even practiced shooting with Abby in ages. McGrady tries moving to another tree farther back, but I follow his movements. I crank the lever and pull off another shot. As I'm firing, Grace drags Lydia into the lee of the cabin. Once they've made it, I duck back behind the building.

I notice Jim isn't here anymore, but I don't have time to wonder where he's gone. Another bullet hits the cabin. Splinters fly into the air.

Grace is kneeling over her sister. "Help me," she says. Eddie hurries inside the cabin and brings out a piece of clothing. He and Grace press the fabric to Lydia's shoulder. There's blood everywhere. It freezes into icy red droplets on the snow.

I peek out again, shooting in the direction I last saw McGrady. But he isn't there anymore. His voice thunders from behind a different tree.

"You should'a stayed out of this, Dinah Weller! You are dead, you hear me? *Dead*!"

Obviously I haven't hit him. I can't keep wasting bullets. He can just sit there and wait for me to run out of ammunition. My pack's in the cabin, and even if I had the ammo here, I'm not sure my hands are steady enough to reload. I have to get closer.

I wait until his next shot strikes the cabin. Then I run for the nearest tree, tripping in the snow. Another comes immediately with a deafening boom. It thuds into the tree right above me. Splinters slice across my cheek, and blood wells and drips down my face. If I hadn't fallen, the bullet would've hit me.

I wait for another shot, but there's a pause. Frantically, I try to count off the shots I've heard. Was that six? I think so. He might be reloading. I bob out from hiding to shoot.

"Dinah, look out!" Grace screams.

The double barrel of a shotgun is aiming straight at me from across the clearing. McGrady's face is behind it, burned and contorted. His lips pull back in a hideous grin.

Suddenly, Jim launches himself at McGrady's side.

I run. The shotgun goes off. I feel the hot sting of buckshot in my right side—my shoulder, my arm, my torso. I fall back into the snow.

Get up, I tell myself. *Get up!*

I can hear McGrady and Jim struggling and shouting. Somehow, I get myself up to standing again. Pain is starting to radiate along my side. My hands come up empty. Shit, shit, *shit*. I've dropped the peashooter in the snow. I look back over my shoulder.

McGrady and Jim each have hold of the shotgun. They're battling for control. Jim's face is turning red from the effort. He's younger and stronger. But McGrady is not going down easy. Spit foams from his mouth. Half his face has been destroyed by fire. For a single, hideous second, I stand there with my gaze fixed on his oozing, blackened wounds.

"Dinah, Edward, run!" Jim yells from across the clearing.

I hesitate. But Grace has found my peashooter in the snow. She brushes it off, pumps the lever. Tears have frozen to her face, along with tiny dots of Lydia's blood. She fires, screaming when the gun recoils. Grace's shot misses McGrady. Yet McGrady's expression shows a flicker of uncertainty. Jim's knuckles are white around the shotgun.

"*Go!*" Grace says to me. "Get help!"

Eddie is reaching for Lydia and screaming, "Mom! Mom!" My mind is a haze of pain and shock. All I can do is take hold of Eddie's hand and pull him away from the fighting.

Night is starting to fall. The snow glows with an unearthly blue, like frozen moonlight. Eddie has stopped crying, but he's still breathing fast. My clothes are sticky, wet with blood and snow. The fabric is starting to freeze stiff. Neither of us speaks.

There's a shotgun blast far behind us. *Grace. Jim.* I glance back.

I want to believe that Jim and Grace stopped McGrady in the clearing. But I remember that demonic look in McGrady's eye, and I'm not sure *anyone* could stop him.

Our boots sink deep into the snow. I didn't have time to get my webs. With each step, it's harder and harder to pull my foot up, keep from toppling over, and then do it again. I take a step and my knee buckles. I land face first in the snow. Eddie puts his arms around my middle and hauls me back up. He has to practically carry me the rest of the way through the woods.

Finally we reach the mining encampment. If it weren't for the snow, we could be on the path back to town in just minutes. But I'm bleeding and wet and freezing cold. There's snow inside my boots, and I can't feel my toes.

There's no way I can make it back to town to find help. But Abby said she'd come.

"Eddie," I say, though my mouth isn't moving right. "I can't. Keep going."

"I'll try to carry you," he says.

"No." I stop his arm from scooping me up. "The bunkhouse. We have to…hide." We both look up at the rotting building. A wave of dizziness hits me.

"He'll come after us," Eddie says.

"I know." But I have a plan. It might be enough to protect us from McGrady. As long as it doesn't kill us first.

54

Millie
1943

I've never felt so helpless, even in all these years since my death.

I watch everything unfold by the cabin—McGrady shooting Lydia, Dinah returning fire. Then Jim and McGrady fighting over the shotgun while Dinah and Eddie try to run.

I want to do something, but everything I try is fruitless. My fingers slip through anything I try to touch.

Grace fires the smaller rifle again, hoping to distract McGrady. She'd do anything to save her son, but she's agonized with doubt. Should she keep firing, though she risks hitting Jim? Charge directly at McGrady, knowing she might distract Jim instead? Every second is endless. Meanwhile, Lydia lies on the ground, shivering and bleeding into the snow.

As he struggles, Jim pictures his twin brother's face— a boy named Mitchell whom he couldn't save.

With a cry of effort, Jim finally wrenches the shotgun away. McGrady falls to his knees, then scrambles upright and runs. Jim fires. The shot goes wide, showering McGrady with bark and splinters. I know that Jim has no more ammunition. McGrady has the rest of the shotgun shells in the pack he carries. Grace fires the peashooter in McGrady's direction, but he's already disappeared.

McGrady is headed back toward the mine. The same way that Dinah and Edward have gone.

As he wades through snow, McGrady pulls another gun from his coat. I recognize it immediately: it's my Edward's Colt revolver with the ivory grip. The gun belonged to Edward's grandfather—and Sean McGrady's grandfather, too. McGrady must have taken it the day Edward and I died. It's the only inheritance that Sean ever received.

McGrady's fingers are shaking as he tries to reload it. He drops the bullets in the snow. Fishes more from his pack. These ones slide home. He snaps the gun back together.

He knew that Lydia was hiding her son in that cabin, and she paid McGrady handsomely to bring supplies and stay quiet. He also knew that she was utterly insane, believed the boy to be her dead brother, but he didn't care. Not so long as he got paid. And he was biding his time until he figured out a way to use the information for even greater gain.

But now, he has no coherent thoughts anymore. No emotion except for a single desire: destroy Dinah Weller and every single member of the Gainsbury family.

The shadow-creatures are still hovering around McGrady, though they can't touch him. I feel their hunger, their attraction, and it disgusts me.

I rush forward to the mining encampment. There must be some way to warn Dinah and Edward.

I'm horrified by what I see. Edward is pulling away some of the boards that block the ground floor entrance to the boardinghouse. They're going to go *inside*.

"Stop," I cry. "It isn't safe there!" If only they could hear me.

The building is severely damaged. Their weight on those old floorboards could be enough to bring the place down. And even worse, McGrady will find them here. They'll be cornered.

I try to grab their arms and pull them away from the entrance. Edward flinches, but Dinah doesn't register the jolts at all. She's terribly weak. She can barely walk. Edward helps her through the opening he's made. They disappear into the darkness inside.

They're ours, the shadows whisper to me. *Ours.*

"Never," I reply.

Minutes later, McGrady emerges from the woods carrying his revolver. He sees their tracks. He's coming.

55

Dinah
1943

We're inching down the hallway. Only the faintest bit of moonlight has filtered into this place. We can't see anything except for amorphous shapes and tilting walls. Eddie's hand is gripping mine; I know how terrifying this unknown darkness must be for him. He's starting to hyperventilate. But we both keep going forward, feeling our way around piles of brick and plaster from walls that have caved in.

"There's a staircase behind the kitchen," I say. "Shouldn't be much farther."

It takes several more agonizing minutes of picking our way through the maze of hallways, but I finally push through the swinging door to the kitchen. High windows let weak light into the room. We pass cold cast iron stoves. Cupboards with doors that stand open, emptied long ago. Thick dust coats the table and shelves. I find the door to the stairwell.

It leads into pitch darkness.

The stairwell at the far end of the boardinghouse collapsed in last year's avalanche. But Nate and I found this secondary set of stairs when we used to explore here. The steps are steep, closed in between narrowly-spaced walls.

"You want to lead the way?" I ask.

Eddie is hugging his elbows and looking around the kitchen. Moonlight has turned his skin a bluish gray. "Not a chance."

I start up. I remember playing on these stairs with Nate when we were younger. We'd close the doors so it was absolutely dark, just like it is now, and we'd laugh like it was all just a game.

The wood groans beneath me. I keep stumbling, dragging on my right side where I'm bleeding. The light from the kitchen fades quickly. I can't see my hand in front of me as I climb.

We reach the second floor. Then find another door that leads up to the third. This staircase is even darker than the last. Eddie moans when he sees it. We head up. I misjudge the distance to the next step and fall forward. My shin bangs the edge of the stair, and I stifle a scream. Pain is shooting up and down my side. I throw out my hands to catch myself, and I sob at how much it hurts.

"You OK?" Eddie asks. He sounds ragged with exhaustion.

I want so much to stay sitting on these steps. My legs are stiff. The wounds on my side and arm are on fire. I could just rest for a moment. My eyes start to close.

There's a noise somewhere downstairs. A door banging open. Then a wild bellow of rage.

McGrady's in the boardinghouse.

We hurry up the staircase, keeping as quiet as possible. We emerge onto the third level. Everything is bright with moonlight and snow. I shut the door to the staircase. Eddie is staring at the far end of the hall, where the building's been torn open. There's a view of treetops and far-off mountain peaks. It would be beautiful if it wasn't so jarring. Wind blows fistfuls of snowflakes in through the massive hole.

"Tell me we're not going down there," Eddie says.

I steer him in the opposite direction. "This way."

The floor is precariously tilted. Old paint peels from the walls. We move as carefully but as quickly as we can toward the common room door. The building whines and snaps. But it's not us. It's coming from the floor below. Another door slams downstairs. The whole building shudders. I practically run the last few steps and grab the doorknob to the common room.

But it doesn't open.

That's when I remember the lock on the other side.

"Shit. *Shit!*" I yank on the doorknob, pulling with all my might. Eddie kicks at the rusty hinges. The lower one breaks.

Then, behind us, the door leading to the staircase bursts open. I know I shouldn't look back but I can't stop myself. McGrady has lunged into the hallway. A floorboard snaps under his weight and he loses his balance, but recovers quickly. His revolver is silhouetted by the moonlight.

Eddie is kicking furiously at the common room door. A bullet smacks into the doorframe, inches from his head. Finally the door gives way under Eddie's foot, and we dive into the room.

Just feet ahead of us, there's a jagged hole in the center of the floor.

Eddie's arms pinwheel. I grab his coat and pull him back. Another shot whizzes past us and smashes into the wall. Plaster flies into the air. We fall to our hands and knees, crawling as fast as we can along the wall. The floor is creaking loudly in warning. A few boards start to buckle beneath us. But we're almost to the other corner of the room, where there's a jumble of old furniture. The bed frame, the stacked chairs, the bookcase lying on its side. Eddie and I can take cover there.

McGrady looms in the doorway. He fires again. I flatten myself against the baseboards, and then wiggle the last few feet to get behind the bookcase. Eddie's right behind me. I'm pulling him in, but there's another gunshot. Eddie cries out. I pull him the rest of the way. His calf is bleeding. I press my hands to the wound. The blood feels hot against my ice-cold skin.

McGrady fires again. My whole body flinches, and there's a thud against the bookcase. Eddie is sobbing quietly against my shoulder. This is a mistake. I thought that the floor up here wouldn't hold McGrady's weight, but I'm wrong. He's going to stand there and shoot at us until one of the bullets finds me, and all the while Eddie's bleeding to death.

"Help us, help us, oh please help us," I murmur uncontrollably, not even sure who I'm asking.

Then something very strange begins to happen.

It starts with the music. The melody is familiar to me now. It's Millie's song. The notes are eerily high-pitched and slow. I peer over toward the wall—the couple of remaining windows are fogging up.

Handprints start to appear on the wavy glass.

McGrady screams and fires. One of the windows explodes. Glass rains down.

Then there's a clicking sound, and McGrady's scream turns to a roar.

He's out of bullets.

"No," McGrady says. "Not you. *No!*"

I look out from a gap between the bookcase and the bed frame. McGrady is still standing at the room's entrance. But there's someone else materializing in front of him. A woman wearing a long dress and a white nurse's cap. She's glowing, and as her outline sharpens the rest of the room dims. As if she's being spun from the moonlight.

McGrady screams in terror and fury. His finger squeezes the trigger again and again, though the chamber is still empty. Then in desperation he throws the gun at her. It simply flies through the air and clatters into the hole in the floor.

The woman reaches out. She puts her ghostly, glowing hands on either side of McGrady's face.

His scream is inhuman.

He takes a step forward, clawing at the woman. Then his face contorts, his horror shifting to a new focus. He's teetering on the edge of the hole. McGrady tries to move backward.

But the floorboards buckle underneath him.

With a huge crack, the floor collapses. McGrady's arms shoot up as he falls. His scream pierces all the way to my bones. Then there's a hideous crash, and his voice is cut short.

56

Millie
1943

Sean McGrady's mangled body is lying on a pile of wood and bricks. His eyes stare upward, and blood trickles from his mouth.

I float down until I'm hovering directly above him. I know he sees me. There's light yet in those irises, though it's growing dim. The shadows are swarming. They're beating their wings and filling the air. They flow out of me, like long trails of smoke.

I feel drained and weak from the show I just put on upstairs. I'm not sure I can stop them.

I'm not sure I *want* to stop them.

He sees the shadow-creatures too. He feels their hunger. If anyone deserves this fate, it's McGrady.

But…there is still a chance.

"Sean," I say. "Listen to me. I know these monsters well. They're drawn to your fear and your rage. You can resist them." Once, a long time ago, I was able to help the dying do just that—clear their minds of their anger and sorrow and dread. So that they themselves could repel the shadows. I thought it was my talent alone. I gave myself the credit. But I was young.

"There must be some goodness still in you," I say to McGrady. "Focus on that. Let the rest go, and these creatures cannot touch you."

With tremendous effort, his gaze meets mine.

Hatred burns there, as fiery as the depths of any vision of hell.

The shadows race out of me and knit themselves around him. I can no longer see his face. I feel myself floating upward, away.

Two pinprick eyes begin to open where McGrady's used to be.

My view of this dark creature dissolves, bit by bit, until it vanishes. McGrady's lifeless body is left behind in the open pit below.

57

Dinah
1943

The bunkhouse is still echoing from McGrady's fall. And then there's a deep cracking sound, as if the very earth beneath us is splitting open. The floor begins to shake.

"Come on," I say to Eddie. "We have to get out of here."

We crawl toward the windows. Eddie is dragging his injured leg. I don't know how he's going to climb down. I can barely move myself.

Rumbles and groans come from the building around us. Boards snap as loud as gunshots.

I get to the windowsill and look out. The snow reaches far higher than it should. Then I remember what I saw before when we passed through the encampment: the snow has blown against the building up to the second floor. It's our best chance.

We're going to jump.

Using my gloved hand, I knock the rest of the broken glass out of the window frame. Summoning strength from somewhere inside me, I help Eddie up. He looks down into the moonlit expanse of snow. With a grunt, he launches himself forward and disappears. There's a thump, a loud cry.

I hang my legs out of the windowsill and follow.

I fall through several feet of powder and land hard on impacted snow. Pain is everywhere, a scream that doesn't cease. I roll down the icy slope and lodge in another bank of powder. Somehow I find my way to the surface. My head breaks through to the open air.

I look up and see the third floor of the boardinghouse slump in on itself. The sound is deafening. Walls crumbling, glass exploding.

I find Eddie and wrap my arm around his torso. "We have to run!" I scream. He leans on me and does his best to hurry, though I'm sure that every step on his injured leg is agony. We careen downhill, tripping over one another in the snow.

The crashing behind us begins to crescendo. We pause and turn, watching as the boardinghouse disintegrates into a pile of broken rubble. Snow and dust and debris hover in the air, blotting out the moon.

My ears ring with the sudden silence. The ground is still vibrating.

Then, there's a low, tremulous rumble from higher up on the mountain. I feel it more than hear it—a primal terror that runs me through like a knife.

Whump.

Fear makes the pain recede. I yank Eddie along with me downhill. We might only have seconds. There's only one place we can go where we have any chance of shelter.

We reach the overturned mining cart.

"Dig!" I say, though I can't even hear my own voice.

We claw at the snow surrounding the cart. I shove Eddie into the small sliver of space beneath. I squeeze through behind him. We're in a tiny black cave. The metal sides of the cart are humming.

There's a crash uphill as loud as a bomb detonating —that collapsed pile of bricks, wood and glass being pulverized by a roiling wave of snow.

And then the avalanche hits us. My eardrums feel like they might burst. My throat aches like I'm screaming, but I can't hear anything but an oppressive roar. We brace our hands against the sides of the mining cart. We're sliding and tilting. The cart's going to tip over and we'll suffocate beneath the crushing weight of the snow. Or we'll slide all the way off the ledge of the basin and into the canyon below.

But the cart doesn't tip. There's a high-pitched whining in my ears. It takes me several seconds to realize we aren't moving anymore.

There's no light in the cave beneath the cart. I feel around with my hands and find Eddie curled into a fetal position. His breathing is shallow. I wonder how much air we have in this tiny space. I try to kick and push at the cart, but it won't budge.

We're trapped here. Buried beneath ice, debris and snow.

58

Millie
1943

After I leave McGrady, I return to the common room and see Dinah and Eddie leap from the window. My hand presses against the wall, leaning out as I watch. They flounder in the moonlit snow. Dinah emerges, and she's frosted with white. She finds Eddie and together they stumble down the hill. I start to follow them, wanting to make sure they're all right.

I don't let myself think about what happened to McGrady, not yet. It's too terrible. And it's too miraculous—am I *free?*

The walls of the boardinghouse are shuddering. The roof folds inward on top of me. The entire structure gives way. I brace myself for an impact, but I feel nothing as the building disintegrates into a huge, jagged pile beneath me.

Then, a strange sound rises in the air. It's like there is an enormous train headed this way, screaming a warning.

The world is suddenly consumed in a swirl of planks, splinters, and snow. The spinning, teeming mass is so dark it looks like the shadow-monsters have returned, obliterating everything in their rage. For a moment I cannot see. But then, in a split second, the remains of the boardinghouse have fallen away, disappearing along with that roiling storm.

I'm left standing in the air, gaping at the wreckage strewn across the basin. Gray snow has filled the nighttime air like fog.

I did not think I had enough credulity left in me to be surprised.

Then I remember—Dinah and Eddie. Where are they?

I float downslope. I sense them: two glowing, humming lives beneath the ruins of ice and debris. In a blink, I'm in the darkness beneath the mining cart with them. They have their arms around one another, both injured and frightened and confused. Every moment it is growing harder for them to breathe. I wish I could offer comfort, but my ghostly touch would only distress them more. They need the sort of help that I can't provide.

I rise above the snow, scanning the landscape. The moon is high. The air is beginning to clear.

There are people trudging up the path to the mountain.

It's a team of almost twenty, most of them women. The Rescue Brigade. They frequently stop to check the path for danger, lest another avalanche dooms their effort. As I draw nearer, urging them on, I recognize Rachel Kohler—Dinah's mother—near the front. She presses onward, thinking only of her daughter.

"Hurry," I say aloud. "You're taking too long!"

The Brigade finally reaches the basin, and a girl around Dinah's age emerges from the group. Dark curls peek out beneath her hood, then a milk-white face with pale pink lips. Abby, that's her name. I've seen her before. Abby runs ahead, and cries out when she sees the terrible damage the avalanche has caused.

"This way," I say, though of course they can't hear me. Some old habits die hard, you might say.

Appearing in front of McGrady was the most difficult thing I've done—pulling all my energy, all my will into that single moment. I couldn't manage that feat again. But there is something I *can* do. I'm quite good at this little trick, in fact, if I do say so m'self.

I start to make footsteps in the snow in front of her.

Abby says, "Mom. Look!"

Tripping over her snowshoes, she follows my trail. I lead her to the place where Dinah and Eddie are trapped. My footsteps wind into a spiral, indicating the spot.

The Rescue Brigade begins to dig.

I witness their efforts. Their fear turns to elation. There are hugs and kisses; relief and wonder. I feel a measure of their happiness, and that small taste is enough to satisfy me. I've succeeded. My existence here has served a purpose.

By the time the sun rises, the entire crowd is gone. I'm alone.

Cherry Mountain is eerily quiet.

I go higher up the slope, above the mess of the boardinghouse and the ruins of the mining encampment. I sit on the ridge, vistas surrounding me in every direction, and I wait.

I think about all that's happened.

There are no traces of the shadow-creatures; their absence is profound. I feel a lightness where before there was a well of hatred and hunger. I wonder if McGrady is now being consumed by that darkness, or if perhaps the shadows drained every last cruel impulse from his soul and left his husk behind, adrift. Is he trapped in a purgatory with them, as I was? Or did I set that colony of monsters free when I gained freedom myself? I do not know.

I'm glad that McGrady's ultimate fate wasn't mine to choose.

I contemplate these mysteries as the sun mounts the sky. Eventually, though, thoughts of McGrady and the shadows pass away from me like melting snow.

Soon, I start to *hope*.

I close my eyes—well, figuratively at least—and imagine myself fading away from here. There must be *something* more waiting for me. Some higher plane than this, where all the people I've loved have gone.

"Mother," I whisper to the sky. "Edward."

Can I go to them? Or will they come for me?

I wait. The wind blows through me.

When I open my eyes and gaze around the mountain ridge, so full of hope, I'm still alone. Ice glistens like cut gems on the surface of the snow.

Has a minute passed? A year?

Now, I see how foolish I've been. Even in death, after all the suffering I endured—both my own and others'—my heart held fast to a childish fantasy of rescue. But no one is coming for me. I don't even have the boardinghouse to call home now.

I wish for sleep—for that utterly destroying darkness. But even that relief doesn't come.

I sit atop the snow, staring out at the endless, bleak expanse before me.

Then, I feel something change. A warmth spreads through the air and caresses my back. I turn.

There's someone standing on the next ridge. He's bathed in bright sunlight.

He walks forward with a slight limp. He crosses the open air just like it's solid ground. Soon, his smile materializes along with the rest of his features—his angular cleft chin, his expressive gray eyes. He's wearing an olive drab wool tunic with a lieutenant insignia.

And he's every bit as dashing as I remember.

Emotion blooms within me—wonder, shock, pure joy—sensations that seem like old friends I never thought I'd encounter again. But here they are, and I remember. I remember so many things. The memories rush back to me all at once: the taste of chocolate and licorice, the comfort of being held in an embrace, the anticipation in that moment before a kiss.

"Millie," Edward says. "It's really you."

He's laughing. He holds out his hand.

I hesitate to take it. I've never seen another like me. He is rimmed with light, his edges shifting like leaves blown by the breeze.

"I've been waiting for you," he says.

"But how?" I ask. "I've been alone for so long." If I were still alive, I'd be crying.

"Have you? I don't know how much time's passed." Edward's features shimmer, blurring and then reforming. "I've been…here, I suppose. It's all a bit of a fog. I couldn't find you, but I couldn't leave. Not without you beside me."

His glowing hand touches my face. I reach out to him. Our fingers don't so much entwine as commingle. I feel a tingling like static electricity everywhere we touch. It's like an electrical charge that buzzes whenever he's near. Yet his presence is also like a pool of warm, soothing water that I can dip myself into.

I'm in awe. He's been waiting for me all this time.

The lines between us are fading, our forms beginning to lose shape. We're being drawn away from here. Like snowflakes pulled by a gentle wind into the sky.

"Where will we go?" I ask.

"I don't know. Find out with me?"

Below us, the mountains are fading away like a dream upon waking. And then, in a blink, they're gone.

Dinah
July 1944

The memorial service is held at midday. The sun beats down on our small gathering. It's like a hot hand against my neck. But I couldn't imagine a bluer sky. Patches of wildflowers have sprouted between the graves, waving gently in the breeze. In the distance, Cherry Mountain is covered in green. It's just the kind of day that I wanted for Millie. No clouds, no rain. Definitely no snow.

The minister says a few words. Briony cries quietly to one side of me, holding a black handkerchief against her face. Abby stands on my other side, her pinky finger linked with mine. There are a few other groupings here, though we're all standing apart from one another. My mother and father. Grace and Jim Gainsbury, who've just arrived from Leadville for the service. A smattering of curious onlookers from around town. Terrance stands at a distance, holding BT by his rope.

We all watch solemnly as the pine coffin is lowered into the ground.

Abby puts her hand on the small of my back and leans in. "I'll see you at the assay office," she whispers. She and her mother are hosting a lunch there in Millie's honor.

The gravediggers are shoveling dirt onto Millie's coffin. I'm the last one there. When I can't see the pine box anymore, I turn to go.

That's when I see Eddie walking toward me. He looks different than I remember. His hair is cut neatly and slicked to one side. He's wearing horn-rimmed glasses, and his face has filled out. He doesn't look as much like his uncle anymore.

"Sorry I'm late," he says. "My father didn't think I was ready to come back here." He nods his head at a man and a younger woman standing way off near the cemetery gate. They're holding hands and watching us anxiously. Eddie's father and sister. I wave. His dad waves tentatively back.

"But I convinced him it was important," Eddie says. "I needed to say goodbye."

Goodbye to Millie. And probably goodbye to a lot more than her, too.

"How are you?" I ask.

He looks off into the distance. Toward Cherry Mountain. "I'm managing. It's been one day at a time."

"How's..." I trail off. I feel awkward. I don't know if I'm supposed to ask.

"How's my mother?" Eddie finishes for me. "I visited her last week. The asylum's not too swell, but not too bad either. It'll be a long time until she's well enough to leave. I just hope that someday it happens."

I nod, waiting for him to say more. But he doesn't. Eddie dips his head. He pushes his glasses back up his nose. "I'm sorry I haven't written. How's your brother?"

"Oh, Nate's OK. He was at Normandy. Pounding away at the Jerries and all that." Barely got off that beach with his life, but I don't tell Eddie that. Nate's been in a hospital, but I just got word yesterday—he's being shipped back to the front soon. I panic every time I think about it.

He lifts his head, his gray irises meeting mine. "Your brother must be proud of you. Because I'd be proud to have you as a sister. For whatever that's worth."

I smile, though my eyes are stinging. "It's worth a lot." I open my arms to hug him, but Eddie shakes his head. For a brief moment, he closes his eyes and tips his head back to face the sun.

"Do you think she's watching us?" Eddie asks.

I know he means Millie. "I think she's...wherever she wants to be." I don't know if that's another place, or no place at all. But I doubt it's Powder Ridge.

"Good." He turns to go back to his family, wading through patches of wildflowers.

Epilogue

August 1945

"Come on," I say to Abby. I have to shout to be heard above the cheering crowd. "The train's already here!"

I weave in between bodies. We're all pushing towards the platform, where a giant Diesel engine has just pulled noisily into Union Station. The train hasn't even stopped yet and men in uniform are jumping from the steps of the coaches onto the pavement.

Abby catches up to me. I'm wearing my work overalls. I came straight from my shift at the Denver Ordnance Plant. The streetcar ride from Lakewood was agony. I couldn't sit still I was so excited.

"Do you see him?" Abby asks.

I'm craning my neck, but there's so many people jumping and hugging and running. "Not yet." Where is he? My heart is jack-hammering like one of the machines we use at the plant.

Mother and Papa will be at the apartment by now, getting a special welcome-home dinner ready. The end of the fighting in Europe has been brightening their moods since V-E Day in May. But if I come home empty handed today, I don't know what kind of reaction I'm going to get.

Papa's been attending classes at the Denver YMCA. He's even applied for several jobs, though he hasn't had any bites yet. As for Mother, I haven't seen her take a drink in several months, though I know she's still struggling. I've heard about a group called Alcoholics

Anonymous, and I've been leaning on her to go. I worry over my parents all the time. But at least Abby's with me; my parents adore her. Abby's taking college classes to become a teacher.

And me? Turns out, being a Rosie the Riveter suits me just fine. Just wait till Nate sees me, all grown up and employed.

We're being jostled back and forth by the crowd. I seek out Abby's hand and squeeze it anxiously. Her eyes meet mine; her smile both thrills me and calms me. "I love you," I say, though I doubt she can hear me. But I can't help myself. I say those words as often as I think them, lest she ever forget.

Then I see a familiar face through a gap in the crowd.

I scream and push my way toward him. Nate drops his duffel on the ground, his mouth stretching into the biggest grin I've ever seen. He grabs me and swings me around and around, even though he's supposed to be taking it easy after being wounded for a second time—a bullet in the side. Clearly, he's feeling stronger. But it was enough to get him shipped home instead of being sent east.

Abby reaches us and we three hold hands as the crowd shifts and sways, all of us laughing.

The war is still raging in the Pacific. Every day I think of those soldiers, hoping—often praying—that they'll make it back safely.

But for my family, the war is over. Nate's finally home.

Thank you

If you enjoyed this book and want to read more like it, leave a rating or review on Amazon and Goodreads. I do read and consider every review. And many thanks to my growing team of advance readers and reviewers— your efforts mean the world to me!

To hear about my new releases and receive exclusive freebies like novellas and deleted scenes, sign up for my newsletter. Go to: http://bit.ly/anwillis

Author's Note

While I'm publishing this book during a pandemic, I wrote the first drafts of *How Much It May Storm* over a year before COVID-19 changed our world. The events of 2020 certainly gave me a far more personal perspective on Millie's chapters. Some of the similarities between the "Spanish" flu pandemic and our own are striking: theaters, schools, churches and other gathering places were closed in 1918 to prevent the spread; mask mandates were controversial then as they are now.

I've tried to present the 1918 pandemic accurately wherever possible. Several towns in Colorado did enforce quarantines, in which visitors were detained and residents forbidden to leave. Nurses did sometimes treat flu victims in private homes (though I doubt they possessed Millie's particular abilities). And numbers of flu cases indeed surged in Colorado in the days after people flooded the streets to celebrate Armistice Day.

If you're interested in learning more about the pandemic of 1918, I highly recommend the online Influenza Encyclopedia, produced by the University of Michigan Center for the History of Medicine and Michigan Publishing. You can find it on the web at influenzaarchive.org.

Where I've taken liberties with history for plot, character, or stylistic purposes—or simply made a mistake—I hope you'll forgive me. This is a fantastical and completely fictional story, after all. There is no such town as Powder Ridge, Colorado.

As for Dinah's story, I'd like to thank the Telluride Historical Museum and the San Juan County Mining Heritage Center in Silverton for their fascinating and inspiring collections of historical artifacts. The ruins of the Tomboy Mine near Telluride served as the inspiration for the Powder Ridge mine where Dinah labors in this book. During the Great Depression, some people did indeed scour old mines like the Tomboy Mine for ore that had been discarded as waste in years before. I'm not sure if these efforts continued after World War II began, but this is one of those liberties I decided to take for the sake of plot.